THE CHRONICLES OF RUSTY

To Viki

I hope you enjoy.

[illegible]

THE CHRONICLES OF RUSTY

W. K. POTTER

TATE PUBLISHING
AND ENTERPRISES, LLC

Published by Tate Publishing & Enterprises, LLC
127 E. Trade Center Terrace | Mustang, Oklahoma 73064 USA
1.888.361.9473 | www.tatepublishing.com

Tate Publishing is committed to excellence in the publishing industry. The company reflects the philosophy established by the founders, based on Psalm 68:11,
"The Lord gave the word and great was the company of those who published it."

Cover design by Jim Villaflores
Interior design by Jomar Ouano

Published in the United States of America

ISBN: 978-1-63063-171-0
1. Fiction / Action & Adventure
2. Fiction / Science Fiction / Action & Adventure
14.02.03

Dedication

To Bucky
For the inspiration

To My Dad
For watching over me

To My Mom
For your continued support

To My Brother
For paving the way

Contents

INTRODUCTION

The universe, as we know it, is a vast collection of galaxies that extend to yet unknown length and depth. We learn more all the time about its energy and unseen physical properties. Our search into the quantum physics realm further builds our curiosity of exactly what's out there and how much more is to be revealed. And yet, in all its wonder and majesty, the universe does not create a thought, it doesn't share a moment, and it cannot build meaning.

Within the universal structure that we can see and understand, reside millions of earth-like planets. Many are much older than the big blue marble on which we exist. What is out there and why? What drives the purpose of all the energy and mass that exists? Does that purpose come from life forces? Does the purpose of our universe rest with those who've come before us, those who are with us both near and far, and those who are yet to come? What happens to the soul when time on earth is done?

This story, told by Rusty, takes us on a journey through all of these issues. It examines our existence through our choices and what we understand to be right and wrong. It looks at what is good, and wonders why evil exists. If we determine the path and purpose of the universe, then where is our existence headed? Do we have help?

The rest of this introduction strives to form the canvas on which to paint *The Chronicles of Rusty*. Read carefully, and then enter the fascinating world of Rusty.

Even if there is only one possible unified theory, it is just a set of rules and equations. What is it that breathes fire into the equations and makes a universe for them to describe?

—Stephen Hawking

Quantum Physics Related Ideas

Objects in our universe are made of filaments and membranes of energy. A connection called super symmetry has been identified between small particles called bosons and fermions.

This connection allows for the possibility of extra dimensions and parallel universes. Existence in one space can also relate outside of that space. Dimensions outside of our recognition then can exist, and possess properties beyond what we now experience. The existence of humanity serves as an explanation and purpose for certain physical properties in the universe.

Multiple Universe Theory

The three dimensions in which we live give us knowledge of the physical presence that is our ever expanding universe. Through that knowledge of time and space, we are able to see the great expanse of it.

Other universes are also within this large framework. These universes bundle multiple dimensions together that are not visible or attainable in our three-dimensional reality. They also possess massive units of energy that require a balance. Therefore; a positive energy and a negative energy reality must co-exist. The two are separated by a dimensional membrane and balance each other, but do not interact.

The universe is wider than our views of it.

—Henry David Thoreau

Creation

We are created into a three-dimensional universe that provides an environment for the soul to develop. It is reactionary in nature (for every action there is an equal opposite reaction). Thus, the soul learns to exist, and develops an awareness of itself and others. It develops in three basic ways; physically, mentally, and emotionally.

Physical awareness: We exist and all around us exist. We have the ability to take action and perform tasks. We acknowledge time as an indicator of that action and the action of all that is around us. Thus, we exist.

Mental awareness: We have the ability to think, observe, and create; the ability to acquire and store knowledge. We reason, investigate and imagine; with that, the ability to build concepts.

Emotional awareness: We are aware of needs, feelings, wants, and desires. We have the ability to relate and determine.

The ability to choose: Through the development of awareness, we establish the meaning of our action. We understand the concepts of cooperation, giving, and love to be the building blocks of creativity; thus adding purpose to the universe. We also understand the concepts of power, acquisition, and conquest as the tools for gaining control.

The Ultimate Question: Does the soul choose to share and create; or does it choose to use and control?

Do you wish to be great? Then begin by being. Do you desire to construct a vast and lofty fabric? Think first about the foundations of humility. The higher your structure is to be, the deeper must be its foundation.

—Saint Augustine

Make friends with the angels, who though invisible are always with you. Often invoke them, constantly praise them, and make good use of their help and assistance in all your temporal and spiritual affairs.

—Saint Francis de Sales

Heaven and the Dark Side

When a life force leaves its host body in the three-dimensional world it maintains its energy and integrity; becoming compatible with the other multi-dimensional realities. As a life force, it passes through the protective dimension and attaches as a new existence in one of the other realities.

There are two multi-dimensional realities that a life force is capable of entering. *Heaven* is filled with positive energy, while *The Dark Side (Hell)* uses the opposite negative energy. Once a soul attaches, it cannot leave the chosen grid.

Positive Energy Reality (Heaven)

In Heaven the life force (soul) enters and connects to the energy web. It unites with other souls who are already a part of the pattern within the energy field. The soul then feeds from the energy, enabling it to learn and grow through events that are shared with other connected life forces. The three-dimensional idea of time is no longer relevant in this reality; only events, opportunities, and outcomes. The sharing of information and the creation of meaning are the ingredients that drive the purpose of this reality, and an infinite amount is possible. Positive energy is focused outward, creating brightness and a willingness to give and share. Event and outcome scenarios from this reality provide information and understanding that become the foundation of purpose for the universe.

Negative Energy Reality (The Dark Side)

Negative Energy has a similar web structure but the properties are different. Negative Energy is focused inward and consumes, creating darkness and the tendency to hoard and possess. It has a structure that permits migrating energy cells that life forces attach to. These cells can clump together to form mega structures controlled by specific life forces; a hierarchy of power then exists. The hoarding of knowledge and information acquired in the negative reality by the hierarchy further creates an environment of domination. New life forces entering the dark side must attach to established structures and become part of that existence. Information is shared with those that the hierarchy chooses.

However, the level of knowledge and understanding in life forces (souls) before they enter the dark side could cause a major concern to the power structure in place. Enlightened souls with better understanding would create a reason for other souls to shift away from current power structures, causing a ripple effect. New patterns of ideas would be established, resulting in the probability of souls migrating toward new structures with higher enlightenment.

Angels

Angels are souls that possess the ability to communicate through the outer dimension of heaven and hell, and into the protective energy dimension. This faculty enables individuals from the three-dimensional world, who possess the same capabilities, to interact with these angels. The connections are rare, but common enough to have limited communication from the realities of heaven and hell with our three-dimensional existence. Mental in nature, the connections rarely possess any physical signature.

Travelers

Travelers are extremely rare and only come from our three-dimensional existence. They have the ability to penetrate the energy dimension that forms the outer layers of heaven and hell, and acquire some of the properties of those existences. This allows for travel back to events in history using the non-recognition of time property associated with heaven and hell. The travel is done with the support of a soul from either of the two realities. The Traveler is able to be placed in a designated period in history, chosen by the host life force. A life force from heaven or hell can only host a Traveler in the time frame of their existence in the three-dimensional world, and then forward from that point. When a Traveler is created with positive energy, there is always an equal created with negative energy.

Worm Holes

A worm hole is a natural space created by the buffering membranes of heaven and hell against each other, and against the protective membrane of our three-dimensional existence. This space integrates the properties of the heaven/hell realities with the distance concepts of the three-dimensional reality; allowing for the possibility of large areas of our three-dimensional universe to be traveled instantaneously. The first challenge for anyone using a worm hole would be stabilizing it. Another would be creating an entry and exit point without ripping a hole in the protective membrane of our three-dimensional existence. Users would have no guidance within the worm hole without some type of signal or beacon. The signal would also provide important location information involving mathematical calculations necessary for exit. Without these specific calculations a rip in the membrane would occur. This would be a catastrophic event, causing the destruction of our world and that of any other world connected by the worm hole.

Knowledge becomes evil if the aim be not virtuous.

—Plato

Six million Jews were killed in the Holocaust; two out of three Eastern European Jews perished.

Legend

Thousands of years ago, the ancients traveled from far reaches of the universe to earth and other living planets. Their purpose was to roam the galaxies looking for life, and creating living keepers of a beacon that would be necessary for future travel using dimensions associated with worm holes. The travelers implanted a gene in the DNA of a man that would provide the future beacon signal; that gene would be passed on through the centuries. The exact person and time of the event were a closely guarded secret that the ancients took with them. The chosen bloodline was created within the early Israelite Tribe.

The dynamics of a cosmic link between worlds in the three-dimensional universe would be a potential disaster for the controlling powers of the dark side. The enlightenment created by such an event would put life forces in a new category of consciousness and understanding. This would greatly threaten the power structure in place.

The dark side was unable to pinpoint the specific bloodline within the Israelite tribe; but historical events created speculation of particular groups to be targeted. The determination was made by the ultimate powers to use all available influences to eliminate the tribe; with specific attention to certain bloodlines.

The designation of the Israelites as the chosen people could in fact have been the expression attached to them as a result of the revelation of the beacon. With it come centuries of persecution and multiple attempts of genocide, generated in part by the dark side. This interference has caused unbelievable human suffering; a measured and careful response from heaven has been necessary at times.

Hitler and his high command came to power by many fortunate moves aided by strategic information provided by the dark side. His alliance with hell came at a time that was perfectly balanced with technology and communication ability to manipulate the masses. The dark side's exploitation helped create one of the most horrific events ever recorded.

The Nazi plan of ethnic cleansing of the Eastern European Jews and Gypsies was the perfect cover for the search and elimination of the bloodlines coveted by the forces of hell. Six million souls were eliminated. Within that evil context, the Nazis had all but finished the job for the dark side. New information provided by a dark traveler had narrowed the search for the final members of the bloodline. This traveler had a specific evil presence about him; a love for killing, a courier of death. His mission was near completion, except for two young children who were unaccounted for.

For every traveler that comes to either reality, there is always a counterpart. The decision in heaven was made to activate the other traveler. The bloodline was down to one family: a young boy named Joshua and his little sister Sara.

> *Non-cooperation with evil is as much a duty as is cooperation with good.*
>
> —Mahatma Gandhi.

> *If it's true that our species is alone in the universe, then I'd have to say the universe aimed rather low and settled for very little.*
>
> —George Carlin

The Book of Ham

Chapter 1 – New Mexico early 1980's

HAM

Ham blew across the New Mexico border as a whirlwind from Texas. He was a free spirit or snake oil salesman, not sure which one. The first time we met was on our college campus. I was an assistant in a work study program checking in new students into Roosevelt Hall, my dorm.

He came blazing down the street in a fourteen-year-old 660 Classic Rambler Station Wagon with horn blaring, made an illegal U-turn and pulled the wagon up on the grass in front of the dorm. His slender frame shimmed out the driver side window with a Budweiser in one hand and a Marlboro sticking out the side of his mouth. Apparently, the door wouldn't open.

He had on a beige straw cowboy hat, and wore a burnt orange Texas Longhorn T-shirt. He also sported knee-length flowered swim trunks, with flip flops to match. Topping it all off with Buddy Holly rimmed sunglasses.

I approached him with my official clip board, but it didn't seem to matter. At the top of his lungs, with an obvious Texas drawl, he shouted. "Can anybody tell me where Roosevelt Hall is?"

Normally that's a fair question, but he was standing right in front of a huge wooden sign that said *Roosevelt Hall.* I took my pencil and pointed at it. Raising his glasses to his forehead, he took a good look at the elusive sign. He smiled, and then as if just remembering something vitally important, he took a defensive stance pointing his Marlboro at me.

"Just gotta tell you, boy; No habla Español."

Confused, I answered; "What?"

He explained. "I don't speak Spanish."

"Either do I," I said.

He asked, "Do I need a passport?"

I was beginning to wonder. "You do know you're in New Mexico?" He just gave me a goofy stare as I continued. "You know, in the USA, one of the fifty states."

He cautiously asked, "So you're telling me I'm ok with no passport?"

I nodded, knowing this might take a while, then asked. "Do you have a driver's license?"

He boasted, "Yes sir, from the great state of Texas."

Taking my opportunity, I joked, "Well not for long if you keep driving like that."

He snorted a quick laugh. Then turning toward the rambler and extending at the arms, he bent and gave it a loving hug, the Budweiser still in one hand and Marlboro in the other. He sighed. "I'd never do anything to hurt this ol gal."

"Name," I requested as I looked down to my board.

He backed away from the wagon, stood straight and pronounced, "Ham."

"Ham," I questioned?

"Yep," he said. He took a long draw off the Marlboro and exhaled while answering. "My daddy was always partial to pork."

By now a fairly large crowd had gathered around and Ham began playing to it. He pointed at the rambler as he bragged. "Yeah this princess has seen the sun come up on the beaches of North Carolina, and seen it set flyin across the Golden Gate Bridge." He went on. "Matter of fact I won this car playing seven card stud at Venice Beach with a bunch of surfer dudes. Sure enough this ol boy thought he had me with a full house. Well I sure enough plopped a flush down on the sand, and drove away with that beauty right there." I didn't have the heart to tell him that a flush doesn't beat a full house; besides, he was on a roll.

His story shifted to the rack on top of the station wagon and the scars left by the surf boards it had hauled. He moved to the back and opened the door to expose four trunks. "These babies right here were owned by four of the most beautiful exotic dancers to ever grace the stages of Vegas. They come complete with pictures that I'd be proud to share, as soon as we get these big boys in my room. Yep, we'll open em up and explore what's inside." He began swaying to some imaginary music that was in his head only.

Being truly impressed with his BS, I decided to play along. "You're in room 312, the door's open."

Ham turned to his audience. "Can a fella find a friend today?" He proceeded to have the station wagon unloaded and all possessions moved to his room without ever setting down the Budweiser or Marlboro. He was very gracious to his moving crew, and told stories that kept them in stitches, congregating in his room till well into the evening.

I was doing my rounds through the dorm noting who had checked in. Passing near Ham's room, I heard him ushering everyone out. "Fellas, you guys are the best, have a good night and adios, muchachos." I had to smile, being fairly sure that was the only Spanish Ham knew.

Oh yeah, me, my name is Rusty. I'm just your typical guy. I've always been your basic standup kind of person. Back then, I was just another ordinary college student having fun and figuring out life. Ordinary, until I met Ham.

He was a skinny, blonde-haired, blue-eyed, would-be playboy, with buckteeth and a strong Texas drawl. Really wasn't all that much to look at, but there was just something about him that drew you in, especially women. Boy was funny now, I'm telling you. Could make me laugh, not just me, he could spin a tale like nobody's business. We would all sit around the dorm and listen to stories and jokes for hours.

Ham and I ended up in the same fraternity. I marveled at his ability to manipulate situations, most of the time the situations involved girls. Being fairly shy when it came to women, I was very impressed at his skill and mastery of the opposite sex, and oh man did he love to tell us about his conquests.

Like the time he bed the mayor's wife back in his hometown. They got to know each other through little league where Ham was an umpire for her son's games. He gave her more attention than her husband had in years and literally charmed her pants right off.

There was the case of the teenage girl who would stop by his dorm room right after she got out of youth group at her church. I know this because I was the girl's youth director at the time. That was a bit awkward.

Once he brought a wayward bartender to a fraternity party and was out dancing with her on the floor. She bent over and began nibbling on Ham's lower stomach. Turning so that everyone could see, he raised his shirt to expose the event. Then, leaning his head back towards the ceiling, began howling like a wolf. Ham actually did that often, howl like a wolf. It was kind of his signature thing.

One full moon summer night, we decided to head out for the sand dunes at the state park outside of town. The dunes were a couple of miles of golden sand. On the outside edges of the park, the sand was dotted with grass and bushes, but in the middle was nothing but mountains of virgin granules built for play. Ham came up with the idea of racing naked across the dunes in the moonlight. Not knowing why, I agreed to the challenge. We stripped down and set the rules and length of the race. Off we ran over the shimmering sand in the full moon glow, free and full of life as we galloped like two stallions snorting in the wind. Ham was fast but I took the lead, mainly because he was trying not to spill the Budweiser in his left hand.

Suddenly there was a beam from a flashlight cresting over the next dune.

"Ham." I screamed in a forceful whisper. I pointed to the light and we both stopped dead in our tracks.

"We need to get out of here!" I hissed in a bit of a panic.

Ham put his finger to his lips to signal my silence, then gave me the hand signal of his palms to wait where I stood. He quietly climbed to the top of the dune and lay down on his stomach, inching up to peer over the top, then scooted back down to report.

"It's the night watchman," he whispered.

We all knew this man as an overweight and retired security guard from the county jail. Walter by name, he was our major nemesis when it came to fraternity keg parties, which were regularly held on the outer edges of the park. He was fairly harmless, but reveled in the opportunity to bust our events and acquire the beer.

Ham looked at me and gave that grin that I hated to see. It was that of an impish rascal, and nothing good ever followed it. "What are you gonna do?" I whispered with trepidation.

"Get ready to run," he said, and turned back towards the crest of the dune.

Abruptly Ham jumped up and thrust his arms high above his head. He began rotating his hips and howling like a wolf. A startled Walter turned his flashlight toward the noise and gazed upon a hilarious sight.

There was Ham, hands and head to the sky, covered in a thick layer of sand, with his Johnson waving at Walter in the beam of the flashlight. Walter had no idea who this creature was but ordered him to stop. Ham jumped back, slid down the dune and was past me before I had time to react.

"I told you to get ready to run," he shouted back as he quickly moved away. Seeing the flashlight beam coming over the dune, I was off with a burst, tracing the path that Ham had left behind. There was no way Walter could catch us, and I doubted he would go to the trouble of calling the Sheriff; it would only make him look bad.

Getting back to our clothes, I found Ham fully dressed and patiently waiting for my arrival. It didn't take long for me to dress and we wasted no time getting to his wagon. Hustling inside, off we sped while looking again for Walter, but he was far in the distance and no longer a threat.

Sand was everywhere and in every crevice of my body. One could only imagine what Ham felt like. It was just a relief to be out of there. "We dodged a bullet there," I said staring down the old dunes road.

Ham scoffed at my statement and brought the wagon to a halt. Swiveling in his seat to face me, he scanned my body up and down. "Not a scratch on you," he analyzed. "We just lived an adventure to tell about for years." He paused to create a more dramatic effect. "Rusty, life is not about dodging bullets." He gave me his best serious look and was really feeling the moment. "It's all about seeing the bullet and kinda leaning into it just a bit."

A big grin spread across his face. "Partner, it ain't about what we're gonna do, it's about what we're doing. We are in the now, you know, the moment; and never should we be in the someday of life."

I pondered his sermon for a few seconds; it was long enough for me to make my own quality of life decision; to get out of the station wagon and remove my clothes once again. Jumping back in, I threw them in the backseat while staring Ham down with a defiant look. I pointed to the open road and declared. "Preach on, brother, let's go have a beer."

Ham got that goofy grin on his face and rocketed out of the station wagon. He proceeded to get naked faster than when he got a quickie from the homecoming queen right before the halftime ceremony of the homecoming football game. He jumped back behind the wheel, let out a howl, and gunned it. We were flying down the road with the windows down and Ham screaming into the night sky. "Hold er steady, Newt, she smells alfalfa!"

Chapter 2–New Mexico early 1980's

LIFE

It was later in our time at the university when Ham and I started to have discussions of a deeper nature. We would each acquire a six-pack of our favorite brew, and to the back roads we would head. Each hill brought a horizon of a new thought. How deep the two of us were back then. We talked about almost anything you could think of, and always got smarter as the sun edged over the hills and out of sight.

One warm summer night we sat on a park bench after two hours of competitive tennis on the courts. We downed a few beers and had begun to talk.

"Ham, have you ever wondered if there is more to life than just what you're doing. I mean some bigger purpose or something you're meant for?"

Ham looked up and smiled. "Partner, I think I'm pretty special every day."

"No doubt," I said in disgust. I went on. "I have this nagging feeling about being part of something special or important, but I have no idea what."

Ham stared into the night and contemplated. "Rusty, what have you not done that you really want to do."

I said, "That's what I mean, there are tons of things I haven't done yet."

He said, "I know, but stuff that would be scary or that would be dangerous to do."

"Now why would I want to do things like that?" I asked.

Ham had that goofy stare as he answered. "I just mean things that you gotta trust or you might die. Like sky diving, that would scare the hell out of me, but I'd be flying. Can you imagine, Rusty? Flying!"

I looked at him knowing the conversation had drifted away from my point, so it was my turn to pretend to be serious. "Ham, you know if you're brave enough you can sky dive without a chute."

Ham's blue eyes got wide. "What?...Really?"

"Yeah," I answered playfully while looking to the night. "You only need a chute if you want to do it twice."

Ham, still with eyes on me, snorted his surprised laugh. He flared his lips and growled through his white buck teeth. "Boy you're funnin me."

I shifted my eyes to him and shrugged my shoulders. "It's the truth."

He let out a howl and charged, tackling me to the ground. We laughed and wrestled until neither of us could breathe.

We often talked about life, and I eventually began to realize that Ham was hiding a vulnerable side. There were times when his mood turned cold, as if a dark cloud had set in over the top of our conversation. We would talk about friendship and love, whereupon things began to unravel for him.

He spoke of his dad, and how cool he was, and how he died in the war. It was a broken promise on his pledge to return. Ham was twelve years old and his dad wasn't coming back.

There was the time with his favorite aunt. They were in the middle of a conversation when she began to feel ill. She suddenly grabbed her arm in pain and stumbled toward her concerned ıllapsing in his arms as Ham screamed for someone to he died with Ham holding on. He was fifteen.

He was a survivor, but at a pretty steep price, forcing his decision to dictate the way he would interact with the world. Ham became a master manipulator, using his ample social skills as tools to insure that all things emotional would go his way.

I attended college to become a teacher. One of my education classes offered a seminar on the topic of bully behavior in schools. The premise was that all of us crave acceptance, and the only way to gain acceptance is through relationships. The instructor identified many different personalities that are present in the natural school setting. The Alpha Male and Queen Bee establish themselves at the top of the food chain, in what becomes the dramatic battle for acceptance at school. All of the other personalities fight for position with, and acceptance from, the Alpha Male or Queen Bee. All except the one called the floater.

The floater is not heavily influenced by the Alpha Male. He would rather socialize with everyone and be friendly and cordial to all groups. That's me, good ol Rusty. All my life I have been a good guy, good in sports, gone to church, and stood up for the down trodden. I'm not exactly the floater because I've got a little bit of the alpha male in me. I'm more of the White Night. I'm the guy in grade school that would go beat up the bullies. I was all about protecting the innocent.

I'm always someone's best friend, and girls loved to have me as a trusted companion. I've been able to see value in fairness and cooperation. It has continually made sense to me to give and share. Friendship has always come easily and I have benefitted from the commitment and loyalty that it has spawned.

Ham was an alpha male; he needed control. The dark side of his personality would surface at times when he spoke so coldly about those who had been hurt by his conquests. His life was about exactly that, conquests, and he struggled to see my side in our discussions on relationships and various aspects of conscience. Never really debating him much, I would still ask him at times about some of the delicate situations he found himself in. Often he would laugh it off and call himself a sinner destined for hell. But, sometimes he would offer insight into his vision of how the world worked.

"Rusty, I have a bit of a problem with heaven and hell."

"Oh yeah?" I questioned.

"Yep. With my track record I don't figure I have much of a shot at heaven."

I questioned. "So you believe you have to earn your way in?"

"Well don't you? I mean if people can just go around doing what they want then what's the point of being good?" He was truly asking.

"I don't think about it that way," I said.

"Oh do go on," he said smugly.

I gave him a fake grin and continued. "You treat people right because it's a better way to live, not because God is threatening you. Making good friends and loving people just feels better and gives you a better life. There is a choice when you get to heaven. You can choose to go into the light or choose not to."

Ham pretended to really ponder my statement. "I sure hope you're right." He turned to me baring his teeth and running his tongue across his lips, "Because sometimes, partner, I just can't help myself." Of course, the wolf howl came next.

He was definitely a live-for-the-moment guy. In his world, the time he spent with a person was judged by the single event itself. He was always proud of the quality time he was able to put forth with an individual, even if history proved it to be a one-sided deal. Commitments down the road did not mean much to him. For Ham, there was pain in the long term. He did not trust relationships; they had always let him down.

Chapter 3–New Mexico/West Texas

DEATH

Ham and I graduated and moved on in life. He, of course, married a beautiful woman right out of college. Good ol Church of Christ girl, and oh my god! Ham became a deacon in the church. He had it going on, rising through the ranks, and two beautiful kids. I really got along well with his wife, and as often as possible would try to get together with them.

Me, I just floated for a while, eventually settling in the teaching profession, met my wife, and started my own family a few years later.

Ham's life eventually began to unravel. His marriage became a sham. The perfect world that he created was undercut by hidden drinking binges and out-of-control womanizing. His marriage eventually ended and Ham was on his own. He was always a pretty good dad to his boys, but his work was suffering, stemming from his life being one big party.

I was cruising along in life, doing ok and teaching kids. Life was good. I kept track of Ham through common buddies, with a road trip or two over the years. It was later, when he moved back closer with a job in his home town, that we began to see each other a bit more, and I saw a major decline in his health.

We made a point to grab a couple of six-packs and head out for a talk. The discussion covered our lives and how they were different than what we thought they'd be. Ham always told me the same old stories and how things were great, but it was obvious that they were not.

On this outing he confessed to me a change of heart. Expressing how badly he wanted to feel like me and see people just for who they were, regretting the wrongs he had committed over the years. Sadness filled the void that once was confidence in his empty blue eyes. He spoke of his boys and how proud he was of them, about how he screwed up his marriage, and how love had escaped him for too long. Searching for meaning, he was in a place where he hadn't been since childhood. His head was full of stories of his mom and dad and the times they shared. I was getting a very bad feeling; knowing this guy, he was getting around to something, and I was pretty sure it wasn't good.

Abruptly ending a story he was only halfway through, Ham's gaze caught mine. His crystal blue eyes were glistening with a tear.

"What is it, Ham?"

"Rusty....buddy...looks like I'm gonna die." He finished the sentence in almost a whisper. His gaze remained fixed with mine but his body slumped into an awkwardly crooked position, with head tilted slightly as if to be wondering about a response from me.

Stunned and not knowing what to say, my mind searched for some kind of supportive response, and I had nothing. Something needed to be said, anything, and then; "Ok...well...shall we stand and sing?"

Ham's eyes widened, and then he blinked. A smirk edged onto his face. I began to nervously giggle, and Ham joined in with a raucous roar, then to his famous howl. Our thoughts both went back to the same thing, a funeral.

A friend of ours had been killed in college in a tragic accident. Hundreds of students turned out for the service at a local church and created an overflow crowd. It was very hot and the tension was high in the room. One of the church members was asked or hired to do the inspirational singing for the service. We had all been there for quite some time and the mood was edging toward restlessness. The man began to sing.

I don't know if it was the situation or the singer; but he was the worst vocalist I had ever heard. Everyone was suffering through the song. Feet were shuffling and many hands were rubbing heads. Finally he was done and took a seat. There was a prayer, and God help us all, he stood up to do another song.

Ham was right beside me and was in agony. I reached for the card holder mounted in the back of the next pew, and took out a prayer request card with the available pencil. Placing the card on my knee where Ham could see, in the prayer request slot I wrote the word *GONG*.

I guess you might have to be from the 70's and 80's to understand what that meant. But all of us at one time or another had skipped class to stay at the dorm and watch Chuck Barris and the *Gong Show*. Strange entertainment acts performed in front of celebrity judges, and if they were horrible, one of the judges would grab a large mallet and bang it against a huge Japanese Gong to run them off the stage.

Ham sucked in a deep breath. Then his shoulders began to shake. His face turned a very bright red and looked like a volcano moments from eruption. He could hold it no longer. Starting as a high-pitched squeal, the laugh expanded to a loud guffaw. Trying desperately to control my own snorting, nothing was working. All around us were stares and whispers. We had the attention of the entire church. The first idea was to do our best to look grieved; unfortunately, no one was buying it. There was only one option left, bolt out the back door.

Now I sat with my old friend and was forced to confront this horrible news. We were staring at each other as death once again had come to Ham's front door. It had crept in even closer; this time it was him.

After the laughter, there was not a lot to say. I asked him about his illness and if the doctors were sure. Determined to find a positive solution, we discussed and I questioned for an extended period of time; finally being forced to accept the situation as it really was. Ham had cancer and the prognosis was grim. I left him that day knowing that his time was short.

I didn't see him for a while after that. He was in treatment and I went back to my life. Often time gets away from us, especially when we try to put something out of mind. One evening at home, the phone call came. The message was to come now, because there was not much time. All of us have had that feeling of dread, when you must go do something, and you know it is going to be emotionally difficult. With a heavy heart, I made the trip.

Entering the hospital was a surreal feeling of isolation. The cold marble walls didn't help my mood. Everything seemed so bleak, from the vinyl furniture, to the hard tile floors, to the nurses who wouldn't smile. I didn't want to continue, but felt as though I were being ushered along the hallway. Almost without effort I approached the room, and there he was.

"Rusty," he shouted in a strained and weakened voice.

I said, "Hi Ham," and the chitchat began. We talked about silly stuff, about almost everything except the reason I was there, to say goodbye. It was inevitable; as time passed, I had to leave. That feeling was back, and already the signs of choking up; the huge knot building in my throat and eyes beginning to tear.

Ham looked at me and said, "Time to go, huh." Not able to speak, I just nodded my head, then moved to bedside and gave him a hug. As we embraced, my words squeaked out. "I love you, Ham."

He pushed me back to see my face as he struggled for voice through his tears. "Rusty, am I a bad man?"

I smiled at him as my tears cascaded down onto the hospital sheets that covered his chest. "You wouldn't be my friend if you were."

I clasped his fragile hand with both of mine. We looked at each other one final time. When our eyes met it revealed his fear. I met his gaze with all the love and belief in my soul; I pulled his hand to my face and gave it a kiss, never breaking eye contact. I spoke one final time, choking out, "Be sure and walk into the light."

Ham offered a weak smile as a single tear slowly drifted down his wrinkled face. He turned his gaze to the window and whispered, "Adios, muchacho."

I squeezed his hand a final time, and let go; leaving the room, it was done.

Ham died a few days later.

Chapter 4 – Poland WW2

JOSHUA

Joshua sat looking out the third-story window of the stark but functional bedroom he shared with his sister Sara, examining the dagger his father had given him as a souvenir from his time in the war. He could see the train as it passed through the Jewish Ghetto, no longer stopping at what once was a busy station on the street below. His family was one of the fortunate ones that had two rooms, a bath, and a kitchen. He supposed it was because his father was an important man, a hero from the Polish/Russian War and a leader among the confined Jewish Poles. It wasn't the magnificent farm house they were forced to leave, but his father made it clear that the family would endure and feel fortunate.

Joshua's father was a leading member of the Jewish Council assembled to run the Ghetto and communicate with the Nazi Command. He received a few special privileges for this duty, mostly the advantage of getting early information on what the Nazis were planning. One alarming fact was that the Nazis were increasing the number of detainees in the Ghetto and building more camps. He knew of the great danger and lethal events that were reported from those places, and had even seen the evidence himself.

Another thing bothered him greatly; he had managed the opportunity to talk with his cousin who was being processed that day. The cousin informed him that all family members had been detained and sent to the Ghetto, while other Jewish families had not suffered such a complete and drastic fate. Joshua's father knew this was a bad sign and was angry with himself for not talking earlier to his boy about the secret. In the first twelve years of his life, he had prepared his boy for just about everything, but he hadn't given him the talk.

It was almost time for his father to get home and Joshua eagerly awaited his arrival; neither Joshua nor Sara was allowed outside unless accompanied by him. Joshua fought boredom every day until it was time to explore. The two of them would venture around the building and into the streets and sewers, looking for interesting hiding places and secret travel ways. It wasn't as much fun as the woods and mountains around their home, but it's all they had now. Finally, he heard the front door open and sprinted to it.

His father saw him approach, and asked with a smile, "Have you done well today, son?"

He was quick with his answer, "Yes, sir."

Sara heard the door and came running in, followed by her mother. The two of them could have been a postcard for the beautiful women of Poland. Sara was a precious platinum blonde with sparkling blue eyes and the spitting image of her elegant mother. She leapt into her father's arms.

"Good afternoon, Father!" she said with glee.

"Hello, my princess, and has your highness been good for the queen today?" He asked teasingly.

"Oh yes, haven't I, Mother?" she pleaded emphatically. Her mother nodded approval with a loving smile.

Joshua butted in, "Sir, are we going to explore today?"

His father could see that Joshua needed to get out, and it would also be a good time to talk. "Yes, Joshua, we will explore something very special today," he said with suspense.

Sara excitedly asked, "Oh, can I go? I really want to go."

He thought for a moment and then smiled as he answered, "Yes, my dear, you should go with us today."

Joshua frowned at Sara and said, "You better be able to keep up." Sara cocked her head and stuck out her tongue.

The strapping man gathered his children and gave his wife a kiss, assuring her that they would be home in time for supper. Joshua and Sara grabbed their coats and prepared to depart. Joshua asked about using the secret passage to leave, and his father agreed to meet them in the basement. He had shown them both how to leave the apartment by way of the pipes behind the adjoined kitchen and bathroom walls. He had constructed a hidden entry through the pantry and taught the two youngsters the way to shimmy down the pipes to the basement. Once there, they could exit via a basement window or through a crawl space into the sewer. His goal for this day was to show the children another hiding spot, this one in the cemetery, and also to talk about the secret.

They met in the dark, musty underground floor, and decided to travel by way of the sewer. It consisted of a large brick tunnel with a deep trough running through the middle of the passage way. There was room to walk of about two body widths on either side. Joshua, ever eager, took the lead with the flashlight provided by his father. The smell was overpowering, but the knowledge gained about the sewer tunnels was more important. Joshua was becoming an expert in deciphering the maze that was the underground system. Sara walked hand in hand with her father, holding her nose with the other. There were noises in the sewer that gave it an eerie feel; a frightening affair for Sara. Joshua was different; he considered the sewer a challenge and was eager to move forward.

Abruptly, he stopped dead in his tracks; in front of him stood a huge, hulking figure. The beam of the flashlight gave him the look of a Frankenstein Monster. He wore a dirty, heavy coat, and a huge beard covered a filthy face. Joshua was startled but did not move. The man mumbled and groaned as he waved his arms at the young boy in his path. From behind him, Joshua's father spoke. "Be on your way, you have no business with us."

The hulking figure looked up to see who was speaking. He hesitated for a moment before shaking his head and turning to leave. As he disappeared into the dark regions of the tunnel, Joshua questioned his father. "What was that?"

His father answered. "He is a creature of the sewer. There are more than him; they live here to hide. They have become outcasts that no one pursues or contacts. They can be dangerous if you have something they want. We need to move on before we encounter anymore."

The group exited through a loosened street vent close to the cemetery walls. The entrance to the cemetery was shut off by strands of barbed wire, so they headed toward a hole in the stone wall around the backside. The complex was massive and extended up a long hill. They advanced toward a building situated in the middle. Many of the graves along the way had been looted and head stones taken or overturned. Most everything in the city was plundered or damaged.

Joshua asked, "Father, where are we going?"

He answered, "Toward that large mausoleum." They quickly made their way to the entrance and opened a massive door. Inside was an empty room that hosted a rectangular stand in the center, where a casket was once mounted. No longer being there, the casket probably had fallen victim to looters. Joshua's father stepped to the mount, placed his hands and pushed against it. Slowly sliding, it revealed a hole beneath. Joshua scrambled over quickly to point the flashlight in the hole. He found a tunnel that extended beyond the walls of the mausoleum, out under the grass and bushes surrounding the building.

The family entered the tunnel together with Joshua in the lead. The sides were supported by wooden beams with just enough space for a grown man to crawl through. It was easy work for the children and they were urged to slow down by their larger father. The tunnel took them to a bigger underground room, probably three meters wide and two meters deep. It was topped by a tin roof with handles extending down. Joshua pushed on one handle as his father did on the other. The covering came free and slid to one side of the big hole. The topside of the tin roof was camouflaged with grass and one small bush, giving no clue to its real purpose as the roof for the secret room. They momentarily scanned the cemetery then swiftly moved the top back in place. The three huddled in the hidden space; it was time to talk.

Joshua's father began, "I must tell the two of you something that can never be repeated outside of the family." He paused in the darkness and pointed the flashlight at both of their faces, wanting to make sure he had their attention. "You carry inside of you a special gift that has been passed down through the family for thousands of years. It will be used one day to save this world. It is our duty to keep it alive within us and pass it on until the day it is used."

Joshua immediately questioned, "What is it?" His father smiled at Joshua's relentless curiosity.

"It is a light to show the way. There will be people from far away that will need it as a signal and a guide."

Joshua was persistent, "Who gave us this light? Where is it?"

His father answered, "It was given to us by the people we call the Ancients. They came to our world long before the time of Moses, and left the light with us as a beacon to be used for the time in which they promised to return. It lives within us; it is a part of us."

He paused for a moment to let the information sink in, and then continued on to make a very important point. "There have been evil people throughout the ages who have wished to halt the life of this light. I believe that is happening now. We are all in great danger and must do what we can to keep the light alive." He put his arm around Sara and gave her a big hug, with his other hand he squeezed Joshua shoulder and spoke. "My brave young son, I am so proud of you. If I am gone you will be in charge of keeping your sister safe."

Joshua's eyes were fixed on his father with laser like focus. He nodded his response while Sara began to cry. She whimpered, "Father, I'm scared."

He took his strong arms and fully embraced his young daughter. "Sara, these are scary times but we must push on. I will need you to be strong and listen to Joshua if need be."

She sobbed sweetly, "Ok."

He changed the subject to brighten the mood. "We must get back, I told your mother we would be home for supper." They exited through the tunnel and placed everything back to original position. There was one more stop that needed to be made. The children had to see the evil that was happening if they were going to fully appreciate the gravity of the situation.

They climbed toward the top of the long hill and out passed the cemetery wall near a tree line. Continuing to climb, they came to the top of the ridge and knelt, looking down onto the valley below. A huge camp was being built. Outside the fence line of the new camp, and toward their position on the ridge, was a mound. It was a mountain of human remains being bulldozed under large clumps of moved earth.

With all looking down upon the atrocity, Joshua's father proclaimed, "This is the evil we face and why we must try to survive." They stared down at a scene that later in history would prove to be one of the worst evil acts ever recorded.

Joshua turned away from the bleak view of the camp and asked his father, "Why would they kill so many people?"

His father gathered Sara in his arms as he spoke to Joshua. "I wish I had an answer for you, son, but I just don't know. I've seen very bad things in war, but nothing like this." They began their journey down the hill toward the city as he further explained. "Hatred is caused by ignorance, but this goes far beyond that. What you've just seen is evil, the same evil that hunts us."

Chapter 5 – Kansas–Current Time

THE DARK TRAVELER

Solitary confinement had become the norm. He really didn't mind; he was always alone with his thoughts anyway. It had to be that way; who would want to have a conversation about the last beat of a heart, or the look on a dying man's face.

His favorite moment of death was watching the eyes, first the recognition and fear, then the resignation and final moments. It was an absolute rush for him the instant that life left the eyes, and fascinating for him to observe a body become a carcass with less worth than that of a cow or pig. Blood was messy, but to watch it pulse from the body after the careful slicing of an artery was orgasmic to him.

He hadn't felt this much excitement in years, maybe ever. Life was not bad, he didn't mind the routine of prison, but memories and imagination can only take you so far. His new friend had come to him again, the only concern being that his friend might not be real. It could be his imagination playing tricks, but his friend assured him it was not.

An angel from hell providing him the opportunity to travel in time and kill again, it was too good to be true. He couldn't have dreamed something as precious as this, yet here it was. A traveler, he was told, was extremely rare and very valuable to the dark forces. He would be used for an imperative mission, and be promised a very important position for eternity in the dark side. That fact really didn't motivate him; the opportunity to kill again did.

His mission was to join with the killing machine of the Nazi organization and systematically eliminate the threat. He would be given a thorough list of families to target, but the angel warned him to be discrete. The cover of the Nazi-caused Holocaust would be perfect, but the danger of unintended consequences was a concern, and manipulating history was always a bit tricky. The traveler was anxious about not getting enough hands-on action. He would be determined to not get stuck being an administrator, and be forced away from his true calling, that of a killer. It would be a priority for him to get some action; what a fertile playground he was about to enter.

As promised, the angel had returned. It was time for the traveler to depart. His wicked dark eyes burned with the flames of desire. Receiving his final instructions, his destiny was back in his evil hands. It would be an occasion for killing, his moment in time.

Chapter 6 – New Mexico/West Texas

FAITH

This is an innocent reminder to you that I am a very normal guy from New Mexico, *the Land of Enchantment*. It truly is an enchanting place, a state where you can go from desert to mountaintop in the matter of an hour.

The beautiful painted bluffs of the Navajo Nation rule the west, while the vast and mysterious Carlsbad Caverns hide their awesome presence under the southeast corner. Many wars have left their mark in the form of old Indian battlegrounds around the Pecos Wilderness, and Fort Union from our nation's Civil War. It's the home of the Lincoln County Wars and Billy the Kid, and the birth place of the Atomic Age in Los Alamos. The White Sands represents the awesomeness of nature as well as the commitment to our nation's defense in the White Sands Missile Range. The Native American Culture is vast, varied, and a signature piece of the state. The proud culture of the Spanish Conquistadors is still present in the capital city of Santa Fe today. I could go on; I'm obviously very proud.

The trip to Ham's funeral required leaving my state and crossing the border into Texas. Let me take a moment to tell you about Randy. He was Ham's employer and the common friend I had mentioned before. He was the go-to guy that took care of everything for Ham at the end, keeping us all informed, and there for Ham during the toughest of times. He organized all the arrangements for the funeral, and it was my intention to attend the service with him. I rented a hotel room with my wife Donna and the kids, and made arrangements to see Randy and the rest of the guys the next day. We had a quiet dinner and settled in for the evening. Little did I know what lay ahead, the night that would change my life.

Sleep came easily, but ended around one in the morning with a sharp pain in my lower back. Cloudiness filled my head, not really a fog, more of a swarming mass of tiny lights. Sensing something more, I felt some sort of presence. Multiple attempts to clear my thoughts were unsuccessful, and the sensation continued. An odd voice entered my head and spoke, "Rusty…Rusty."

Not being sure whether to speak or think, this was bizarre. I kept trying to wake myself, but was clearly up. Looking at Donna sleeping peacefully, my decision was not to wake her at this time. I focused and formed the question, "What?"

The voice answered, "How are you?"

"Who is this?"

The voice answered. "It's Ham."

It was definitely time to wake up. Struggling to my feet, I painfully worked my way toward the bathroom, turned on the light, splashed water on my face, and took a good look in the mirror. Secure in the fact that I was now truly awake, another attempt was made at returning to bed.

On the way, once again the voice spoke, "It's really me; I need to talk to you."

Turning back around and wincing in pain, I retreated to the bathroom, turned on the light and shut the door. I took a seat on the toilet and analyzed myself in the mirror. I appeared ok, but was not ok. Goose bumps covered my forearms and thighs, showing signs of stress. Clueless on what to do, I once again gave in to the presence in my head and formed another question. "What is this?"

The voice answered, "We're talking like always, buddy, just different."

I pleaded, "Please leave!"

"Rusty, I need your help," the voice was insistent. "It's really me, Ham; I'm an angel."

At that moment, despite the bizarre nature of all that was happening, the thought came to me that God must have a sense of humor. Ham an angel. I had no idea what all of this was about, but that was just funny.

"Look, I don't know if any of this is real, this is stress or something. I can't see you, and if you really are Ham, what in the hell kind of angel would you be?"

"Just an ordinary angel, that's all there really is. Ok, we got that straight," he declared.

I protested. "No, no, no; we have nothing straight at all."

"Well, you know you're talking to somebody, so why can't it be me; Kinda funny huh?"

"None of this is funny, Ham. Why are you here?"

He said, "I need your help."

I whispered, "Why me?"

Ham replied, "I can't talk to anyone else, but I can to you. You have a gift."

I said, "Great, Ham, I get to be the weird one, what about all the other guys?"

He said, "You're not listening; they can't do this. Like I said, you have a gift."

I retorted, "I don't feel very gifted."

"Well you are," he said. "That's why you can talk to me, plus there's more, but let's just stay with this for now. You have something special and you need to learn to use it."

I bristled. "I don't know if this is real; nothing is making sense."

Ham knowingly replied, "I did a little something to help with that; to make this a bit more believable. Your back is in pain, right?"

"Yes," I said.

He boasted. "That's me, I'm causing the pain. Now I can take it away. I figured you would need some tangible stuff to help you believe. Go ahead, check it out."

In an instant, the pain was gone. I was reeling; this apparently was Ham, but nothing like this had ever happened to me. I was pretty sure that fact had just changed. Not being sure what to do, I decided to cooperate. "Ok, so now what?"

"Sorry about the back, but you're hard to convince sometimes; I had to do something."

I grumbled, "Gee, let's see, I'm thinking of quite a few things you could have done."

Ham said, "Hey, I'm sorry, it's all I could think of at the time."

I was curious. "So you can go around causing pain in people?"

He said, "No, no, just you."

"That's some good news." I answered sarcastically. Ham chose not to respond.

I was ready to get to the point. "Ok, why are you here?"

He laid out a series of things he wanted me to do and say on his behalf to friends and family at his funeral.

"Oh man, you have got to be kidding, the entire place is going to think I'm nuts."

"You can handle it. This is important stuff. Rusty, you have a gift that you can share. With your help they might understand." He had a point, but I still had some reservations.

I said, "Randy will never go for this, and either will your mother."

"They will both be ok; it's just a matter of you getting up and talking."

My thoughts centered around all my friends and other people who would be there, and how stupid I was about to look.

Ham knew what I was thinking and addressed it. "Some will believe and some won't, but the people who need to hear will hear. You will be using your gift, and that is an important step."

The conversation went on through the night, resulting in a written series of things to be said at the funeral. The conversation then turned to information about being an angel. He said angels have a special ability to communicate with people on earth who possess the same gift, explaining that angels only try to help, and don't have the ability to change things. He was confident that my role at the funeral would provide understanding for many people. That made me feel good, but I still wondered and was suspicious of what Ham was really up to.

The next day had to start with an explanation to Donna. This was not going to be easy. I wasn't sure how to start. Before I could begin, she worried, "Something has, happened hasn't it."

I glanced at her and nodded my head. "Ham," is all that came out of my mouth.

"I knew it," she said. "I sensed it. I just had this feeling."

She listened intently to the story, and hung on to every word. I was flabbergasted to hear her support. "You need to do this," she said.

"Everyone is going to think I've lost it," I moaned, desperately looking for a reason not to proceed.

She said, "Well, maybe not everyone."

"Everyone," I insisted.

We ended the conversation with her supporting whatever I decided to do. It was time to go see Randy.

I rang the bell at Randy's house. That feeling of dread was back, how was I going to start this conversation? He answered the door and invited us in. Still getting dressed, he asked me back to the bedroom to talk while he finished.

We entered, and I began the conversation with a concerned apprehension. "This is kind of important."

He paused and sat on the edge of the bed. "What is it?"

I blurted out, "I talked to Ham...last night."

Analyzing me intensively, he searched my face for more information. "Are you sure?"

"Pretty damn sure," I said, and told him the whole story of what Ham had asked me to do.

"Damn," he said.

"Yeah," I answered.

"Randy, I'm really worried about looking stupid in front of everybody."

"I don't blame you."

"Thanks," I said sarcastically.

"Rusty, if this is something you need to do then we should see about it." He was trying to be supportive but there was doubt in his voice.

I was defensive. "Randy, look, I don't want to do any of this, but I told Ham I would."

"No, no, Rusty, I get it… this is just way out there."

"You're telling me," I answered.

Randy continued. "We need to head over to where Ham's mom is staying and talk to her."

It was amazing; he listened to what I had to say, not trying to talk me out of it, or call me crazy. He might have thought it, but bottom line, he was ok to push on. He finished getting ready and joined us in the car for the trip to see Ham's mom.

As we approached the house where she was staying, the knot in my stomach came back again. After all, this was Ham's mom I was about to go in and tell this story to. Randy entered first to talk to her. A few moments later he came for me, and in we went.

"Rusty, it's good to see you," she said with a warm greeting.

The tension was getting to me and my emotions were on edge. I just nodded my head. She was sitting on a big fluffy sofa dressed in a light-blue blouse and comfortable white pants, and asked me to sit down with her.

"Now tell me what you need to talk to me about," she gracefully reassured. Her presence was stunning, so warm and inviting. There had been so much to prevail through in the last year, yet she found a way to comfort me. I didn't want to tell her. I wasn't going to tell her.

"Ouch!" My back was struck with a lightning bolt of pain.

"Are you ok?"

"I'm fine, just a little reminder about something I need to do." Although sure Ham was abusing every rule that governs angels, the message was received.

So I began my story, trying my best to sound sane. As the part about Ham coming to me approached, tears began to trickle down my face. I felt a heavy burden, talking to her about her departed son. I got through it and sat there drained and feeling defeated, knowing I had not made my case.

The elegant woman leaned forward and softly took my hand. She soothingly responded, "I want you to know how much I appreciate you being a part of Ham's life. If Ham told you this needs to be done then you do it."

She turned to Randy and asked him to make me a part of the reception after the service.

Humbly I answered, "I don't know what to say."

She said, "It's nice to have you here. You were an important part of his life. There isn't necessarily anything that needs to be said." She leaned over and gently gave me a hug. Her manner gave me a lift, and reinforced my commitment to Ham's plan.

The funeral itself was a blur. I couldn't tell you one word that was said. And sooner than expected, I found myself at a table with my friends and family. It was the reception, and it was time.

I would love to tell you that I was magnificent and eloquent. I would love to tell you I was even functional. But what I was, even after all that had happened, was still undecided. Randy served as a master of ceremonies, and when it came time, he glanced back. He was giving me time to make a decision. I looked at him and pleaded with my eyes for help.

Stepping back, he turned and whispered with a hint of impatience, "It's up to you."

"Really appreciate the support," I fraudulently murmured.

I was expecting another lightning bolt, but it didn't come. It was as if Ham had brought me to this point and was leaving it up to me as well. I thought about Donna, Randy, and Ham's mom. In an odd but real way, their faith was resting with me. They had all given the green light to follow through with this and I was just about to bail. Everything was ready, but still lingering was the commitment to take the plunge. I thought back on my history with Ham; we always had each other's back, and I knew what had to be done. Standing, I stepped to the middle of the floor, gathered all available courage, and pulled out the prepared speech.

The reception hall was set with tables and chairs semi-circling the open area in which I was standing. The chairs were filled with family and friends, all of whom were curious why some guy might be addressing them.

It had to begin with a short explanation. "I have a short speech that Ham asked me to read. We wrote this speech together." I paused. "Thing is, we wrote it together last night."

The room began to buzz with whispering, and then a big man angrily stood up. "What the hell is this, and by the way who the hell are you?"

Randy stepped forward with his hand up. He insisted, "Bob, sit down and let him finish." The big man shook his head in frustration but returned to his chair. Randy gave me a nod to continue, and Ham's speech began.

"Hello everyone. By now you've met Rusty, and I imagine he's not feeling too welcome. So, Bob, unlock that jaw, Cynthia, get that look off your face, and Tracy quit him/hawing." I quickly scanned the room and saw a few smiles, then continued.

"I've grown up with most of you and know you well. Hell, I've been playing ball and taken showers with you boys all my life. There

are no secrets, I've seen you naked. Now that I think about it; I've seen just about everyone in the room naked."

At that point, there were many women staring at the floor, with plenty of uncomfortable foot shuffling and throat clearing throughout the room. One woman dressed in a bright flower-print dress, adorned with a grand yellow Easter hat, sat smiling.

I pushed on. "*I figure everyone is a little uneasy. Well, except you, Doris, I know you're smiling, and I have always appreciated your free spirit. I asked Rusty here to do this. He has a gift, and I want him to use it, but I also wanted to talk to you all.*

"I walked into the light awhile back and found something I never could before. Mama, I always knew you loved me, and now I understand how. It is the pure purpose of a mother's love, the selfless gift of accepting grace.

"All my life I could do things, but I'll be damned if I knew why I wanted to do them, didn't have much regard for consequences. Now I do, and you know, all of you need that too. I call it stuff; you just need more stuff. It's not what you know that is important; it's what you understand about what you know."

Raising my eyes to check the room, it was apparent that all eyes were on me and focused in. The tension had calmed a bit, so I pressed on.

"You see, understanding is to knowledge, as soil, water, and sun, are to a seed. Once you understand something it will blossom, then and only then will it reveal its full beauty and the benefits of its purpose.

"Boys, I'm telling you, if you love a gal but you don't understand her, there's going to be a lot of pain, no matter. But if you understand her, she will bear the fruit of love beyond what you ever imagined it could be.

"If a man willingly gives another man a hundred dollars and understands why, and that man takes the money, appreciates it and uses it with great purpose, the resulting outcome will have value at the bank and in the heart. Those boys will be tighter than stink on a stockyard.

"If you use something, it will produce its worth. But if you share the same, you will feel the strength of common commitment and reap the benefits of enlightened purpose. All I'm sayin, that's stuff.

"You can know all there is to know in this world, but you're only as good as what you understand about what you know. Now just be good to each other. Honor and reach out to those who need it. Do another man a favor, without asking anything in return. Grab your partner and share with them something that you should have said a long time ago; that's stuff. Get out on the floor, give it a whirl and just talk about stuff."

After giving Randy the prearranged queue, he punched a button for music to start, and the signal for the end of the speech. Ham had requested Willie Nelson's rendition of "Remember Me" to be played. People took the floor around me as if I weren't there. I anonymously left, dodging dancing couples and making my way toward my final destination.

That last stop was Ham's ex-wife and boys. On approach, I congenially said hi, having always been friends. Speaking apologetically, I said, "I know this is all hard to believe."

She smiled saying, "Well, yes it is."

I pulled the speech out from my pocket and continued our conversation. "There's one more part to the speech, but it's just intended for you." She seemed surprised, but gestured her ok to go on.

I began. *"The best likeness I ever made was of you to the most beautiful flower ever grown. I am so thankful our boys have you to guide their path. I celebrate the happiness that is your life; if only I could catch that first tear you shed because of me and mend it to your heart. You are a treasure, and I finally understand."*

Looking up, my eyes found her struggling for composure. Tears were attempting to escape their mascara-rimmed containment. She gently laughed through her response. "That boy always could talk."

"Yes, Ma'am," I said.

There was one more job to do; I needed to talk to the boys. With permission to do so, my attention shifted to them. There really wasn't much to say to them. The task was simple, put my hand on their hearts. I approached the oldest with his mom by my side, and feeling more calm than I had all day.

I explained. "Your dad asked me to do something with you."

The boy was very aware of the situation, having watched my performance earlier. Considering all that he had witnessed, it was brave of him to nod his ok. The palm of my right hand slowly lifted towards him and gently landed on the chest area of his heart. His eyes flared wide as he caught my gaze.

I said, "I don't know what this means exactly, but your dad asked me to do this. He said you would know." He smiled with appreciation, his eyes lit with recognition. I heard the tiniest of whimpers and turned my head to see tears rolling down his mother's face. She gave me a wondering look.

I was missing something here; Ham had not given me complete information. I turned back to the boy. He waved for his little brother to come, then reached around at the shoulders and embraced him with his arm. His other hand moved around my wrist. Taking charge of my hand, he placed it over his little brother's heart. The little one had his attention on me, seeming confused but excited.

The older boy spoke. "It's Dad. He's here."

The little boy gripped my hand as hard as he could squeeze, he wasn't sure whether to smile or cry. It must have been apparent that I was clueless to what was going on; the older boy began to explain the story of his dad leaving home.

When Ham moved out of the house, there was a final talk with the boys. Wanting them to know he would always be there for them, he placed his hand over their hearts and told them even though he would not always be around, he would always be right there, in their hearts. Over the years, this had become the standard way that Ham would greet and say goodbye to the boys when they were together. I had to laugh; just like Ham to steal an idea from *ET*.

My mission was complete. I got a big hug and thank you from Ham's ex, and said goodbye to the boys. One final scan of the room, as if in the final scene of a movie. It was a rap.

Knowledge vs. Understanding

Finding Donna and Randy, we made arrangements with all the others to meet at a restaurant, then left the scene; the scene of what exactly? Well, I wasn't sure.

At the restaurant, I reflected on the past two days and being part of some bigger picture than just being contacted by Ham. Was this some kind of faith-building opportunity for me? Was my duty actually being a witness, or was I learning something about my gift? I had been given an opportunity to communicate ideas he thought were important, but I sensed it was more of a test for me. There was more to it.

It was time, and a long drive lay ahead. I found Randy to say goodbye. "Gotta go, my friend. Thanks for your help."

He offered, "That was a hell of a day." He continued with a question. "Are you comfortable with everything that happened today?"

I answered, "Comfortable? No I'm not comfortable; there's more to this. Ham has more in mind, but I don't know what."

He laughed. "Oh brother. Well it won't hurt my feelings if you leave me out of it."

I grinned. "I can't guarantee anything, but I'll see what I can do." We hugged, then taking my seat behind the wheel, I drove off into the night.

Driving home was going well. I was wide awake and everyone else was sound asleep. I was listening to the radio daydreaming and relaxing after two tough days. "Rusty....Rusty!"

"Nope, I'm not answering. I'm tired, Ham."

"Come on, I thought it went great, didn't you?"

I said, "Great? Most of greater West Texas thinks I'm nuts."

Ham proclaimed. "You were tremendous."

I admitted, "It was special for your boys."

Ham said proudly. "Yeah, they're so sweet, you did good buddy."

I asked, "Ham, what was all that about? What was it all for?"

He contemplated. "Well let's see, you helped a lot of people think, and a few understood. You turned sorrow into love because of your selfless act. But most importantly, you were able to use your gift and see the benefit of courageous action with purpose."

He was definitely giving me a sales pitch, but it did make me feel good. We drove on for a while and I was waiting for what was next.

"Rusty! Hey, there's something I need you to help me with."

The other shoe finally dropped. I obliged and asked. "What exactly requires my help?"

"First, you need to understand," he said cryptically.

"What's that supposed to mean?" I groaned.

"There's going to be tons of stuff for you to accept, and if you don't understand you won't trust, and if you don't trust you won't help." We drove for a while, and nothing was said. I figured Ham was giving me some time to myself to think. It had been an exhausting day and I really wasn't in an understanding mood.

He continued. "Rusty I need to tell you more about your gift. You truly are very special."

I said with a yawn, "Yep, that's me, Mr. Special."

He insisted. "I'm serious, you have a gift that very few have ever had and the world is going to need it."

I questioned, "The world is going to need my gift of talking to you?"

Ham gave an obligatory laugh. "No, knucklehead, it's way more than that, but I know you're tired. The rest can wait for now. Rusty, just think about this: if you could help more people than you ever could imagine by using your gift, would you do it? Would you be willing to accept and use that gift even if it meant your life would change forever? My friend, there is much to think about. But for now, I will leave you with that, and talk to you later. I am out of here; adios, muchacho!"

That was it; he was out of my head as quickly as he had come in. I drove the rest of the way deep in thought over what Ham had said. We made it home. The family piled out of the car, into the house and plunged into bed.

I woke late the next morning and trudged to the kitchen for some coffee and mental decoding while sipping a well-made cup of brew. Was I crazy? No, there was enough evidence to know this was real. The ensuing question was the important one. What would be next? I guessed that would come out when he contacted me again. What could be so important?

Chapter 8–Poland WW2

Family Divided

Joshua, Sara, and their father left the cemetery, making the decision to stay on the streets for the trip home. Block after block, the haunting buildings loomed on either side. The boarded-up windows and yellow stars sloppily painted on doors reminded them of the horrible context in which they lived. The three- and four-story buildings cast an ominous shadow over the path as the family navigated the deserted streets.

Up ahead, Joshua could hear gunfire and turned with concern to his father. They stopped to listen and evaluate; from a rooftop Joshua heard his name. He looked up and saw Daniel, one of the boys that lived in the neighborhood close to them. Daniel began franticly climbing down the drains and window ledges of the building. They moved toward him. He was in a panic and spoke rapidly. "You must turn around, we need to hide!"

Joshua's father helped Daniel down from the ledge and tried to calm him. "Ok, Daniel, tell me what has happened."

He blurted out, "The Nazis have raided our building and are taking everyone."

With great concern, the man took Daniel by the shoulders and stared intently into his eyes. "Tell me what they were saying." He was speaking very sternly and it sent a chill through Joshua.

Daniel began to tear as he pointed toward the camp. His voice was a whimper, "They are taking them there." Daniel continued, shaking his head in confusion. “I don’t know anything else; my father sent me to the roof to hide.”

Joshua’s father was deep in thought; he turned to his son with a grave look. He spoke to him as if he were an adult. “I must go to your mother.” He took his young son’s shoulder in his firm hand, his eyes determined yet strained with emotion. “This is the time of which we spoke, you must watch over Sara and be prepared to take action.”

Joshua tearfully nodded and threw himself into his father’s arms. The strong man embraced his son and battled to stay composed. Releasing him, he turned to Sara; her beautiful blue eyes were stained red, tears streaming down her delicate cheeks. He knelt in front of her and took her hands, no longer able to hide his tears.

“Sara, you must promise me that you will follow your brother’s lead.” The little girl acknowledged him, then gently collapsed into her father’s chest.

She gushed. “I love you, Father.” He gave her a big hug and reached for Joshua to gather them both together.

He affirmed, “Your mother and I love you both so very much.”

Time was an issue; he knew he must refocus and get the children in a safer place. Turning to Joshua he commanded, “Take Sara and Daniel to the sewers and wait at the hiding point near our building. Give me three hours, and if I don’t meet you, move to the cemetery.” He stood and motioned for them to be on their way. Joshua stood and drew a final gaze from his father; it was strong and full of strength. The boy accepted it with the slightest of bows, and then turned to Sara and Daniel. With authority in his voice, he urged them to move out. Their father stood heartbroken as he watched the children leave; he knew it would be for the last time.

Chapter 9 – New Mexico/ late 1990's

ADVERSITY

Knowing Ham too well, his last visit confirmed that the funeral was secondary to what he actually had in mind. Yes, he was sending a message to his friends and family, but he was definitely using that opportunity to educate me. I wondered about a gift that could be so special, and I worried about his statement about my life changing forever. I kept coming back to Ham's mantra about understanding; "*It's not about what you know but what you understand about what you know.*"

So I got it; the big picture is about greater understanding, which can take you far beyond what you initially perceive. The unsettling part was taking that and applying it to myself. I was beginning to realize the depth of experiences it took to know something well enough to claim understanding of it. Whatever Ham had in mind for me, whatever my gift would turn out to be, he was adamant about my understanding of what it meant and what was at stake. With every thought of it came the knot in my stomach.

Life was going well for Donna and me. We were cruising along while watching our children gradually learn the basics of life. It was one of those days. We had the kids in the car headed for supper at a pizza joint. Our car entered an intersection at the same time as a truck going a hundred miles an hour.

"Hello, Rusty." It was a women's voice. I felt very strange. The room was swirling and my head wouldn't focus. A terrible headache dominated any concrete thoughts. A bed was beneath me, but felt as if it were airborne. Being completely disoriented with no idea where I was forced a mental question. "What is going on?"

The woman beside me asked if I could hear her voice. The room continued to swirl and I wanted to vomit. Everything was a blur. I tried to speak but to no avail. The voice told me to relax. She mentioned an accident and being in a hospital. Fatigue consumed me, and my eyes could not stay open.

I sensed myself drifting... drifting, further and further down a path. I came to a warm and very comfortable spot. On one side was an inviting bright light, warm and peaceful. To the other was a pulsating dark presence. There were two paths; one leading toward the peaceful light, the other into the alluring darkness. The light was so serene, while the darkness oozed with energy. I began to drift toward the light; it was so beautiful and inviting. I thought to myself that I would just stay here.

A voice came to me: "Rusty, go back." I couldn't tell where the voice was coming from and wasn't sure if it was a man or women. It was just a voice. I didn't want to go. The voice repeated, "Go back, you have much to do."

The room returned along with a massive headache; this time I could see. There were curtains all around and the constant beep of a monitor. I remembered being told something about a hospital. "Welcome back, Rusty." A nurse grabbed my hand. "Can you feel that?" she asked. I tried to answer but realized a tube was in my mouth. I blinked my eyes, and she got the message. "Good, I will be right back with the doctor."

He entered the room and came to my bedside. "Rusty, you have been in a very bad accident. You have been asleep for two weeks. It's nice to have you back. Please don't try to talk right now. Stay awake as long as you can but don't strain to do so. You are making very good progress. I will check with you often. We are very glad you're back."

He left the room with the nurse, and I was alone with no idea what had happened, not remembering anything. "Where was everyone?" It was time to investigate what was wrong with me. I could move my hands and feel my feet, but couldn't seem to move my legs. My head was held stationary and bandaged all over. I realized that I was pinned down and imprisoned on the bed, and began to panic. The monitor beep began to increase; in rushed the nurse to check. She examined my eyes and could tell I was scared. Encouraging me to relax, she told me to focus on breathing, assuring me that I was doing fine, but it was important to stay calm. She was going to increase my medication. I felt myself relax and breathe more easily; very sleepy.

I woke up to see a nurse standing next to me. "Hi, Rusty, glad you're back." She seemed genuinely happy to see me awake. "We're going to take your tube out tomorrow."

I tried to talk and was able to gag out a question. "Where is my family?"

She understood me but hesitated to answer, then decided to speak. "Rusty, I'm so sorry, your wife and kids are gone. You had a terrible car accident and they are gone." My head felt like it was going to explode. The nurse became concerned. "Please, Rusty, you must relax." I tried to kick my way out of the bed but I was still pinned down. She apologized again and adjusted my medication.

The next thing I remembered was in the hospital room with no more tube in my throat. I had a brace around my neck but could move and feel all parts. There was a cast on my left leg. I was still heavily bandaged around the head and felt as if a very bad nightmare was finally coming to an end. Finding and pushing the call button, the nurse came promptly in to see me. "Good morning, Rusty. It's good to see you awake."

"How long have I been here?" I asked.

"This is you're third week in the intensive care unit," she answered.

"My family, where are my wife and kids?"

"Rusty, I am so very sorry, but they were killed in the accident."

"What accident! I don't remember an accident. I don't know what you're talking about." Confusion reigned, a nurse telling me my family was dead. I was sure there had been a mistake.

"Ham!...Ham, you get in here!"

The nurse was holding my hand. "Rusty, there's no one here but me."

"No, no, no!...Ham, you answer me now!"

"Rusty, you've had a traumatic head injury and I really need you to calm down."

I screamed, "Calm down! Ham, you son-of-a-bitch, get your ass in here right now and fix this!"

The nurse moved toward my medication. "I'm sorry, Rusty, but I must keep you calm."

Another room, it looked more like a hotel room, not a hospital. A man walked in the door and greeted me.

"Rusty, I'm your physical therapist. You have been moved to a rehab hospital. My name is Hal."

I asked, "Why don't I remember moving?"

"You've been under some very heavy medication over the last six weeks. Your doctors felt that it was best while your brain recovered."

"How bad is it?" I asked.

He said, "Quite a bit of swelling and memory loss. We won't really know until you get to work in your rehab." He smiled. "That's my job."

Chapter 10 – New Mexico/ late 1990's

STUFF

The task of beginning rehab was daunting and a job all to itself. A crushed leg and a brain injury were all consuming, so my new work devoured much of my day. There was a great deal of swelling in my face, and no memory of the accident. Add to it, a faulty memory over the last two months, remembering only bits and pieces of my intensive care time, and you have quite a mess. Being told that I was near death made me wonder if that was the path and warm spot that I had experienced.

Avoiding everything and being vacant of emotion was easier, so I refused to face the world. Just to crawl up in bed and sleep until it was time for rehab was my goal; contact with the outside world was the nurses and Hal.

I actually liked Hal a lot. He worked me hard but was very patient, especially with my memory rehab. After finishing physical therapy for my leg, we would spend long periods of time going through all procedures associated with strengthening brain function and memory retention. He understood my unwillingness to socialize, but would always try to gently push me out into the world. "Rusty, you have to get out there sooner or later."

I countered, "I just don't feel like it. There's nothing out there I want."

Hal frowned. "I don't think that's true."

"Hal, I'm not the same guy. I don't have anything to say."

"Whatever," he sighed. "You talk too much when I'm around," he said, smiling.

Hal was good to me but definitely the guy in charge around the wing, giving out orders and always making sure the staff was doing what they were assigned at all times. One day I kidded him, "You're kind of a hard ass aren't you?"

He laughed. "You're just now figuring that out? You're not as far along as I thought."

If a day went by and I didn't mourn Donna and the kids, a guilty feeling filled my next day. I was getting better physically, but emotional stability was really a struggle. It was just easier not to confront anybody that wanted a reaction from me; who should tell me how to feel? Nothing, that's what I wanted, feel nothing and express nothing.

Three months had gone by and exercise progressed to walks outside. Some lost brain function was returning, still there was memory loss and cognitive problems, but I had made dramatic progress. Anger toward the accident remained, and with it was my anger at Ham.

I was there for him time after time, and when I needed him most, he was AWOL. It was always all about Ham. I had to force myself not to think about it; if I did, all that was accomplished was anger and pain. So I did my work and kept my routine.

Chapter 11 – New Mexico/ 2000

Reality Check

Hal came to the room one morning with some news. "Rusty, we are going to move you to a new facility in Albuquerque. I will be transferring with you."

I was confused. "Why Albuquerque?"

Hal sat down and got comfortable to explain. "You have made great progress but there are still holes in your memory and your retention. We believe your brain function has a chance to return completely with continued therapy." He paused to give me time to question.

I did question. "Ok I get that, but why Albuquerque, why can't we do that here?" Hal shifted uneasily in his chair.

He leaned forward for emphases to speak. "We are putting you in protection."

I gave Hal a flabbergasted look as I asked, "What in the hell are you talking about?"

He continued. "Rusty, there is a lot you can't remember about the accident and details that you don't remember before, during and after the crash." He became very serious and official. "In fact, it was not an accident; you were targeted."

What do you say to something like that? What in the world? I had a million questions flying through my head. Who would want to kill me? Why was a physical therapist talking to me about protection? Now that I thought about it, Hal was always around. So who was he? I decided to start with some answers from him.

"So who are you, Hal?" I was staring him down.

He sat back in his chair and tried to explain. "Rusty, I've been assigned to help you and also protect you. That's all I can say."

I stayed on him. "You say assigned, by whom?"

"I'm not at liberty to tell you, but you've got to believe me, Rusty, I'm on your side. The only thing I can tell you is you're a high priority, or I wouldn't be here."

I went silent, desperately needing to think. Nothing was making sense; this was just like another bad dream. I continued to search for a clue to why anyone would go to the trouble of trying to kill me. Why would I be a high priority to anyone? There had to be something that tied all of this together. Finally it hit me: Ham.

I asked Hal a question already knowing the answer, "Do you happen to know who Ham is?"

He said, "Never heard of him."

Shaking my head I said. "Of course you haven't, and you're not going to tell me if you have." I thought to myself, *If I could just get my hands around Ham's little pencil neck.*

I probed with another question. "Ok, let's just say I go to Albuquerque; what's the plan?"

Hal was ready. "We will continue therapy until you are ready to return to teaching. Then, we are going to change your name and get you a job in the Albuquerque area."

I was shocked. "Change my name? No way!"

Hal was trying to be gentle. "Rusty, tell me your last name."

I gave him an odd look and then opened my mouth to speak. Oh come on, I knew my last name, just say it. Oh my god! How do I not know my last name. All this time and I didn't realize that? I looked at Hal speechless.

Hal took the opening to hammer home a point. "Rusty, do you realize that you've never asked about family and friends? You have not asked about visitors. When you began rehab with me we had extensive conversations about family and all you could come up with were Donna and your children. Further, you have no recollection of those talks. You don't remember huge parts of your history."

Hal was trying to explain the situation I was in. "You're in great danger, and now is a good time to make an adjustment like this. We believe your mental abilities will return, and you will get back normal function; but we also must keep you alive."

I sarcastically quipped, "Hal, normal has left the building."

He smiled and continued. "We will locate on the Air Base in their specialized treatment center. I think in six months to a year you will be much better. After that, it's back to work with your new identity."

I was concerned. "Hal, who is trying to kill me?"

He consoled. "Rusty, everything about you is highly classified from the highest levels. I don't have anything to tell you; even if I did, I couldn't."

I asked, "Is this for good? Will I ever be able to see anyone that I remember?"

Hal said, "As far as the rest of the world knows; you died on the operating table after the accident. You've had extensive plastic surgery to your face and have a much different look. As far as who you remember, if you haven't remembered by now, the chances of any more returning are minimal."

Stunned and confused, I had not accepted the full consequences of the accident, and now nothing would ever be the same. A new identity and a new life; I felt very alone. Venting some frustration with Hal, I mockingly asked, "What happens when I go back to work? Are you guys going with me to class?"

Hal stayed patient. "No, you won't see anyone but me when you leave the base. You will get a place to live and I will be your contact."

I kept my sarcasm. "Are you going to dress up as my mother?"

"Better," he said smiling. "I think I'll be your brother."

Chapter 12 – Poland WW2

THE HUNT

The Nazi organization was a perfect fit for him. He had so much power, and so many around him willing to kill. His good fortune had led him to the Jewish Ghetto. It was time to clear the city and send the remaining Jews to the camps. He was so excited; after all, he could kill on a whim with very little apprehension from those around him. Staying focused was a key; he knew his real job and what needed to get done.

The family had been tracked to this apartment building, but only the mother was home. Interrogating the woman would come first, but he doubted that would provide much information. She was a beautiful blonde, and he had thought about having his way with her, but as always with him, the seductive thought of killing clearly had more influence than sex. It would be a waiting game to see who or what might turn up.

There was a commotion at the door and he turned to see. *Perfect,* he thought. The husband had conveniently returned, but not with the children. It was time to go to work, so he approached the man, his body pulsated with adrenaline. What a wonderful opportunity to take life. He felt so dominant. There was sure to be terror and fear.

He addressed the husband. "Your children, where are they?" He wasn't expecting an answer; in fact, he hoped to not get one. Slowly walking towards the wife and removing his pistol from its holster, he pointed it at her head and spoke to him again. "I think you should tell me where the children are."

Joshua's father stood motionless with a violent stare toward the window. The Traveler smiled at him with almost a giggle. The husband reasoned. "There is no need to kill her; she does not carry the gene."

The traveler was impressed. "So you know why I'm here; you're right, she doesn't have to die, but I must have the children."

The wife commanded her husband, "Don't you dare say a word."

The traveler let out a chuckle. The woman's words ended her life. The pistol shot resonated throughout the building and to the streets and sewers below. He most wanted to see the reaction of the husband, but it was disappointing; he stood stoic with eyes closed.

His victim lay lifeless on the floor, and he paused a moment to frame the incident in his head. Experience had taught him to savor these precious occasions; this one with the added spectacle of the husband watching. Alas, it was time to move on, and he raised his eyes to his next victim. Slowly he moved, looking for any type of fear. He desperately wanted to know what this man was thinking.

"Spare yourself the torture and tell me where the children are." The man said nothing. The Traveler continued. "Spare your children this life of running; if you give them to me they will die with no pain. But if you don't, I will hunt them down like rats."

Joshua's father shifted his eyes for the first time to meet the Traveler's stare with an overpowering one of his own. He had one final thing to say. "You will pay one day for what you have done. I gladly give my life for my children to live on."

The Traveler was uncomfortable with the intensity of this man. There was no drama, and where was the fear? He let out a long sigh; all he had planned was ruined. *Oh well,* he thought, then lifted his pistol and fired.

A noise came from the kitchen. The Traveler alertly pointed his finger in that direction; the soldiers quickly moved to investigate. They reported the noise as coming from the wall.

He ordered, "Rip it apart." The squad slammed into the wall with the butts of their rifles, ripping through the plaster and exposing the vertical tunnel that housed the building's pipes. Immediately the Traveler ordered his men to deploy. He sent two to the roof and the rest to the streets and sewer below. He was close, and felt the anticipation of the kill.

Chapter 13 – Poland WW2

FUGITIVES FROM EVIL

Joshua held Sara's hand as they entered a main corridor of the sewer; Daniel followed closely behind. Joshua's mind was racing with questions and worry; the look on his father's face had been strong, but Joshua saw the sadness in his eyes. They came to a spot with a large beam crossing the sewer trough; their destination was a cavity behind the merging tunnel wall on the far side. The crossing would be tricky. The tunnel was dark and moist and a false step could plunge them into the blackness below.

Joshua took the lead and shot the beam of the flashlight downward to guide his progress. Carefully he placed his foot on the beam to check the surface. His analysis was wet but not slick. Turning to Sara and Daniel he asked, "Are you ready?" Daniel nodded; Sara gave her brother the look she always gave him when he tried to baby her. They crossed without incident.

A sudden noise from around the corner in the adjoining tunnel put Joshua on alert. Someone was there. Joshua motioned everyone toward the wall. Slowly he made his way toward the intersection of the two tunnels. It wasn't a patrol; it could be a rat; he was about to find out. Flashing his light around the corner, he spied a pair of boots jutting out from the cover of the wall. Strangely, no reaction came from the owner. Joshua made a decision to turn the corner and shine his light on whoever was at hand. There stood a boy, Joshua figured about his age, dressed well enough in a coat and wool hat.

He asked, "Who are you?"

"Joseph," was the reply.

Joshua continued to look him over, then asked, "Where did you come from?"

Joseph answered with tears welling in his eyes, "They took my family, but I ran."

Joshua knew he was talking about the Nazis and had to make a quick decision. "Come with me," he said. Joseph followed him around the corner to where Daniel and Sara waited. Joshua gathered the group and guided them to a specific area of bricks on the tunnel wall. The adhesive mortar was loose or missing on some of the bricks. Placing his hands on two of them, he pushed. They toppled into a space on the far side. He repeated the act until the opening was wide enough to squeeze a small body through. The hiding spot behind the wall was a small cavity formed by a large concrete support for the two merging sewer tunnels. The space fell between the sewer support and the foundation of the building above. Joshua settled the group inside and turned his flashlight on Joseph for more questioning. "Who is your family?"

Joseph answered, "We are gypsies from the river. The Nazis surprised us while we were trading goods near the city. They forced us here and took my mother and father. That's when I ran. My father told me to."

Joshua pointed to the other two. "This is Sara and Daniel. Sara is my sister and Daniel is our friend. We are all running, but I have many places to hide."

Sara stuck her hand out toward Joseph. "Nice to meet you," she said. They shook hands, as did Daniel. Sara asked, "Where did they take your family?"

Joseph answered emotionally, "I don't know. We were brought to the city and came to a check point. My father attacked one of the guards and told me to run. I was able to get to an alley and jump in the sewer. I've been down here ever since.

Daniel asked, "How long has that been?"

He responded, "I think about two days, I'm not sure." The boy was in shock, and with a bit of desperation in his voice declared, "The rest of our clan doesn't even know where we are; we live on the river at least three valleys away. They will never find us. I must find my parents."

Joshua counseled, "Not a good idea right now. It would be better to stay with us until we know more."

Sara added, "Stay with us and my father will help you find your parents when he comes for us."

Joseph was weak with dehydration and hunger. Sitting on the concrete floor signaled that he was accepting Sara's offer.

The conversation reminded Joshua that his father was past due, which prompted his decision to go take a look. He informed Sara, "I'm going to go look for Father. I will be back soon."

Sara grabbed his arm and pleaded, "Please be careful."

Joshua nodded his pledge and then addressed the group. "When I go, put the bricks back in place. Nobody leave until I return, and stay silent." He waited until he had assurances from all three, then crawled out and began his trek toward the building where he hoped to find his mother and father.

Being on his own allowed for quick travel, and he soon shined the flashlight on the makeshift entry point to the apartment above. His decision to enter through the pipes was based on the unknown situation in the apartment.

He proceeded with caution into the opening that led to the pipes. Once there, he positioned himself between the wall and pipes and began to shimmy his way up. As Joshua got closer, he could hear voices, then a gun shot. Fear raced through him, not for himself but for what might be happening in the apartment. He hurried his climb and came to the opening at the kitchen. The voice of a man was speaking in the room just beyond the kitchen.

Joshua recognized it as his father's voice and was struck with terror. His father spoke of dying for his children. The ensuing gunshot stunned Joshua, sending him clanking back against the pipes. His head was swimming with worry and confusion. The order to deploy alerted him that he had been discovered. Gathering himself, he instinctively sped down the pipes. Common sense told him it would be a race with the Nazis to escape the sewer. There was no time to think about his parents; he had to make it to Sara and the boys and get them out.

Joshua hit the sewer in a full sprint; dangerous travel in the wet darkness. He was quickly approaching the group and began shouting. "Sara, let's go! Daniel, Joseph, let's go!" First to peek from behind the wall was Daniel as he pushed the loose bricks onto the pathway. He could see the flashlight beam bouncing as it rapidly approached. Joshua yelled, "Come on, get moving."

Daniel waved for the other two and came out to join Joshua in the sewer. Joshua explained with hurried breath, "The Nazis are right behind, follow me out. We must hurry." Joshua grabbed Sara's hand and led her across the beam, and the boys came right behind. Holding Sara's hand, Joshua increased the pace to a trot, knowing they had to exit the sewer soon or be trapped.

The group came to a vent located fairly near the cemetery where Joshua wanted to exit. The boys climbed the exit ladder side by side and worked as a team to move the large vent grate to one side. Joshua climbed to street level and took a look. He was developing a plan in his head, anticipating that Nazi patrols would be approaching. It would be wise to have a decoy to draw attention if need be, and the only man for the job was him. He looked down into the sewer and alerted Sara. "When I take off give me thirty seconds; then move everyone to the hiding place in the cemetery."

Sara nodded that she understood. Joshua knew they must not delay. "Ok, here we go." He sprinted out to the middle of the street and headed in the opposite direction of the cemetery, running until he reached the adjoining street and turned the corner. At the end of the block stood the Nazi patrol and the Traveler. Joshua stopped in his tracks and immediately turned and sprinted in the opposite direction. Not wanting to lead the patrol back to Sara and the boys, he turned the corner and continued away from the group.

The Traveler ordered, "Shoot him." The soldiers raised their rifles and fired. Joshua heard the bullets slam into the bricks of the building as he made his turn. Speed was his ally to avoid the patrol. His other thought was to move up and out of sight. He sprinted hard for the alley further up the street and made a quick turn. Like a monkey, he began to climb the fire escape attached to the alley side of the first building. It would be crucial for him to be on top of the three-story building before the patrol came into view.

Joshua made the top just as the patrol crossed the alleyway. The Nazis paused for a moment to make a quick scan of the area. Finding nothing, they advanced up the street in search of the elusive boy. Joshua caught his breath and peeked over the edge of the roof. He saw the patrol on the move and heading onward. Now it was possible to back track and head for the cemetery. It wouldn't take him long; he just hoped that Sara and the boys had made it.

Racing across the connecting rooftops, he reached the street adjacent to his destination. Carefully making his way down, he checked for street traffic, then quickly crossed. The next obstacle was to climb over the tall rock wall that guarded the gravesites on the far side. With ease, he shimmied his way to the top and then hopped to the ground. Once inside, he weaved his way through the gravesites toward the mausoleum, and entered through the large door. Crawling down the tunnel, he was very relieved to find the group waiting for him.

Sara gushed, "Joshua, I was so worried." She leaned forward and gave him a big hug. She continued, "Where are Mother and Father?"

Joshua could not look at her. She asked again. "Joshua, where are mother and father."

He had been too consumed with the escape to deal with the tragedy until this moment. His heart was breaking and he could only mumble his response in anguish. With eyes closed he said, "They are gone Sara; just gone."

Chapter 14– New Mexico/ late 1990's

CONFRONTATION/ ACCEPTANCE

And soon a year had passed after the accident, and with it a standard routine had developed at the base. It was apparent that I was stronger in focus, getting physically in shape, and feeling good. Still, there was a huge hole in my heart. But I was functional and able to put a few things into perspective, knowing many important areas in my life needed to be addressed.

There was also a lot of conflicting emotion about the accident, or as now was evident, the attempt on my life. Did I get my family killed? Not feeling responsible, I suspected who was, and wondered if Ham would ever come around again. There was so much to be accounted for, and anger brewed within me.

It was time to go back to teaching. There was a feeling of insecurity about my memory, but the scores of the content test in my science subject area came back just fine. It was a matter of jumping back in and getting after it. Hal arranged a teaching and coaching position for me on Indian Reservation just outside of Albuquerque, on land that nestled up beside the Rio Grande River.

It was a beautiful and lengthy stretch of river that was edged by what is called the Bosque. The river spawned the growth of large trees and foliage in this area that guarded the banks for up to half a mile on either side; in stark contrast to the barren landscape of the dessert climate outside of the river's influence. The entire river valley was framed by the towering and majestic Sandia Mountains, truly a beautiful place to locate. It was also isolated, and the underlying reason why Hal had made that choice.

Hal posed as a federal environmental specialist in charge of protecting and conserving the resources in the Bosque. This gave him the opportunity to work closely with tribal leaders as well as law enforcement from the state and the tribal police. There would be no new faces around that he would not know about.

One of the officers on the force of the Tribal police was Jonah Washington. He and sister Tinley were from the tribe, but were orphaned early in life when their parents were killed in a tragic DWI vehicle roll over near Santa Fe.

An unusual man-and-wife team stepped in and adopted them. The couple worked as missionary ministers for the Lutheran Church, and ran a compound right on the reservation in a small adobe church with adjacent housing. The unusual aspect of the two came in the fact that they were Alaskan Eskimos. How they arrived in New Mexico on a Pueblo Indian Reservation was a whole story in itself; but they were genuine at heart and made an excellent set of parents for the two youngsters as they grew to adulthood.

Jonah became good friends with both Hal and me. He had been a top athlete in high school and often stopped by the gym during basketball practice and games. A natural athlete and adventurer, Jonah was a perfect fit as a friend for Hal. They both enjoyed the outdoors and often trekked out to hunt along the back spaces of the river toward Bandelier National Park. Tinley was also a gifted athlete and outdoor person. She would try to accompany the boys on their trips if she didn't have work responsibilities for the tribe, as she was the director of the community center.

The interesting thing about both of them was the blending of their Christian faith with the naturalistic beliefs of their tribal heritage. Being Eskimo, their mother and father were not foreign to Native American culture. They always presented the children with the foundations that represented each belief. It gave the Washington children an interesting and rounded perspective of the world.

Both Jonah and Tinley attended church every Sunday, and they also danced in many of the religious ceremonies of the tribe. New Mexico is famous for its Indian Dancers, and there are many Pow Wow dance groups that perform during certain times of the year. I asked Jonah once if he danced at any of the Pow Wows. He was dismissive of the question, answering, "Pow Wows are just for showoffs."

His dancing was for religious purpose only, and it was very personal for him. Hal and I were privileged to be invited to the fall harvest ceremony on occasion. I was fascinated with the purpose, detail and the elegance of the dancers. They told a story, and it was a story through dance that had been told for hundreds, if not thousands of years.

Jonah glided with the grace of a master of ballet, totally out of normal character. Until he vaulted skyward and stomped the ground in a symbolic showing of the sacred power of the rain storm, which seemed a bit more like him.

The ceremonial dress was magnificent, none more apparent than when Tinley flowed out for her part of the presentation. Stunning is the word that described her, in a beaded feather head dress and full length buckskin dance gown. Her beautiful face was aglow with painted accents lightly brushed on her high cheek bones.

The passion of the ceremony could be seen through Tinley's eyes. One moment, a look of the obedient young maiden honoring the god of the river that brings life; next, a sultry gaze while representing the female role in the fertility dance. Her entire facial picture, framed by the beautifully beaded deer hide straps that dangled from the headdress, which pressed against her silky black hair.

It was then that I became aware of the attraction and connection between Tinley and Hal. The ever-alert Hal was totally mesmerized by the movements of the beautiful and elegant Tinley. A train could have run through the middle of the ceremony and Hal would not have flinched.

They eventually began seeing each other, and after a couple of years of casual dating, became seriously in love, beginning a quiet relationship there on the reservation. Both kept separate housing and maintained a low profile, but their commitment to each other was undeniable.

Jonah was a laid-back free spirit of sorts. A handsome man, but not a ladies' man; probably because of upbringing, and his respect for the individual. These qualities made him quite popular, but he would always shrug off any compliments sent his way.

Being a very alert and shrewd police officer made Jonah invaluable to the tribe. Add to that the qualities of a great ambassador, through his disarming since of humor and non-threatening way, and you get Jonah, one of the most interesting men I had ever met.

He would often make up humorous Indian sayings and speak them in the Indian lingo of the old Hollywood Westerns, always funny and clever. A huge movie and TV historian, his preference was a John Wayne movie or *I Love Lucy* episode rather than some dumb reality show. Needless to say, he was an unusual and loveable character.

Jonah often wondered about the relationship between Hal and me. Once on a camping trip with the four of us sitting around a good fire, he brought it up. "What is the deal with you two?"

I sipped the coffee in my cup and questioned, "What do you mean?"

He pointed at me from across the fire, and then at Hal. Wagging his finger between the two of us, he accusingly said, "You guys come to the res. and act like you don't know each other. But, it's obvious that you do and did."

I asked, "Why does it matter?"

Jonah was unusually agitated. "Because I'm an investigator and I don't want you two thinking you've pulled something over on me."

Hal was sitting with Tinley draped on his arm. He began to chuckle while Tinley buried her head in his shoulder, feigning embarrassment.

Jonah looked at them incredulously. He put his hands up in a questioning pose. "What?" He continued his quest for the truth. "Tinley, what do you know about this guy you're holding on to?"

I had to admit, I wanted to know that answer as well. She was not about to say anything incriminating, and just shrugged her shoulders.

Hal offered his light-hearted response. "Jonah, there are a few times in life when you just have to let things go."

He contemplated Hal's statement for a moment, then took a long stick and poked at the fire. Stepping away and capturing a theatrical pose, he decreed, "The beaver builds his house on what he believes is the safety of the river. Yet, the wolf waits outside his door. So goes the man who builds his life with deception, the wolf awaits." He said all of this in a voice somewhere between Clint Eastwood and Mel Brooks.

We all began laughing but it was too much for Tinley to take. She sighed with a giggle. "Good god, Jonah; just shut up!" That was Jonah, a serious investigator one moment, a comedian the next, always able to adjust to the moment.

The Washingtons were the perfect medicine for my soul. In fact the whole Indian culture was a blessing for my wounded heart. The slow pace and devotion to mother earth brought a warmth that I was missing and was a natural conduit for friends on the reservation. I was not considered to be one of them, but that was not necessary. They gave me their friendship and trust as a gift. It was Jonah who tagged me with a name on behalf of the tribe: "The one who understands." I could not have been more honored.

I lived in one of the apartment houses provided for teachers on the reservation, close to school and the river. It was a good set up, and I liked my new job, quickly becoming part of the staff as a science teacher and basketball coach for the freshmen team.

In an office in the gym after a game, it was late and I was watching video results of the game that night, getting statistics, taking notes, and analyzing corrections that would need to be made at the next practice.

"Rusty!" The voice startled me and I jumped in my chair; then realizing who it was, anger began to build.

"Just go away. For your sake and mine, just go away."

"Come on, Rusty, we need to talk."

There would be no excuses and I let him know. "We could have talked a year ago! Now, just go away!"

"That's why we have to talk. We couldn't talk a year ago." He wasn't pleading, but there was true concern in his voice.

"Why? Did you have too many important things to do out there in the cosmos? Something more interesting I'm sure."

"Rusty, I was here. I've been here the whole time." Now he was pleading.

"Bull! I was calling for you, begging for you, and you weren't here." I was really angry now. He was trying to weasel out of it.

"Rusty, you couldn't hear me. Your crash was very bad and really messed up your brain. You lost your gift for a while."

I refused to let him off the hook. "Ham, it's always just about you. When it came to crunch time, you weren't around. Why not, Ham? You got my family killed!" I was screaming into the darkness.

Ham kept coming back. "Buddy, there is absolutely nothing more important to me than you and your family."

Sadness was replacing my anger. "Where were you, Ham?"

"Rusty, I was right here. I can't predict the future, I had no idea what was coming. Dude, I owe you everything. If it weren't for you, I wouldn't have understood the meaning of the light. You helped me understand; because of you I trusted the light."

I was numb and just sat there as Ham continued. "All of us have been rooting for you to make it back. Do you remember the voice that urged you to go back?"

With irritation I answered, "Sure, you told me to go back and do more things for you."

"No, Rusty, I didn't tell you to go back." Ham paused.

I questioned, "Who did?"

Ham answered soothingly, "Donna did."

That staggered me; never had it crossed my mind that Donna and the kids were alive. Guilt flooded over me. I threw my hands to my face and unleashed a scream of anguish. "I got them killed!"

"No you didn't, and Donna knows that," Ham counseled.

I lashed out, "Then who killed them, damn it, I need to know!"

"Rusty, stay with me, buddy. Everybody is ok and mostly worried about you. You were about to cross the threshold when Donna stopped you. Any further and you couldn't have come back. We have a lot to talk about, and will get to all of it."

I just sat there and listened. Ham explained that history can be changed, and through a series of events, I actually went through that intersection twice. The first time safely, but the second time a deadly collision. "Rusty, your history has been tampered with and has put you in what is called a paradox. You are writing one history over the top of the other. There is an evil presence out there that has attempted to eliminate you. That is why you've been hidden for all of this time."

He continued to dwell on one particular point. "Rusty, it is really important to Donna that you move on with the rest of your life."

I wasn't convinced. "Really? She doesn't want me out there with her?"

Ham explained., "She sees a bigger picture, and understands how important you are. She knows you must use your gift."

I bristled. "My gift, my gift, I am sick of hearing about my gift."

Ham was sympathetic. "Rusty, this hasn't worked out the way it was intended and I know you are angry and frustrated. Just give me a chance to fill you in. There is a vitally important issue that must be addressed, and your gift will play a major role."

I was ready for some answers. "Ok, Ham, tell me about it."

He began. "There are realities within the universe with many extra dimensions. These dimensions intertwine and form the existence that I am in. The dimensions in your reality form your vision of the universe, like the multiple dimensions do in mine. All of this stuff coexists in the same universal space, but is separated by a protective dimension. You are what is known as a traveler, and have the ability to enter that dimension. While you're there, you adopt many of the properties that go with it, like the non-recognition of time. You can be taken by a host from my reality and be placed in events that have already occurred. That means you can travel back in time."

I just shook my head. "You're kidding with me for some reason, aren't you?"

"No, Rusty, not at all. You have a gift that is extremely rare. It is the reason you needed to come back."

The conversation had left my comfort zone. "Ham, you are freaking me out."

Ham counseled, "Just hang in there with me and trust in what I'm telling you. Your gift is vital to everything that matters. When I come back, it will be very important for you to be ready to use it."

I said, "What do you mean come back?"

Ham said, "The timing of events must be correct, and that time hasn't arrived. When it does, things will move very quickly."

"How long do I have?" I asked.

"It will be years before the time is right. Your travel must coincide with future events."

I asked, "Are you going to give me some details?"

"It's a very delicate matter in how much you know and when you know it. You will become part of events that have already happened and we must be careful of what you influence. There have already been very serious unintended consequences."

I asked, "Do you mean the attempt on my life?"

He answered earnestly. "Yes, and that's just the beginning."

I asked, "So are we talking a year, five years?"

Ham was careful. "It will be years before the time will come. Rusty, it is important that you don't know too much too soon. Please trust me on this. When the time is right, you will know what you need to know."

I felt his concern. "Ok, Ham, I'm willing to wait. I guess it will give me time to get used to the idea."

"You're a good man, Rusty. We are lucky to have you on our side. There are important times ahead. When I do come back, your life will change dramatically, you will need to be ready for that. I wish I could tell you more but there is so much at stake. One more thing my friend: be aware, you are still in danger. Stay with Hal and stick with the plan. For now, adios, muchacho."

I stated meekly, "Bye, Ham."

After he was gone, I sat there for quite some time thinking. There was just so much I didn't understand. My future was such a mystery. I was going to be a time traveler? What had that boy gotten me in to?

Chapter 15 – Poland WW2

Growing Up Quickly

Sara took the news of her parents' death very hard, crying for hours, and now sat silently staring at nothing. Daniel and Joseph waited quietly in the small room hoping for some clue from Joshua on what to do. It crushed Joshua to give Sara the news of their parents' death. He was torn between sorrow and responsibility. The little boy in him wanted to mourn his parents, yet he knew he had to step forward and lead the group if they were going to survive, just like his father had told him to do. His decision was survival.

Turning to the boys, he began his role as leader. "We will go out after dark and I will show you the remainder of the hiding spots." Joshua put his hand on Sara's shoulder and squeezed. "We will make them proud. We will survive; it's what Father told us to do." Sara said nothing, but Joshua didn't expect her to. His stomach churned inside with grief, nevertheless he pushed on. Any emotion he felt was secondary to the responsibility of survival for the group. Realizing he was the one that could, he was ready to shoulder the load. *Yes,* he thought to himself. *I must do this.*

A month went by and Sara was recovering. Joshua put together a brilliant series of procedures and routines for the group to follow.

The time his father spent with him teaching survival skills was paying dividends. The group was eager to follow his lead and Joshua was a natural teacher. Ultimately, his ability to lead and think ahead would be the most important ingredients of the survival chances for the group.

The boys were becoming very proficient in the art of escape and acquiring goods. Joseph had a gift for catching fish along the river. His background as a river rat came in handy. Being very athletic brought an added gift as that of a performer, doing stunts for the group that were learned from living among the entertainment-oriented gypsies.

Daniel was the organizer. His gift was logistics, quickly learning how to hide and store bounty that the group acquired, and placing equipment and food in various strategic locations identified for him by Joshua. This proved vital for the group's ability to relocate quickly and efficiently. Another role was to serve as a sounding board for Joshua's ideas. Rarely was Joshua ever countered or confronted, but it was good for him to have Daniel to discuss with.

Sara stayed close by Joshua's side, becoming his number one assistant and aide for every operation that the group undertook. She was an excellent lookout and developed numerous signals that were undetectable to outsiders, but alerted Joshua and the boys when they were in operational mode.

Sara also had a gift of making everyone feel good, taking the mothering role and always having a nice thing to say. She had a knack for getting the boys to play make believe with her. During down time when they had to stay hidden and out of sight, the boys would often adopt roles in Sara's make-believe plays. Being an avid reader, she would also read aloud from books that Daniel had acquired from the various dump sites in the city, bringing the characters to life and giving them her special touch. Most literature was unimportant to the Nazis and was cast aside for convenience.

The loyal band had begun its journey as children, but was rapidly developing into a well-oiled survival machine. The months began to add up and eventually became a year. This particular day, they were on a rooftop in a well-conceived and hidden den. Joseph was juggling broken bricks while Sara read quietly to herself. Joshua was contemplating, aware that the war was winding down and many changes were ahead.

He relayed his concern to Daniel. "We must be prepared when the Nazis leave. All routines that they have established will change, and we must change with them. We should also be prepared to leave the city before the Russians get here. They could be worse than the Nazis."

Joseph had been listening and halted his juggling to speak. "We can go find my people on the river and live with them."

Daniel asked, "Are you sure they're still there? Do you think they survived?"

Joseph shrugged his shoulders. "Can't say, but if anyone could survive it would be my Uncle Sebastian."

Joshua was interested. "Following the river could be good. It's a way out of the city and would provide a source for food and water; if we find Joseph's people, even better."

Joshua, sensing the proper moment, became reflective as he addressed the group. Sara noticed his seriousness and laid down her book to listen with the others.

He began. "I am proud to be one of you. I consider each of you a family member. We owe one another our lives. I will protect and serve this family forever, and never forsake it. Will you join my pledge?"

Sara piped up immediately, "Of course we will, Joshua."

Joseph announced, "I will fight to the death."

Daniel's response, as always, was simple and sound. "We are family forever."

Joshua commanded, "So be it."

Chapter 16 – New Mexico/ Current Time

THE MISSION

As the weeks went by, I thought often about Ham and my being a time traveler. It never completely left my mind. I worried about having responsibility in such an important situation and knowing little about it; also using a gift that had yet to expose itself. What was it going to feel like? The coach in me wanted to practice this time travel. Coaching logic told me that was the only way to master it.

I contemplated often about how the universe was structured, and theorized that everything done on earth has a purpose of teaching us about how it all works. I could kind of see how our concept of heaven had developed over thousands of years. There were so many questions for Ham. I wasn't sure how willing he would be to answer them, but I damn sure was going to ask them.

The weeks turned into years and my life continued on its predictable pattern. It was about spending time with my players and students, and pretty much staying on the reservation for any social outreach. I did spend time at the golf course next to the lake that controlled the flow of the river. It was a beautiful setting, laying just below the big mesa and overlooking the lake and river valley. A few beers here and there with Hal and Jonah, and the rest of my life was a quiet existence waiting for Ham's big event, which I assumed would eventually come. Hal had become my best friend, even though he was a nuisance at times, constantly checking up on me.

Jonah and I bonded when Hal began spending more and more time with Tinley. On one occasion, an important member of the tribe had died. Jonah asked me to attend the funeral ceremony with him. It was a huge event and tribal members converged on the community center. Tinley was busy with responsibilities and recruited Hal's help. That left Jonah and me to attend by ourselves.

The process of the burial itself had been ongoing for a few days. Much like a president, the body lay in state in the community center gym. Hundreds of pueblo members, from multiple reservations that reside along the lengthy stretches of the Rio Grande, came to pay respects and to say goodbye. I was informed by Jonah that this process was not reserved for important members only, but was a wake that was performed for every tribal member. The spirit is given time to say goodbye to loved ones before the ceremony to release the spirit is done. In that ceremony the body is placed so the spirit can see the mountain and the Sacred One who awaits the spirit at the top. At the end of the ceremony the spirit is released as a light that only tribal members can see. While the light rises and makes its journey, the body is burned to enable its return to Mother Earth, and a continuing contribution to the circle of life.

The burning of the body these days was symbolically represented outside the community center by a bonfire. Jonah and I walked out together as the large stack of wood was being lit. The head medicine man held a ceremonial pottery urn that contained the already-cremated remains. He positioned himself between the fire and the towering mountain, raising the urn to the sky, as the medicine men chanted the song of the dead.

I stood silently among the hundreds that filtered outside to participate in this final burial act. All faces were reverent as the group answered the chants of the medicine men. Eyes were trained on the sacred mountain. It was near sunset and the slopes had turned to their watermelon red color. I noticed many making methodical hand gestures toward the mountain, as if they were acknowledging an act that was happening. I assumed it to be the ascending light that I was unable to see.

The medicine men brought the ceremony to a close with a final prayer for the sacred one to accept the ascending spirit. As people began to leave, Jonah and I walked to his police SUV to wait for the traffic to clear. I was curious about the ceremony so I asked a question "Jonah, did you see the light go up the mountain?"

He turned his head and looked at me. He smiled as he hesitantly answered, "Yes, Rusty, I saw the light." He paused to see my reaction.

I asked, "Who waits for him at the top?"

Jonah was matter of fact with his answer, "The same one who waits for you and me." He cocked his head with a shy smile and continued. "I'm sure that's hard for you to believe."

I countered immediately, "Trust me; I have no problem accepting that at all." I looked at the floorboard, shaking my head as I lightly laughed. "If you only knew."

The investigator came out in Jonah. "Why don't you tell me? I've wanted to know for a long time." He gave a wry smile, hoping I would come clean.

I smiled back with an apologetic answer, "One of these days, my friend…one of these days."

I was enjoying myself and life was good. As the years passed I would occasionally reflect back on Ham and how our conversation had ended years before. There was something big out there waiting for me, but it had been so long. The question was when would it all go down?

From outside my science classroom came the ring of the lunch bell. I opened the mini fridge on the table behind my desk, picked up my sack lunch and headed outside. Eating outside at lunch was a pleasure. It allowed for escape from the teenage pace at school. The breeze was a cool one. It was November and fall had set in. The school sat on top of a hill that gradually sloped in the direction of the river. I walked down toward the Bosque and to an empty bench that was framed by a rock wall and covering canopy. It had a terrific view of the river, and that's where I chose to have my lunch escape. The leaves on the trees were turning beautiful shades of red, brown, and yellow. The geese were preparing for the winter and making their presence known. I had the beautiful view of the Bosque on one side, and the towering Sandia Mountains looming on the other. It was a relaxed setting and my day was going very well.

"Rusty," the voice chirped. "Rusty!"

"Boy, you do know how to screw-up a beautiful day," I growled.

"You're sure right about that, it is beautiful," Ham said.

I said, "So you're back."

This unfortunately prompted Ham to give his rendition of a Gloria Gaynor hit.

"That's right I'm back, from outer space,
I just came in to find you here with that look upon your face,
You've got all your life to live and I've got all my love to give,
We will survive; we will survive, hey hey."

As usual, he made me laugh, but it was absolutely awful. So I encouraged him to stop. "Ok, ok, I get it; you're back."

I was relying on the fact that no one could hear him at school. I also hoped they didn't see me talking to myself.

He managed to contain himself and move on to why he was there. "So are you ready to go on your mission?"

"It's a mission now? Ham, how am I supposed to do a mission? I haven't heard from you in years and all of a sudden I'm supposed to just take off. I can't go in and tell the school there's a mission to go on; I have to justify my time."

Ham responded, "Your time gone will be relative only to this mission; you won't miss any time here at all."

"Huh," I uttered sarcastically.

Ham explained, "Time travel is a move back in time; no current or actual time will be involved, only time in the past."

Ham was insistent. "So, are you ready to go?"

That was it. I'd had enough. "No, I'm not! I'm not going anywhere until I know what I'm supposed to do and where I'm supposed to do it."

Soothingly he said, "Yes I know. I'm getting to that. But most importantly, you must be emotionally ready to go."

I retorted with a little frustration. "Ham, give me a break, I've been very understanding about all of this but I need information right now."

He was forthright with his answer. "Fair enough, but I warned you that things would move quickly when I returned, so here it is: You're going to be placed in Poland during World War II. You are traveling back to help a young boy and girl."

He paused for a moment to check my reaction. I didn't give one, so he continued. "You are a traveler, and that comes with a certain amount of protection." Ham sounded almost motherly. "You will be ok, but you're going to a bad place. If something happens, you will revert back to the energy dimension, and then back to current time. This one won't be much fun, but it is critical."

A couple of things bothered me about his statement. I didn't know exactly what was going to happen, but I was getting the idea that it was going to be heavy. The other notion might even be worse. What did he mean by this one? Did he mean there was more to come? I was pretty sure Ham wasn't going to tell me if there was.

He continued to rally for his cause. "Rusty, you can do this, but it's going to get tough. I can tell you this: you will go to help the boy and girl survive. They're what are left of a very important family."

I made a comment that needed to be said "Ham what if I don't want to go, are you going to make me?"

Ham was sincere. "No, Rusty, I can't make you go, but do you remember our talk years ago about your gift?"

I acknowledged. "Yes, I remember."

Ham continued. "We talked about the opportunity to help more people than you could ever imagine. This is that time."

I added, "You also said it would change my life forever."

Ham's answer was honest. "Unfortunately, all of this has already changed your life forever. Rusty, you are in the middle of this, whether you want to be or not."

I thought about that. He was right. One way or another, my life had led to this moment and this gift. I asked, "Will you tell me a little more about the children?"

He obliged. "Their names are Joshua and Sara. You will go to help them stay out of harm's way. I should tell you that these children possess a gift that is very important to the world and universe as a whole. They are your concern and nothing more. There will be a role for you on arrival, of which you will be aware and have knowledge of."

He had another important fact to tell me. "Rusty, being a traveler, you are protected as I said before; with one exception."

"That's interesting," I said with caution.

Ham continued. "The exception is if you encounter another traveler. You would be vulnerable to him as well as he being vulnerable to you. The two of you would be from the same time period and interaction between you would be relevant to current time."

I stated what I figured was the worst-case scenario. "So that means we could kill each other and it would stick."

"Yes," Ham answered.

I was concerned and curious. "What are the chances of us meeting?"

"Very likely," Ham conceded. He went on to clarify. "Rusty, there is a traveler sent from the dark side, he is there to eliminate the children, and he is the one who has already tried to kill you. He will stop at nothing."

I voiced my insecurity. "Ham, this sounds like a very big deal. I don't feel qualified for this job."

He answered sincerely. "Buddy, I can't think of a better person for it. Believe me, my friend, we are fortunate that you are the traveler; it's your heart that matters most. More than anything, these children need what you can give."

There was silence for a time, neither of us knowing what to say. It was becoming apparent to me that I really had no choice. I thought back on my life to this point, and questioned what this might mean for the rest of it. Always wanting to help, my decision came as a surge that went through me from head to toe. It's that feeling when you commit and just know. I declared, "Ok, I'm ready."

Ham affirmed. "I know you are, pal. It's time to go." His voice began to drift from me, much like going under anesthesia for surgery. I remained very alert, you better believe it. I could still see the Bosque below and the mountains above, but a blanket of silence fell over all of it. Not a sound. Then, a sea of pulsating white brightness flooded over and through me; suddenly, nothing at all.

The Book of Joshua

Chapter 17 – Poland WW2

BACK IN TIME

"Ok, I'm cold, really cold." I found myself in bed, a bunk bed in a small room, or more like a hut. It was all wood on the sides with a tin roof. A lantern hung on the wall and a box of stick matches rested on the wooden ledge next to it. There was an iron potbelly stove in the middle of the room. A metal smokestack rambled from its top toward the ceiling and out.

I was dressed in long flannel underwear and covered with a wool blanket. There were additional clothes draped over the lone wooden bench in the room. I got up and dressed in a long-sleeved wool shirt and heavy wool pants. Socks already being on, I slipped on a pair of brown work boots. A thick jacket hung on the wall by the door along with a floppy wool hat to go with it. I quickly put them on and stuck my hands in the pockets for warmth.

"Ah yes," I said discovering gloves in the pockets, and slid them on my freezing digits, while looking around the room to see what else might be available. A small window with wooden shutters was holding back what must be assumed was morning light. Opening the shutters revealed trees that were nestled on a hill in the near distance. The weather appeared to be overcast, and a significant amount of activity seemed to be going on outside beyond the wooden door of the hut.

This is what I knew. It was Poland, just outside of the city. The time was World War II and the German Nazis were occupying the country. The Nazi labor and death camps were just a few miles down the railroad tracks that were located right outside my door. The Jewish Ghetto, created by the Nazis, had been emptied a year before. Thousands of Jews and political prisoners were transported to the camps. A train would leave every day loaded with prisoners headed most likely to their doom.

The air was cold and had a strange kind of thickness to it. I opened the door and strolled out to face the day. What I thought to be overcast was more like a haze. There was little wind on this gray morning, and a foreign smell filled my nostrils. I couldn't place the odor, but something about it made me uneasy.

I was in charge of a pull cart that sat outside the door. My job was to sift through belongings taken from Jewish and political detainees, and transport in my cart, the sellable items back to shops in the city. Most of the larger valuable merchandise had already been taken by the Nazis and stored in warehouses awaiting shipment to Germany. The rest of the bounty was used to generate a little capital in the city, attempting to counter the black market activity there.

The area around my hut looked like a stockyard. Gates and fences all designed to herd the prisoners into holding areas where they were stripped of almost all clothing and possessions. From these holding pens, they were loaded onto boxcars for the trip to the camps. On the far side of my hut was the hilly wooded area that was in view from my window inside. There were walking paths leading to the hill and beyond to the barracks that had been constructed for the Nazi troops.

Armed guards, stationed all around the area, monitored my movements. I was allowed into only one area where belongings were piled. From there, the trains and the people being loaded were in view. Watching them day after day made this atrocity unfathomable, in its total disregard for human life.

They came to the pens from many directions. Some under Nazi guard, others under direction from men in civilian clothing.

The people all displayed the same air of sadness, with a common gait to their walk. A march of sorts, or more of a trudge, eyes fixed to the ground and shoulders slumped.

The guards barked orders and the prisoners dutifully responded. Huge numbers of people were guided into the pens in male and female groups, then stripped. The piles of belongings were gathered and brought to the area where I stood.

While loading the cart for my trip to town, I watched the people. Fear lived in many eyes, but some were merely windows to a vacant house, all hope was gone with no evidence that a soul still remained. The prisoners were all so thin; it looked as if they had not eaten in some time. But the heartbreaking totality of the setting was the prevalent sadness of them all.

The train's arrival sparked the guards into motion, barking orders for the detainees to board. Young and old were stuffed into boxcars with little room to breathe. I was stung by the terror and sorrow as the train began its trip, the final journey to the camps. I wanted to turn away but couldn't escape the frightened eyes of the children, while separated mothers desperately screamed out their names. The men were mostly silent with eyes cast at the ground. The hopeless nature of this horrific scene had more than taken their dignity, it had disarmed their will.

The guards were varied in approach with the prisoners. A few were harsh and threatening, pointing cocked pistols at heads and threatening to shoot. Some did shoot for no apparent reason at all. Others were silent, systematically prodding the prisoners along the designated route. For the guards, this process went on day after day. I wondered how any man with conscience could do it. The thought came to me, that there are many victims in an atrocity such as this, some more apparent than others.

I was generally left alone to do my work, loading the cart and taking it to one of the entry stations. The cart would be checked for content by the officer in charge. His real motivation was to ascertain value of anything he might want. Then, the cart was allowed into the warehouse area for a clerk to document the load. I was given an official invoice to be used when reaching the designated destination.

Trips each day to the city differed, heading for various delivery locations every day of the week. The trips took from three to five hours to complete, depending on location. The procedure was usually the same, presenting my manifest to the clerk in charge, and then unloading the items on the document to be checked off. I then was led to the back for payment, it coming in the form of food from the kitchen that existed in most of the makeshift stores.

Available food was prepared and then taken to the front for sale or barter with customers living in the city. Clothes, furniture, and personal items were also available at these locations. I was given a small credit every time the cart delivered its content. It was enough to eat on and still be able to take a little with me for the evening or next morning. Sometimes I had to decide between essentials or food, because of the small amount of credit that was allotted to me.

The trip back was a bit easier with an empty cart. I often took different streets to investigate new areas, and possibly anything lying around to take and burn in my stove. If no material for fuel could be found to burn, then time had to be spent in the trees at the hut looking for wood. It was a race of time to get back and start a fire before the bitter cold of the winter night set in.

The city was a maze of concrete and brick, with mostly three-story buildings framing the grid. The streets were usually empty of any casual observers or pedestrians. Most of the activity was due to military traffic or some other sort of official business. The Polish resistance was waging a guerilla war with the Nazis, so strict curfews were in place.

When darkness arrived, very little light was available in the city. Most of the street lamps were non-operational, and light from the buildings was minimal at best. The streets were barren.

Any usable items had already been taken by the remaining residents or by the Nazis; it was a stark and bleak place.

The curfew was put in place after dark. Nazi patrols increased their rounds during curfew hours. I always tried to be out of the city by that time, but had permission to travel after curfew if there was a valid reason. It was dangerous to deal with the patrols, especially if I had anything of value with me in my cart.

The Nazi ruled the streets; they were commanded by the captain of the guard. He had power, but more importantly, was the most consistent one to deal with. The Nazi soldiers had the authority of shoot to kill, and it was critical to deal with the proper patrols, and if at all possible, the captain.

The empty Ghetto had been partially repopulated by Polish families that were trying to find work in the factories. Some Jews were allowed to remain if they were a vital part of the factory system. But at dusk, it was as if the entire city was empty, doorways locked and heavily braced, and windows fortified with any available material to prevent entry.

It had been a long day and I was on the way back to my hut, still in the city and night closing quickly. I had bartered a loaf of bread and was looking forward to it, plus wood acquired from some old crates. This would heat my hut nicely that evening and possibly enough for the next morning.

Being approximately six blocks away from being out of the city, the night overtook me. I grabbed the small lantern from its hook on the cart. This was an important decision; having very little oil to use. The moonless night stressed the need for light, or it would take me forever to travel in the pitch black. The decision was made, and I lit the lamp. The cold was penetrating and I needed to get back.

The lamp provided enough light to see the street in front and created dark floating images on the buildings along side. It was an eerie sight that also made me nervous. I could be seen, but could see very little, which promoted my desire to continue the journey as quickly as possible.

The only sound originated from the wooden wheels of my cart colliding with the hardness of the street. Then, I began to hear noises, little rustling sounds of movement, but couldn't ascertain the direction. *Whoosh!* Something rushed by my cart from behind. I turned and saw nothing but black. Suddenly, a loud clatter came from the street in front of me. Turning, I held my lantern high. It sounded like a rock hitting the pavement. *Whoosh!* Something from behind me again!

"Who's out there?" I demanded.

Silence from the darkness; I checked the cart and was missing some of my wood. *So that's what's going on,* I thought. They were stealing my wood. It was obvious that there was more than one of them out there. Why didn't they just overpower me and take it?

It was time to get out. I picked up the handles of the cart and began to pull as quickly as possible, dousing my lantern and going for it in the dark, my thought being, at least I couldn't be seen either. Hurrying over the pavement, I could see small bits of light coming from the buildings, which helped with my bearings and keeping the cart in the middle of the street.

Bam! The cart was rammed. There was a high-pitched wail, then the thud of something sharply hitting the street. Stopping to listen, I heard a faint whimper from what sounded like a tiny voice. I cautiously reached for my lantern and lit the wick to regain my source of light. Circling behind the cart, I held the lantern out. A small figure lay on the street next to a big crater that I had somehow missed with the wheels. The figure indeed was a little girl. She could not have been more than ten years old.

"Are you ok?" I asked, moving closer.

She said nothing and kept her face hidden from view. I lowered the lantern for a better look. There were cuts on her arms and elbows, most likely from the collision and fall that I had heard. Moving the light toward her leg revealed an ugly sight.

The shin had a huge gash, and her foot rested at a strange angle. It was in fact a badly broken leg.

"Oh man," I gasped as I reached down. She attempted to scoot away, wincing in severe pain but making no sound.

I warned, "You have a broken leg. I need to take a better look at it."

"Leave her alone," a voice demanded from the dark.

It was impossible to determine the origin, but the voice was that of a boy.

"This girl needs help," I demanded.

"We can take care of our own," he declared.

I reasoned, "The leg is badly broken and she has deep cuts that must be treated. She should see a doctor."

"No," was the answer from the now urgent voice. "That can't be done. Just give her to us."

"Do you know how to set a leg? Do you have ways to treat these cuts?" I asked.

The voice didn't answer immediately. Finally he said with a little less conviction. "We must go; give her to us."

He now had indecision, but was determined to get her out of there. That told me they were undoubtedly on the run.

I said, "I know you need to leave, but this girl is in trouble if she doesn't get help." I suddenly thought of Ham and the children I was supposed to help. This might be them; what other children would be out here?

I reasoned with him again. "Just tell me if you can get her treatment. I don't care who you are, I want to help her."

"Why do you help her? Why should I trust you?" His tone was different now; he was trying to figure me out. He needed help, but wasn't ready to trust me.

"She's a little girl," I pleaded. "Her leg is broken and those cuts will get infected if they're not treated. I think I can set her leg, but it must be done soon."

Voices came from the end of the street. Looking up, I could see light from lanterns moving toward us. I glanced back at the girl, sudden fear flashing in her dazzling blue eyes. The lanterns meant danger to her. She began struggling to move but was stymied by the pain in her leg.

The boy urgently insisted, "It's the Nazi patrol. We must take her now." Out of the darkness stepped a young boy in a wool cap with jet black hair jutting out from under it. His big brown eyes were ablaze with determination. He looked to be a little older that the girl, but could not be more than twelve or thirteen.

"If she stays, she dies," he contended as his eyes burned into mine.

He was right, but I didn't know what to do. If he took her she would be in severe pain and they would have to move very slowly. The chances of her leg setting correctly were almost zero and the chance of serious infection in her wounds was certain. The voices and the light were getting closer. It was time to make a move. I looked around the street.

A plan came to me as I spoke. "She can't be moved like this, but I have an idea." The boy was looking at me waiting impatiently for more information. "I need help to move her over to the side of the street by that gutter. It's deep enough to hide her in the dark."

My plan was to move the cart in between the gutter and the rest of the street. I would talk to the patrol and explain about being on my way back when I hit the big crater; then I'd clarify that I was simply checking for damage and would get back on my way.

The boy was out of options. He nodded his head to affirm the plan, then turned and whispered a quick signal into the night air. Immediately, two boys stepped out of the darkness awaiting instruction. I motioned them over to help. As a unit, we lifted the girl and carefully moved her to the gutter. I tried to position her leg to the best possible angle for comfort, but she was in severe pain.

The boy hunched over her and gently took her face into his hands. "You must stay silent and completely still. You must, Sara, you can do this, and I will be nearby." He kissed her on her forehead, gave her an encouraging smile; then all three boys came to me. I motioned to the cart and we moved it into position by the curb.

The light from the patrol was getting very close. I could hear voices communicating back and forth, checking the streets and reporting back to their commander. This would not be good if they were making sweeping rounds of the entire street. Sara would be seen for sure. An additional plan was needed to get their attention on something else. I whispered into the darkness for the boy. He quickly came out with a worried look.

"I'm going to tell the patrol that someone up the street attacked me and tried to steal my wood." He acknowledged my idea and I continued. "If you and the other two can make some noise, then maybe the patrol will leave quickly and chase you. You would need some kind of escape plan." Rolling his eyes at me, he answered, "We have plenty, we will be ready."

I continued. "I will keep Sara with me and move her in the cart to my hut." A thought came to me and I said with worry, "But, you won't know where to find me."

He assured, "We know who you are, we will find you." And then he was gone, like a ghost into the darkness.

I grabbed the lantern and positioned myself on the street side of the cart, waving it like a distressed citizen and crying for help. The patrol responded, moving quickly toward me.

I shouted, "Hurry, they are getting away." The captain of the patrol was first to arrive and began the questioning.

"Why are you on the street after curfew?" he demanded.

"I'm on the way back from my drop for the day," I said with a rushed voice. "I've been attacked!" I emphasized.

"Who attacked you?" he questioned.

"I'm not sure, I couldn't see in the dark. They were trying to get my wood," I said motioning to the back of the cart.

The captain raised his lantern and walked toward the cart. The rest of the patrol began to look around in the street. This was not good; it would not take them long to spot Sara. With almost perfect timing, a broken brick flew in from the darkness and crashed into the street; then another, and another, until the patrol was ducking for cover.

"Halt this," ordered the captain. "Who goes there?"

One of the soldiers anxiously fired a shot from his rifle.

A voice from the darkness yelled, "Run for it." The sound of footsteps echoed in the street.

The captain gave the order for the troops to deploy in a search-and-pursue formation. He looked back at me and said, "Move on to your hut, I will deal with you later." He turned his attention to the street and his troops, and gave the order to move out in double time.

I watched them sink into the night, and had a suspicion that they were wasting their time trying to catch those boys, but the plan had worked. I redeployed swiftly around the cart to where Sara was hiding and put the lantern down low to the ground so I could see her face. Her blonde hair lay sprawled on the pavement. Her cheeks were bright red from exposure to the cold, and her blue eyes brimmed with tears as she gritted her teeth against the pain.

"We must move rapidly," I urged. She answered with a nod of her head. Circling to her far side, I tried for the best angle in which to pick her up; gathering her shoulders with one arm, and with the other, doing my best to support her broken leg.

As I lifted, an intense whimper escaped her clinched mouth. She could not have been more than fifty pounds, and I moved her gently to the cart, placing her in the back. Shifting the wood around made it possible for her to lay flat. I then stacked the wood in a fashion that shielded her from view.

Placing the lantern on its hook, we were now ready to be on our way. It was important to make the journey as smooth as possible, because Sara would feel every bump. Time was of essence, the leg must be set very soon, and she was probably going into shock.

The plan of getting her to the hut had a problem, which was passing through a guard station to get there. The whole deal would rely on the relationship that I had established with the guards. They were familiar with me, and hopefully that would provide enough discretion to get past them without Sara being seen. They usually paid no attention to me when I was pulling an empty cart, but the wood might be an issue.

We were getting close and I advised Sara to be very still. Stopping the cart one last time, I checked to see if any part of her was visible. Then, lifting up a piece of wood covering her face, said encouragingly, "Here we go." I gave her a smile and put the wood back in place, knowing her life depended on me. I didn't stop to think of the consequences that might be facing me if the Nazis found her, and that was probably a good thing.

"Greetings, gentleman," I said on approach.

The soldier in charge stepped forward to address me. "You are later than normal."

"I had my long trip today and found this wood, so it took me more time," I explained.

The guard glanced at the wood in the back of the cart and demanded, "Where did you get this?"

"I bargained for it in the city," I said proudly. He began to circle the cart, inspecting it.

"This is very cheap," he chided, as he came back to face me.

I explained, "I intend to burn it in my stove tonight. I need the fuel and it is too late to look in the trees."

"We also have a fire," he said, pointing to the fire pit next to the guard post. It was obvious what he was implying. I needed to be very careful here or he would request the whole load, and that would be the end for Sara.

"I would be glad to give you some of this wood to help your fire make it through the night. I will stack it with the rest of your pile as I go by."

"Very good," he conceded, and stepped back to let me pass. As I did, he stared directly into the cart. My heart was in my throat as I kept my eyes cast toward the ground; I did not want to challenge in any way the authority of this man.

"Halt," he ordered, approaching me with a questioning look in his eye. Suddenly, a rock came out of the night and landed at his feet. He whirled around and peered into the blackness. He began barking orders and the guards all drew their weapons. Another rock rained down, and then another. The guards nervously began firing rounds. The soldier in charge ordered them to stop. Turning to me he ordered, "Move on, and don't forget the wood." I nodded and aimed the cart toward the woodpile. The soldier deployed his troops and ordered them to spray the area with gunfire. It was my sincere hope that the boys were long gone by then. But, the Nazis were occupied, and that made for my opportunity to move on.

I unloaded a big portion of the wood, doing my best to keep Sara concealed, but she was in view if anyone came close to the cart. Moving quickly, the goal was my hut, which was only a hundred meters away. I reached the front door and backed the cart right next to it. Opening the door, I came face to face with the boy. Jumping back with fright I gasped. "How in the world did you get here?" I continued while regaining my composure. "You scared me half to death."

"I'm here to help," he answered, ignoring my original question. And with that, he stepped out of the hut and slid into the cart with Sara, pushing the wood aside and kneeling next to her. He soothingly said, "Everything will be fine now, you will be ok." She nodded her head and they both looked to me.

I urged, "Let's get her inside, we should not waste time."

We picked her up and carefully moved into the hut and over to the bunk. I held Sara and the boy supported her broken leg. Placing Sara on the top bunk, I braced her leg with my blanket. It was now time to set it, something I was not looking forward to. The boy climbed up on the bunk and moved around toward Sara's head. He put her head in his lap and held it with his left hand, then placed his right arm over her chest for support. It was apparent he knew what was coming.

I gave a look of concern to Sara and warned, "This is going to hurt, but it is very important to stay as quiet as you can. There are soldiers everywhere." She nodded and looked up at the boy. He gave her a knowing nod and then shifted his attention to me.

"We are ready," he assured.

I maneuvered the leg into its proper position and applied side pressure, then pulled. Sara squeaked in pain and the boy covered her mouth with his hand. He hugged her tightly and whispered for her to hold on. One more tug and I could get it. There, it moved into place. I checked Sara; tears were streaming down her face. She had shown tremendous courage. The boy smiled and wrapped his arms around her. He looked at me with a question on his face.

"What next?" he asked.

I craftily answered, "Well, we are going to tie support to her leg; then, Joshua, we are going to talk."

I had caught him by surprise. "You know my name?"

Chapter 18 – Poland WW2

Change of Plan

The Traveler was frustrated. He was too busy to effectively look for the children in his current position. He had too many duties that had nothing to do with finding them. He did enjoy the killing, he could not have asked for more, but he had to stay focused on the reason he was there. His only choice was to change his status and move to one of the street patrols. From there he would be able to consistently search with the aid of the dogs. He would have to answer to the captain of the guard, and he did not like that, but it would be worth the opportunity to search.

It had been over a year since he traveled back in time. The war was winding down and he feared the possibility of running out of opportunities. He knew the children were still in the city, coming close to their capture multiple times, but they had proven to be quite elusive. Sooner or later he was sure to have them, and knew he must. It would not be wise to disappoint the powers of the dark side. The job would be finished, he thought, if he had been given complete control. But the insistence of the dark angel to minimize unintended consequences had slowed things. It was frustrating to deal with time that was already part of history. He had to remain patient and avoid as much nonessential contact as possible.

He had been told about the other traveler and had taken steps to eliminate that threat. The only thing to do was stay focused on the children and deal with other issues as they arose. He would find them, kill them, and be done with it.

Chapter 19 – Poland WW2

Best-Laid Plans

There was much yet to do around the hut to secure Sara's status, so the answer to Joshua's question about how I knew his name would need to wait for the moment. Remembering some cord in the cart that I used to tie items down, I exited to retrieve it, then back inside to Sara at the bunk.

I made a request to Joshua. "We need water in that bucket in the corner. There is a pump about fifty meters to the south." In an instant he was up with the bucket in hand. "Hey," I warned. "Be very careful, there are many eyes out there that can see you." He cocked his head and looked at me with disdain, then vanished.

I turned to Sara. With the exception of her chapped red cheeks, she was very pale. Reapplying the blanket from the bunk, I spread it over her. "How do you feel?" I asked.

"I'm ok," she whispered. Her beautiful eyes were full of determination and curiosity. "What's your name?" she asked.

"Rusty," I responded.

"That's a strange name," she said with a weak grin.

"Yes, I guess it is," I said, smiling while continuing to work on her. "We need to get your cuts cleaned up."

About that time Joshua came bursting back into the hut with the water, setting the bucket at my feet. I acknowledged his quick work with a nod of gratitude and a smile.

"I have one piece of cloth that we can use with the water to clean these cuts," I said as I pointed toward the end of the bunk. Joshua grabbed the rag and dabbed it into the water. Lifting the blanket off of Sara's legs, I began to clean her wounds, one severe cut and a few abrasions.

I advised, "For now, cleaning the wounds will have to do; tomorrow we will need to come up with a plan for bandages and ointment."

Suddenly, there was a commotion outside and a voice. "Cart Man, come out of the hut." The patrol had returned and the captain was there to speak with me as promised. Joshua plastered himself against the wall. I turned to Sara and gave her the signal with my finger for silence. I quickly covered her with the blanket and edged her gently across the bed away from the door. Then using the wood from the floor, I piled it on the bunk to disguise anything that might look like a human form.

"Coming out," I yelled. As I walked out the door, Joshua was edging toward the window.

The captain stood waiting for me in an official stance. "Have you been attacked before?" he asked in a very short tone.

"No, I've never been that late on the street," I said.

"You have no idea who it was?" he questioned with a disapproving look.

"None," I answered with innocence.

The captain commanded, "I must look inside." Pushing past me toward the door, he stopped and drew his pistol.

"I assure you it is only me and my wood," I said as my heart pounded in my chest. If Joshua was still in that room, all hell was about to break loose. He opened the door and entered. I could not see around him so I watched his body language. His head scanned the interior. The hand which held the pistol began to drop and his shoulders relaxed. Joshua had made it out. The captain walked to the middle of the room and I hurriedly followed him in. He glanced at the window and then at the stove. His eyes turned toward the bunk. He stared at it for a moment and then looked at me.

"So this is your home," he said with just a shadow of a smile settling on his face.

"Yes, this is my palace," I quipped.

He moved towards the door. Trying my best to stay out of his view and breathe normally, my hope was to not show any signs of stress. As we made it outside, he stopped to study my face. Again, as if on cue, there was a disturbance about two hundred meters to the east. The captain's attention was summoned by gunfire and loud voices, followed by more gunfire. He made a hand gesture for his troops to deploy, and they did in an instant.

The captain briefly returned his attention to me. "A very busy night that seems to be following you, cart man."

I pleaded my innocence. "Captain, I have no idea." I raised my palms and shrugged.

He spoke with a distrusting smile, "Good bye for now." He then turned and followed his troops.

I moved back to the hut and waited outside till they were gone. Giving a big sigh of relief, I felt myself relax for the first time. The captain was right; trouble was following me around. That trouble was in the form of Joshua, and I had no doubt that he was leading the Nazis on another wild goose chase.

I went inside and over to the bunk to uncover Sara, clearing the wood to reveal her angel face; one that you only see in the movies.

With an impish grin she declared, "Good job."

"Thank you," I answered. Then with concern I expressed, "I'm worried about Joshua."

"Don't be," she boasted. "They will never catch him." I was beginning to believe that to be true. Who was this boy superhuman?

I got back to the task of cleaning Sara's wounds, trying to keep the blood on the towel to a minimum; I didn't want to explain it later. With the cleaning done, all that was left to do was brace the leg with wood from the crate. I had to figure a way of tying it around her for support.

Sara teased, "I hope you know what you're doing?"

"You better hope I do," I said. She was beginning to relax around me and I was seeing a sweet and funny little girl, who was very curious about what I was doing. She possessed a seemingly natural curiosity that sparkled in her eyes.

"Where do you live?" I asked.

"We live everywhere," she responded, shrugging her shoulders.

I probed. "So do you live in buildings?"

She answered, "It's too dangerous to live in the buildings, the Nazis would find us."

She went on to explain how they constantly stayed on the move, and about the two other boys who had banded together with them for survival. Their parents were either dead or in the camps after the Nazis had cleared the ghetto. The group had found each other and Joshua was their leader.

They used the sewers for travel during the day and the aid of darkness at night. The river was a mainstay for them, washing and cleaning themselves, fishing, and trapping game to eat. Joshua had arranged an intricate pattern of places to use for rest and sleep at night. There were many empty buildings in and around the ghetto area since the Nazis had cleared it. Some of the buildings had hidden areas either on the rooftops or basements that the group used. Joshua picked the sites based on escape ability if they were discovered. The cemetery was close by and it had many buildings and monuments that were good for hiding. Wherever they stayed, Joshua had multiple escape routes available.

Staying warm was a big challenge for the group. They had blankets and coats but had to stay very mobile. Joshua and Daniel kept hidden stashes of supplies around all of the designated spots where camp would set up.

Camp was never longer than a day before moving on. Cooking was a problem because a fire gave away location very easily. The group cooked outside in the woods when the wind was blowing in a safe direction. Sometimes they would cook in the sewers even though it was damp and smelled awful. Only one person did the cooking, it was too dangerous to have the whole group around a fire together. Usually, Joshua would do it; he had the best chance of escaping if something were to happen. He would then transport the food to the location of the others.

"Where are they hiding tonight?" I asked.

Sara gave me a suspicious look. "I should not tell you."

"That's fine, I was just curious," I said. There was a noise at the window. I turned to look and saw a stick pushing the shutter out and up on its hinges. Quickly, a little body slithered through the opening. Joshua was back. He was covered in mud, his face completely black. Those piercing brown eyes were framed in mud and stood out even more dramatically than before.

"Hello," I said. Joshua nodded his head and fixed his gaze on Sara.

He gave her a warm smile and said, "Looks like you're feeling better." She grinned and nodded her head.

I had been thinking about what should be done next. Sara needed to stay still for at least a few days; she also needed some kind of crutch to walk with once she began moving. I told all of this to Joshua. He listened intently to what I had to say. I suggested that Sara rehabilitate within the hut. He was not comfortable with that idea, but I assured him that it was necessary. I also felt it was the safest option available.

Joshua was puzzled. "Why do you help us?"

I wanted to answer correctly; what could I tell him that would make sense?

Joshua continued, "Nobody helps the Jews."

I was trying to find the words to explain. "Joshua, I am here to help; it would be hard to explain everything to you. I want to help, you need to trust me."

"We trust no one." His voice was tinted with anger.

He shot a stern look at me as he remembered his original question. "How do you know my name?"

Ham had warned not to give out too much information. “Joshua, I have been sent by people that want to help you. For now, you must trust this to be true.”

Sara spoke, “I trust him, Joshua.” She was up on an elbow and looking at me. “I can see it in his eyes, he doesn’t hate us.” Joshua walked over to Sara, bent to her ear and whispered. She shook her head with conviction. “I don’t care, we can use him and he wants to help.”

Joshua was in a bind. He didn’t like the idea of leaving Sara behind and he didn’t like the thought of depending on, or trusting me. He was clearly worried about Sara. “You are my sister, I can’t leave you behind.” He was taking a stubborn stance, but the facts did not support his position and he knew it. He looked at me long and hard. “How long must she stay?”

“A couple of days to let the leg set a bit better,” I said. “She will also need some kind of a crutch to aide her once she does start walking again.”

Joshua assured. “I can take care of that.”

I wanted to change the mood. “Why are you so muddy?” I asked.

“Harder to see me and it helps throw the dogs of my scent,” he said with a sly grin.

Joshua was a warrior in the body of a little boy. He had a commanding presence about him that promoted confidence in what he said and did. The fire in his eyes gave insight into the soul of a survivor. He would not be stopped. The way he moved, everything about him had a purpose. His mission for the moment was to take care of Sara. We began planning the next few days.

Sara would stay in my top bunk while I kept her hidden. Joshua would arrange for the crutches and an exit plan once she was ready to move. He had a brilliant mind when it came to strategy and planning, with detailed knowledge of the area in and around the city. He knew the routine of the patrols and when it was dangerous or safe to travel.

There was increasing unrest in the city caused by the resistance. This made Joshua nervous and he voiced his frustration. "They should all just go home and wait for the end of the war. The Nazis are beaten, but the resistance causes more patrols to be put out and a lot of unnecessary danger."

He was right; the fighting in the streets had made many of my trips unpredictable and dangerous. It was clear that the Nazis were beginning to move things out of the city, but the fighting kept a large contingent of Nazi soldiers in the area. I made arrangements with Joshua to meet during the day. My trips were becoming less and less important to the Nazis, which aided our effort. Sara would stay in the hut, with me checking on her once during the day. Joshua was going to teach me the routines of the group and show the strategic havens where they located.

The next day we were to come together outside the cemetery. I pulled my cart there in case it might be needed, and headed back toward a mausoleum where Joshua had told me to go.

"Over here," came a call from behind a monument near the mausoleum. I could see no one but I knew it was Joshua.

"Do we need this cart?" I asked.

"Bring it towards me," Joshua yelled. I could see an arm sticking out and waving from behind the marble slab. Bringing the cart around the far side, I almost stepped into a cavern.

"Good gosh, what is this?" I gasped. The ground on the backside of the monument was gone. In its place was a huge hole, big enough for a hiding place and makeshift living quarter.

"We can roll the cart into the hole for now," suggested Joshua.

"Why do I need to hide it?" I asked. "I haven't had to hide anything."

"Now you are with us and we absolutely hide everything until we need it," Joshua said. "We can't be seen."

So the cart was rolled into the hole and covered with an intriguingly deceptive camouflage on top. It was a large flat wooden frame with a thin tin cover that roofed the top of the large hole. The exposed top of this large tin sheet was camouflaged with dirt and shrubbery identical to the grounds of the cemetery, making it impossible to be seen. It was very impressive.

I was curious. "Doesn't it bother you to be living among the dead?" Joshua scoffed a laugh.

He motioned for me to come along. "I want to show you something," he said.

We walked to the far side of the cemetery and jumped the stone fence then hiked up a hill through the trees. The smell that I had been wondering about for all of these days was getting stronger. The odor was intense and I finally recognized it as the smell of rotting carcass.

"Joshua, what is this, where are we going?"

"Not much further," he said without breaking stride. We crested the hill and looked down upon a valley of death. Thousands of bodies lay half buried in the soil below. I was astonished, the picture could not possibly be, but it was. All of my years of teaching and the knowledge of the Holocaust did nothing to prepare me for this mass murder scene. I dropped to my knees in dismay.

"Oh my god, Joshua, how many?"

"More than can be counted," he said. The boy had answered my question about living among the dead. He went on to tell the story of this murder collection pit. Many of those killed in the city and camps over the last two years had been dumped out here or burned. Thousands upon thousands had been killed for various reasons, and most of the bodies were Jews.

Joshua's gaze met mine. "My parents and all of my relatives are out there. Now it is just Sara and me." Joshua stared at me with those penetrating eyes as he made a proclamation. "We will make it. We will survive."

"Joshua, that's why I'm here," I affirmed while looking up at him.

He reached down and offered me a hand up, and pulled me to my feet. "Why do you say that, Rusty?"

I explained. '"Joshua I'm not from here."

"No kidding," he said with a smile.

"Obvious I guess," I acknowledged. "But I've been sent here for a reason and it's to help you and Sara." I looked at Joshua and his face was puzzled.

"Why us?" he questioned. "We are two without a family just trying to survive."

"I know," I said. "The two of you are very important to many people; do you have any idea why?" He shrugged his shoulders. I felt like he might know more than he was letting on, but it was time to get back to business.

He said, "We must hurry and cook, it won't be safe here much longer." Joshua had stashed food out here before sunrise, explaining that he often cooked in this area because no one ever ventured this way, plus the smell covered up the smoke.

His father had spent years in the woods teaching him the skills to survive in nature. Those skills had served him well for survival in the streets. For quite some time now, he had been the man in charge.

Joshua explained how Joseph and Daniel had come along when the ghetto was cleared out. I knew that Joshua had organized this current band of survivors that they had become. It was truly amazing to watch the team operate under his leadership.

Daniel was the organizer and Joseph more athletic and strong. The two boys had total loyalty to Joshua, and trusted his decision making, creating a team that could think on the run; a well-oiled machine.

Sara provided the mothering role to the operation, being the one who always had a kind word and a warm heart.

The key to success was Joshua himself. His best leadership quality was the simple willingness to do the toughest or most dangerous job; always putting himself in the line of fire first.

Now the war was almost over. The Russians were moving ever closer to the city and the Nazis were preparing to leave. The resistance was fighting almost every night, making travel difficult and dangerous.

The Russians were another problem. They were not going to be overly sympathetic to four Jewish kids; plus Joshua's father had never trusted them. There were many Jew haters in Russia, and the army on its way was going to pillage what the Nazis left behind. His final move in this war would be leaving the city by way of the river. Joseph's gypsy family was out there somewhere, and he had convinced Joshua that they could be found.

Finishing the cooking, he buried the fire in soft dirt. From over the hill came the sounds of large equipment working. We edged toward the top of the hill. Joshua motioned me to the ground. Then together, we crawled toward the top. The Nazis were organizing a massive operation to uncover the bodies. "What are they doing?" I asked.

"They're going to burn them," Joshua said.

"But there are thousands of bodies," I said in disbelief.

A cold penetrating darkness flooded over me, my eyes fixed on the callous scene below. The best description to be made was a massive attempt to hide pure evil. Joshua must have sensed my repulsion, grabbing my arm and shaking it forcefully.

"We must go quickly," he urged. We scurried down the hill, Joshua snatching the bag of food as we left. No matter how hurried he became, there always time to check before entering any open area. We meticulously made our way toward the cemetery. Soon enough, we were back, and it was time for me to go check on Sara. Approaching the monument, Joshua gave the signal of arrival. The top slid back and there stood Joseph and Daniel by my cart.

Joshua gave the order, and we lifted the cart up and out. Before leaving, he gave me food for Sara and myself. It was fish, and some other meat that I dared not ask about.

"I will be at the hut tonight; be careful in the city. There are very few good people there right now." Joshua was giving advice like a veteran master sergeant, which I was glad to accept.

I left the band of brothers and headed toward my hut. The journey went without incident. Approaching the hut, I noticed that all but two guards were absent from the post, and soldiers were hurriedly moving around.

I asked one of the guards what was happening; he told me that the camps were preparing to be moved. It was official, the Nazis were moving out. The Russian Army was close, and he also informed me that my hut would be dismantled in the morning. This was obviously very bad news; Sara needed more time to heal.

I entered the hut to check on her and looked towards the bunk. As planned, there was no sign that she was there.

"Sara it's me, Rusty." The bedding went flying back and there laid a smiling blonde treasure.

"Greetings, Sir Rusty, what brings this pleasure?" She was so joyful that I just had to smile. I didn't want to ruin the moment and tell her bad news, so I didn't. Instead I played along.

"Your highness, I am at your service." I stepped back and bowed with my arm extended to the side.

Sara giggled and extended her hand with palm down. "You may kiss my ring, kind Sir, and prepare me some water to quench my thirst."

I hadn't thought about it, but Sara had not had water to drink for hours. "Immediately, Madam," I groveled. Proceeding to the bucket, I dipped the wooden ladle to bring forth her request. She grabbed the handle and quickly downed the water.

"Slow down," I cautioned. "You are very dry and the water could choke you if you drink too fast."

"It tastes so good," she said with begging eyes for more. I obliged her and filled it again. Finishing the second cup, she brought the cup down revealing a questioning look on her face.

"Rusty, what is going on outside? There has been yelling and trucks passing by all day." I hesitated and looked at her with concern.

She questioned, "What is it Rusty?"

"The Nazis are leaving and they will tear down the hut in the morning."

Sara didn't blink an eye. "Good, I'm tired of lying here. We will make a plan tonight and be gone before they know it."

I smiled while responding, "As you wish, your highness." I bowed my head and sent my hand in a sweeping motion. Sara let out a giggle and then corrected herself by putting finger to lips. She knew it was vital to be quiet, but her effervescence momentarily overtook her.

We conversed for the rest of the afternoon, awaiting the darkness that would bring Joshua. Sara was such a bright little girl, and despite her circumstances, was so very positive about life. It seemed as if she cherished every moment and made me want to smile, which felt so odd in the setting that we were in.

She was a dreamer, knowing exactly the house on the river where she would live. It was just down the road from her home where the family lived before the war. Her dream was to be a baker, and make the finest breads and cakes right out of the kitchen overlooking the river, just like her mother had done. I could have listened to her through the evening, but we were interrupted by the rattle of the shutter as it swung open.

Joshua slithered through; going directly to his sister and kissing her forehead. "How are you?" he asked.

"Joshua, I'm fine, quit worrying about me," she whispered in a short tone.

I interrupted. "We have a problem." Joshua turned and searched my face for information.

I said, "The Nazis are leaving; they will tear this hut down in the morning." I could see the wheels turning in his head. His thoughts had moved immediately past any conversation about moving Sara; that had already been assumed. Planning and thinking through possible scenarios were in his head, which strategy to use.

Joshua said, "I noticed the number of guards around the compound has been reduced. But, there is more traffic in the streets." I nodded my head in agreement.

I said, "The guards told me that many of them would be busy moving supplies."

Joshua said, "It would probably make sense to wait till later in the night and give things a chance to settle down. That will give me time to get Daniel and Joseph and be back here to make the move."

He addressed me. "You will handle the cart and move as we clear the path. The move must be made in small segments according to where the cart will be most hidden." He turned and spoke to Sara. "The route we must take will be very bumpy; it's going to be painful." Sara was offended by his pampering tone, giving him a dismissive look and sticking her tongue at him.

Joshua smiled. "I will be back in a few hours." Then tucking his floppy cap down tightly to his head, he left by way of the window, with the flash of a Marvel superhero. The general had spoken; it was time to ready ourselves to leave.

I began by gathering everything and placing it by the door. There really was very little besides what was covering Sara. I ventured outside to the cart, maneuvering it closer to the front of the hut. While there, I noticed foot traffic beginning to dwindle. Soon, it would probably be down to just patrols.

Time seemed to be moving slowly as we waited. Sara must have sensed that I was getting nervous. "Rusty it's going to be ok. Joshua will take care of everything."

"I'm sure he will," I said. I walked over to Sara and began checking her leg and the splint holding it in place. My eyes caught hers, and she gave me a big grin.

"You are a very good person, Sir Rusty."

"Well thank you, Your Highness, but how do you know this? I'm sure someone such as you has met many pretending to be good but end up bad at heart."

"Of course," she said confidently. "That's exactly why I know you are good. I can tell by looking in your eyes. I know good, and I know bad; I know love and I know hate."

"You are a wise one, Princess Sara." I was infatuated with this little girl.

"I'm curious, Sara." I looked at her seriously. "When you look into Joshua's eyes, what do you see?"

"I know he seems so serious, but he is just protecting me," she said, shrugging her shoulders. "I see love. I've seen his eyes all of my life. I see when he's happy, I see when he's angry, and I see when he's worried. But I always see love." Her eyes questioned me.

"Why, what do you see?"

Thinking for a moment, "strength," I said. "And also courage, I get this feeling when I'm around him of such focus and commitment; the word that comes to mind most often is courage."

Sara could not contain her grin. "See, I was right. You are a good person. You see Joshua as he is; just like our father did." Sadness came over the little girl's face as she reflected.

Joshua's timing was perfect. The window flew open, and in he slid.

"We are ready," he assured.

I moved to the door to take a look outside; things were quiet. I turned to Joshua. "So tell me the plan."

Joshua began. "Daniel has two hiding places ready on the way to the cemetery. He will be a lookout as we move. We shall make a push for the first hideout, and then wait for the best opportunity to move from there. I will stay with you and Sara and help with the cart. We might need to move the cart very quickly, so it would be better to have two of us. Joseph will also be watching. He will be ready to be the decoy if we run into a patrol."

I asked, "What's the plan when we get to the cemetery?"

Joshua answered. "By that time we will need to stop and regroup. We will stay at the cemetery and wait for darkness tomorrow night, then work our path to the river. Daniel made two rafts and has them hidden and waiting. We will float the river in the darkness. Joseph knows the woods downstream; that's where we will find his clan."

Joshua had a good plan but I was curious. "Then what, where will you live?"

He didn't hesitate. "We can survive until we get to Joseph's people; sooner or later we will find them."

Joshua was getting anxious. "We need to go. The longer we are outside the greater the danger." Going to the window, he swung it back and forth as a signal to the boys that we were about to be on the move. A rock hit the hut. Apparently Daniel had gotten the message. Joshua looked to me for guidance on moving Sara to the cart. I supported her leg with one of my arms and wrapped the other arm around her bottom. Joshua held her shoulders.

I checked with Sara. "Are you ready?"

She responded bravely, "Let's go."

We lifted, and I knew the pain would be intense. The little girl closed her eyes and bit her lip, not making a sound. Together, we carried Sara out of the hut and slid her in the cart. Quickly piling all clothing and blankets on top of her, we were off.

The first heading was set for a burned-out building right on the edge of the city, about a mile away. Our challenge was staying off the roads, using only small walking paths and open fields full of rocks. The lone light came from a crescent moon; that was good for cover but made it very difficult to see the rocks and the path.

Once the building was reached, the plan was to angle through the streets until reaching a particular opening in the sewer. The boys would scout in front of the cart as we navigated through, ensuring the coast was clear. Our exit would come near the cemetery, and then the final short push for the hideout.

The journey began in almost full darkness. It was rough as expected and I knew Sara would be very uncomfortable. We were making decent progress and had come to the middle of a field, when shouting started and a commotion ensued on the road to our side. Suddenly shots rang out; a Nazi patrol had crossed a resistance group and a fire fight began to rage. A bullet whizzed by my head. We had a problem; we were in the line of fire.

"Joshua, we need to get out of here," I whispered franticly. He nodded and began to push hard on the cart. I picked up the pace and the cart crashed over the protruding rocks. Bullets continued flying our way and one slammed into the cart.

From the darkness came Daniel and Joseph, they recognized the dilemma and began pushing alongside the cart. The pace was to rough and the cart was in danger of breaking up. I motioned for all to stop. I quickly checked the wheels and they were still intact. I pulled back the clothing that covered Sara. She was in tears but was otherwise ok.

"I have an idea," I said.

I motioned for everyone to pick up on the cart from underneath. The boys all nodded that they understood. We lifted and the cart cleared the ground. Another hundred meters had to be made before we would be out of the field and out of the line of fire. Bullets were flying all around us and we were in great danger. The weight was very difficult for the boys but they pushed on.

Joshua urged them. "Keep going, we can't stop. We must do this."

Reaching the edge of the field, Daniel and Joseph collapsed on the ground. I moved to the front of the cart and grabbed the handles. Joshua pushed from behind and we were able to move the cart to the cover of the trees. We were finally out of direct line with the fire fight. Joshua jumped into the cart to check on Sara.

"We made it," he said. Sara grabbed his hand and squeezed it. She smiled at her brother, not wanting to speak and reveal her pain.

Joshua reorganized the crew. He sent the two boys back to their support positions. We were under cover of the trees and should have a safe path to the first stop.

We reached the building without incident. I had water in a pouch and shared it. Everyone needed some rest and refreshment. Sara sat up and took a drink, even in the darkness I could see the puffiness around her eyes from the tears.

Now our challenge was different. Moving in the streets would be easy and swift, but the danger was being seen. The plan was basically the same; Daniel and Joseph would be scouts and decoys. Joshua would help move the cart and be the final decoy if needed.

We worked one city block at a time. The cart stayed close to the buildings and made a move across streets when the coast was clear. We were doing well until two blocks from the sewer opening. A Nazi patrol was headed straight for us. The other problem was that they were probably going to go through the sewer for a security check.

As planned, the boys deployed. Joseph revealed his position and took off. Two from the six man Nazi unit quickly followed. Seeing that, Daniel jumped out and took off in the opposite direction. Two Nazis followed him.

Now we were down to Joshua. He turned to me and whispered.

"I will take the final two. You go in the sewer and I will meet you near the cemetery." I nodded and Joshua ran to the middle of the street. He waited till they ordered him to halt and took off down the street. I was positioned in the shadows as the Nazi soldiers raced by in pursuit of the fleet-footed Joshua.

Pulling the cart out of the shadows, I hurriedly moved for the opening into the sewer. I had never been in a sewer before. The smell was overpowering. It was pitch black and I was going to need some light. I asked Sara if she could reach the lantern. I heard her fumbling around looking for it; finally her tiny voice.

"I've got it," she said.

I moved closer to the sound of her voice and felt around until my hands came across the lantern. There were matches in my pocket and I lit the wick. The lantern gradually brightened enough to see the immediate area around the cart, but not much more. Looking to the side of the cart away from the wall, I gasped. The wheel was just inches away from a ledge that plunged into darkness.

"Sara, don't move," I warned. If I would have taken one more step, we both would have been over the side. Grabbing the handles of the cart, I gradually moved forward until it was centered on the narrow path. Now I had another problem. I needed both hands to move the cart, but there was also a need for the lantern up and forward to have light to see. One mistake and we would be over the edge, and I had no idea how deep it might be.

There was only one thing to do. "Sara I'm going to need your help."

She responded, "Tell me what to do."

"I need you to move as far forward as you can in the cart and sit up. I can't get around the cart to help you. You will need to hold the lantern for me so I can see the path."

"Ok, Rusty," she said bravely.

"Sara, it's going to hurt a lot."

"I know, just give me a moment." Little by little I saw her petite frame scoot toward the front of the cart. One last scoot and she had her shoulders and arms resting over the top of the front rail.

"Ready," she said. I gave her the lantern and put my hand warmly on her shoulder. She gave me a victorious look and I smiled back at her; then turned my attention to the task in front of us.

Focused concentration would be needed to keep the wheels from the edge. The path was so narrow that I was scraping the wall as I pulled. The pace was slow but we were making headway. Not sure how far to go, I trusted Sara for direction; and that Joshua would be at the exit point to meet us.

Suddenly a deep voice spoke from the darkness. "I'll have that cart." A large shadowy figure emerged into the dim light.

"Who are you?" I questioned sensing danger. The daunting figure drew out a large knife as he moved closer.

He mumbled through dirty teeth, "I said I'll have that cart." The man was filthy, with a scraggly long black beard. I reached back in the cart and pulled out about a 3-foot-long 2 by 4 that I had plucked from out of the hut.

"You're not taking this cart," I said.

The man growled with anger and took a step towards me. Just then a large rock struck him in the middle of the back. He gasped for air. Another rock plunked him in the back of the head. He staggered, I swung the 2 by 4 as hard as I could and hit him in the shoulder. He staggered and stepped off the side of the ledge to the darkness below. I heard him hit and begin to moan; I still didn't know exactly how deep the trench was, but the man was still alive. Out of the darkness appeared Joshua.

"Quickly," he said and pointed down the path. "There are more of them." Joshua took the lantern and we headed toward the exit. I could hear more voices and breathing, but nothing was in our immediate path. The sewer had me spooked and claustrophobic. The shadows created by the lantern were one monster after another to my eyes. Sara put her hand on my shoulder and squeezed. I could tell she was frightened, and briefly put my hand on hers, but quickly moved it back to the handle of the less than stable cart.

Two torches appeared, coming right for us. My hands began to sweat as I gripped the handles of the cart tightly, and prepared for a fight. Joshua pushed on. Huge relief engulfed me when I saw the faces of Daniel and Joseph holding the torches. They had checked the path ahead and said it was clear.

We continued out of the sewer as a group. The boys extinguished their light just before exit so the flames would not attract any attention. One more burst to the cemetery and we had made it; a three hour journey that seemed like an eternity.

The cart was stowed with Sara still in it. There was just enough room for her below the cover of the hide out. We all crawled in and made it a very snug fit. It was cold outside so the body heat from all of us was helpful. Joshua poked his head up to where he could see his Sara.

"Are you ok?" he asked.

She smiled and answered her brother. "I'm fine."

I said, "I need to check her splint and her leg." Joshua slid down and I maneuvered around him and up to Sara.

"Hi, Rusty," Sara chirped. I blew her a kiss, and she pretended to blush. The leg looked ok but the splint had loosened.

"Sara I'm going to tighten this splint and it might hurt a little bit."

"Well, if it only hurts a little bit that's nothing compared to earlier," she said with a big grin. This was the most resilient little girl I had ever been around. I made quick work of the splint and slid back down in my slot.

It was time to rest for a few hours, and then the team would go out and bring more supplies in before the sun came up. A long day of hiding was ahead of us before we could move again the next night.

I did my best to sleep but had to settle for just resting off of my feet. My mind was full of thoughts about these unbelievable kids, and what I could do to help them. The atrocities they had faced were mind numbing insights into what evil could be. I was going to do anything possible to get them through this.

The next thing I knew Joshua was shaking my shoulder. I guess in fact I was able to sleep. "Time to go," he said. The boys readied themselves and prepared to leave the hideout. Daniel and Joseph slid out first.

Joshua turned to me. "Rusty, stay with Sara, we will be back soon."

I acknowledged the command and Joshua followed the two boys. I moved up to the level of the cart to check on Sara. She was sleeping, and that allowed time to study her precious face. Her blonde hair was a dirty mess, but still framed the face of an angel, so beautiful and peaceful in her dreams. I smiled knowing that when she awoke, her feisty little self would return.

Time was hard to judge sitting in a dark covered hole, but it would be daylight soon and the boys were expected back at any time. Suddenly, Joshua was back. He pulled open the cover and slid into the hideout with a distressed look on his face.

"What's wrong?" I asked.

He was thinking as he answered, "The Nazis are at the far end of the cemetery. I overheard them planning to sweep through looking for valuables." He paused as he continued to think. "That means they will be overturning head stones and digging around."

I knew what that meant. We had just lost our hiding place.

Joshua continued. "We must leave now before the sun comes up."

I became very concerned. "Joshua, that means we travel through the city in the daylight."

He impatiently explained, "We have no choice; there are no more places to hide. If we don't go now we will still be on the run, and risk the chance that someone will find the rafts at the river."

He was right. The Nazis patrolled the river often. We were going to have to make a move.

I questioned, "The boys?"

"They are in position to support the move out of here, decoys just as before. One more thing, the patrol has a dog, so we must give ourselves more room and try to stay downwind." Joshua moved up to talk to Sara.

"Did you hear all that?" he asked.

"Yes, and I'm ready to go," she answered.

He took a quick look outside and decided the time was right. The plan was to get the cart to an isolated alley about three blocks outside of the cemetery. We had to make it out through a hole in the cemetery wall, and then be exposed in the street for half of a block, before turning the corner and out of view of the patrol.

Joshua would help me get the cart to the wall, then position himself to be the third decoy. We moved the cover off of the hole and rolled the cart out. Joshua signaled the other two as we moved the cart in position. It was important to hurry because light was only minutes away.

I was at the hole in the fence with my hands tightly gripping the handles. Just then, Daniel and Joseph bolted through the cemetery and out the far side. The dog got the scent and tried to follow. The handler held him back and the commander of the patrol sent two soldiers instead. That still left the commander, two soldiers, and the dog; not good news. Joshua made the decision to be the next decoy.

He turned to me. "Wait till the dog pursues me, then go quickly before any of them turn around to look." There would be great danger in what Joshua was about to do. He was going to run perilously close to the patrol to insure they would come after him.

"Joshua, please be careful," I pleaded.

"Always," he answered with firm focus. With that, he was gone.

He stayed inside the wall of the cemetery until in full view of the dog. It got his scent and jerked the handler forward. The commander gave the ok to release him and the Shepherd came charging. Joshua held his ground until the dog was thirty meters away. He sprinted for the stone fence with the dog closing quickly. Planting his foot in the slot of a missing stone, he leapt high to the iron rail at the top of the six foot fence. Grabbing the rail, he swung over in one move landing on his feet; then ran up the street parallel to the patrol, with the dog stuck on the other side of the fence.

Now was my time. The patrol was focused on Joshua. I pulled the cart out of the cemetery and on to the pavement; then pulled hard for the corner just ahead. The patrol was now in full pursuit of Joshua who had turned down the next street, and was swiftly heading away. I made my corner and was moving parallel to him about three blocks away. The dog was barking loudly in pursuit, but I was pretty sure it was too far behind to catch the master of escape.

I came to the intersection of the next street and moved close to the near building; then peered around the corner to check traffic. The coast was clear so I crossed as quickly as possible.

Joshua turned into an alley and jumped for the ledge of a window on the side of the adjacent building. His foot planted firmly and he grasped high for an iron bar that was attached to a mangled fire escape. It dangled loosely but still connected all the way to the top of the building. His right hand gripped the bar tightly, but the force of his weight prompted the loose iron to swing away from the edge on which he was standing. Joshua became airborne; swinging out and away from the building, but gravity sent him headed straight back in on a collision course. He knew the impact was going to be severe, and also knew he must hold on, because there wasn't much time. The collision jolted him hard enough to knock his breathe away. Gasping for air, he focused hard to not relinquish his grip. The sensation finally subsided and he began to breath. Looking upward, he rotated left and reached with his hand, securing the next rung. Repeating this procedure, he went right hand over left until able to place his feet on the ladder. Now Joshua could race to the top. The dog and the patrol were closing in; only moments away. If he were seen, they could call for another patrol and trap him on the rooftop. He reached the top and threw himself onto the rock and tar covering of the roof; then jumped up and sprinted away.

The patrol reached the alley at that exact moment. Fortunately, none of them had their eyes up, and the dog became confused on the location of the scent. One in the patrol scanned the buildings in great frustration. He was so close and only needed one shot.

His eyes glowed with the burning desire for the kill; feeling it would be today, he just knew it.

I made it to the alley where we had planned to regroup. Momentarily I heard movement coming from above. Joshua was climbing down from three stories by moving from window to window, using any kind of hand hold available. Jumping down from the final eight feet, he was breathing heavily; also indicating he needed water.

Sara was sitting up and handed the water pouch to me. I walked over to where Joshua was sprawled on his back and offered my hand to help him sit up. He took a big drink and expressed his thanks; then looked at his sister and smiled.

"Well that's a start," he said.

Joshua was now breathing normally. I was curious about Daniel and Joseph. Joshua kept them out to form a wider perimeter, wanting to spread our advance as we approached the river. So if need be the patrols would have more than one group to worry about. They had already been misdirected in three different ways, and still with no knowledge of the cart. It was a good plan. The boys would meet us at the rafts.

We decided that Joshua should continue to lead the way, and insure that the coast was clear. With the cart, I would stick to the alleys as often as possible and use the coves of the buildings as a way to hide. Joshua moved to the end of the alley and peered around the corner. He waved me forward, and I advanced the cart with Sara as my passenger. He sprinted to the middle of the street and made a quick analysis; then gave me the signal to move.

I pulled on the cart with all available force and jerked it into motion, hoping that Sara was ok in the back. Pulling hard across the street, we made the cover of the next alley. My heart was pounding as I checked to see if Sara was ok. Her eyes were wide with intensity and she nodded excitedly, letting me know she was fine. We continued this process for many blocks; Joshua checking the street for traffic, then signaling me to cross.

He came back from this particular street with a worried look. "We are close but the traffic is very heavy. Our entrance to the river is in the middle of the next block." He said, pointing across to where the road dipped down toward the water. He continued. "There is a patrol with a dog at the top of the street that crosses our path, and a road block setting up down the street in the other direction, stopping all vehicles. We must move now or be trapped."

Joshua was running out of options and the concerned boy knew it.

I asked, "How far to the water after you make the turn at the alley?"

"About a hundred meters," he said.

We decided on a plan of diversion to occupy the patrol with the dog. I would take the cart to the top of the street and engage them, give the dog my scent and keep their attention on me. Joshua would time his journey with Sara according to the activity at the road block, and attempt to avoid any detection. They could basically stay out of view of the road block by hugging the buildings. The big issue was with Sara now needing to walk. Their pace of movement would be slow. If the street could be crossed, they should be home free.

We moved Sara out of the cart and on her feet for the first time in a couple of days. She was a little unstable and unsure of her footing. Joshua secured the crutch and placed it under his little sister's shoulder. They practiced briefly with Joshua helping her along. Ready or not it was time to go.

I moved the cart out of the alley and along the side of the large brick building; not wanting to be seen until contact with the patrol, which was about fifty meters around the corner. As quickly as possible I made the turn and approached. Taking the moment, I engaged them in a hardy and thankful hello. It was the Captain and his squad. "Captain, thank goodness it is you."

"Cart Man, what are you doing this far in the city?"

"I'm looking for safe shelter, but between the fighting and the patrols I've had to keep moving." While talking, I slowly moved beyond them trying to encourage their turning toward me.

I spoke to the captain. "I thought if I could get to the river or over that way, I might find a spot." I pointed up river and in the direction I wanted them to look. The dog had taken a keen interest in my cart and in the jerky I had been smart enough to stash in my pocket.

Something had flushed Joshua and Sara out of the alley, and they began making their way slowly across the street. I continued talking and pointing toward my pretended destination, trying to buy time. They were fully exposed from both sides. I pushed my pockets forwards toward the dog trying to keep his attention totally on me.

"Cart Man, there is no safe area in the city right now, you must leave and find shelter elsewhere," the captain said.

"I will, Captain, but I would like to go up here and cross at the bridge if possible." I continued to point up river and away from Joshua. They had made it across and were moving out of sight.

"No, Cart Man, you will not have clearance to cross the bridge. You must turn around and go back." The mission had been accomplished. Joshua and Sara had made their crossing. I gave a look of disappointment but agreed to go back, and turned the cart around slowly, attempting to buy more time.

Joshua leaned Sara against the wall of the building just inside the alley. He looked her in the eye. "How are you doing?"

Sara was in a lot of pain but she told her brother; "I'm doing fine."

He adjusted the crutch and moved himself into position to support her for the last leg of the trip. When he looked up he came face to face with a little boy.

He was dressed in a heavy coat and hat, and was not more than nine or ten years old. Joshua was stunned; the boy had come out of nowhere. Around his neck was a string with a whistle attached to it. The Nazis had used this in the past. They hid young children in alleyways and streets. When the children saw a violation, they blew their whistles to alert the patrols.

Joshua addressed the boy while pleading with his eyes. "It is just the two of us, we haven't hurt anyone. We just need to get to the river. No one will know, just let us pass." The little boy stared at them both. He looked at Sara and she gently smiled back at him. He looked at Joshua up and down, and then he spoke. "You are Jews."

The words came out as he reached for his whistle. Joshua released Sara and desperately lunged for the little boy; Sara went toppling to the ground. The boy and whistle were just out of his grasp, and the sharp shrill of the mechanism echoed off the buildings and down the street into the ears of the Shepherd.

The patrol came to immediate alert status. The dog turned toward the street and scrambled off with his handler right behind.

Joshua got to his feet and forgot about the little boy; it was too late. He gathered up Sara and the crutch and made a desperate move toward the river. He carried most of Sara's weight as she used the crutch for balance on her far side. The dog made the corner, and the big Shepherd was bearing down on the fleeing pair.

I left my cart and ran along with the Nazi patrol, turning the corner in time to see the Shepherd sink his teeth and claws into the back of Sara's thick coat, dragging her down. Joshua leapt over Sara and attacked the dog with the handle of his trusty knife, knocking him off, then drew his knife back and swung at the snapping dog. Sara popped off the ground and grabbed her crutch. She continued her struggle to walk toward the river.

The incident was flashing past me in slow motion. An eager Nazi soldier raised his rifle to fire. My scream of "no" seemed to take forever to leave my throat. He fired, and my eyes moved down the street. Sara's delicate frame lifted off its feet and fell lifeless to the ground. The captain gave the order to cease fire and the patrol moved in. Seeing Sara, Joshua dropped his knife and collapsed to the ground. The Shepherd was told to release and retreated to his handler.

Joshua rose to his knees and turned to his baby sister. He moved his head down to hers, tears streaming from his eyes. In a whisper he begged her to get up, stroking her hair and pleading with her. He hugged her lifeless shoulders and collapsed on top of her, laying there not moving. The soldier who had fired on Sara raised his gun for Joshua, his eyes ablaze with passion. I had moved into position behind the patrol and had to act quickly or Joshua would be dead.

"Captain, this boy could be of good use to you. I've seen him work, I've seen him around." I moved toward the soldier and got between the rifle and Joshua, trying to direct all attention towards me.

"Cart Man, how do you know this boy?" the captain asked. He motioned the soldier to bring his rifle down.

"I see many things on my trips and I would often see this boy, always working; he is strong and smart." I knew none of this was going to make much of a difference to the captain, but I wanted him to think for a while before he made a decision. I looked right at him; our eyes met and he knew I was trying to save the boy. He walked around to the other side of Joshua where he lay holding Sara.

"He doesn't seem to want to live," he said dismissively, gesturing with an open palm to the non-moving boy. The captain needed a reason to save him and he was leaving it for me to give him one. I had to get Joshua on his feet.

"Get up, boy!" I shouted at Joshua. "Boy, get up and live." There was no movement. "Boy, I'm here to tell you to get up and live." I got down on one knee where I could see his face. I spoke at him with fierce passion. "Listen to me, get off this ground." I moved closer and whispered. "Get up, Joshua. Sara would want you to get up."

There was a slight movement to his head. He slowly turned and focused his eyes on mine. They were dark and unsettling as he glared toward me.

"Bury her," is all he muttered. Joshua rose to his knees, then gradually stood, keeping his intense stare on me. I nodded to acknowledge that I would take care of Sara. He turned and prepared himself to move with the patrol.

"Cart Man, I will take him to the camp, and can only guarantee his safety until that time." The captain walked closer to me. "The camps are breaking up and moving toward Germany. It will be very dangerous and many will die." He nodded to me and turned toward his patrol, giving the order to move out.

I noticed the soldier who had fired on Sara; he glared at Joshua with malice in his eyes, gripping his rifle tightly, as if he had unfinished business. His eyes met mine, and in them lay evil intent. I knew Joshua wasn't safe as the patrol turned the corner and headed out of sight.

A debilitating feeling of loneliness suddenly engulfed me. The scene was brutal. Little Sara lay at my feet and the great Joshua was being led off into harm's way. The mission I had been charged with was in shambles.

I knelt down next to Sara and ran my fingers through her golden hair. My eyes filled with tears as I sat upon the hard cold street. Gathering her up, I hugged her tightly to my chest. Not being able to hold it in any longer, I lashed out. "Ham!... Ham!... Damn it, why does this little girl have to die?" Rocking her back and forth, tears flooded down my face. "Why did she have to die? She had so much to offer, she was so good."

I lost track of how long I held her, but eventually, rising to my feet, I carried her to the cart. Joshua's knife rested on the street where he had battled with the dog, and I took the time to retrieve it, then commenced on what amounted to a funeral march toward the cemetery. I was trying to make sense of what had happened, but I couldn't. Angry and disillusioned, I walked, searching for answers along the way. There were plenty of questions heading Ham's way, and I was hoping he was hearing all of them. My thoughts drifted to the innocence of Sara, and grief engulfed me again. I could not except that she was gone and would not except any reason for her death. There was no purpose that could possibly justify this tragedy.

I had very little memory of what was encountered on the way, but before me were the gates to the cemetery. The wire that had secured the entrance was gone. Pulling the cart through, my journey continued toward the mausoleum, no longer caring if I encountered a patrol. I unlatched the door of the shed that was adjacent to the structure and walked inside; unearthing a shovel and rake that Joshua had buried under the dirt floor. Grabbing them, I then walked outside and encountered Daniel and Joseph standing before me. The boys stood motionless with tears in their eyes, peering at me, and no doubt wondering what was next in their lives. Seeing them sent an awkward feeling of warmth through me. I had felt so alone, it was very good to see them. I also realized that they were waiting for my direction.

I spoke solemnly. "We must bury her properly. It's Joshua's wish."

We sorrowfully moved the cart toward the monument and positioned it at the edge of the hiding place; it was time to say goodbye. I pushed back the blanket to exposed little Sara lying quietly, her hands on her chest as I had placed them earlier, her golden hair framing her still and angelic face.

Daniel was first, gently positioning her head in his hands, as he lovingly bent to kiss her forehead. He whispered a personal thought in her ear, as tears rolled off his cheeks and onto Sara's quiet face. Pulling his head back, he paused for a final look, then gradually stepped back, never letting his eyes leave her.

Joseph rushed up and gathered her little body in his arms. He wailed as he rocked her. "I'm so sorry, Sara." He would have held her forever but I had to step in. The two boys were still in danger, and we needed to proceed.

I was absolutely humbled by these two boys, having survived so much; still love flowed from their hearts. Their ability to say goodbye in such a sweet and loving manner, soothed the wounds of my aching heart.

It was time for my goodbye. I looked out to the horizon and noticed the burning had stopped. The ashes no longer billowed up over the hill. A ray of sun broke through the haze and seemed to illuminate the area around the cemetery. Looking down at Sara, I thought about the sweet ray of sunshine she had been in my life. Tears rimmed my eyes as I spoke. "Ok, Sara, it looks like your ride is here. May God and every angel out there be with you always. I know one that better be."

Leaning down, I kissed her forehead and gently placed my hand over her heart. I whispered passionately while hovering above her precious face. "Ham, you take care of this little girl." I backed away to view her for one final moment; then nodded to the boys that it was time. Wrapping the blanket around her, we lowered the cart into the hole that would serve as her resting place, as it had for all of these days. We began the sorrowful job of filling in the grave. With every shovel full of dirt, my thoughts drifted to memories of Sara, which eventually brought me back to Joshua.

His wish that Sara be honored properly had given us purpose through our grief, but now we had to move on. The boys needed direction and a plan. We finished filling in the dirt and found a head stone for the grave. With the point of Joshua's knife, Joseph etched out the letters of Sara on the stone. We all stood for a moment absorbing the significance of what we had just done. I broke the silence and motioned the boys back to the storage building. We buried the tools and sat down for a conference.

I took charge of the meeting. The plan was to continue on with the original idea of the rafts and using the cover of darkness. The boys would leave the city by raft and use the river and woods as their refuge until they found Joseph's people. With his familiarity of the countryside, Joshua had already mapped multiple sites for hiding and cooking. The boys were skilled at trapping and fishing, and if they were careful, they could survive until they found the gypsies. That was the plan, and I wanted to make sure they were going to follow it, and not try to help Joshua.

That was to be my job, and I knew there was nothing they could do to help. It had been a long day and we had used it all. Night was falling quickly and it was time to move. I turned back toward the boys. There they stood, in their heavy coats and hats, looking like two that might be in *Spanky's Gang* at the movies. There was no clue to lead one to believe that these two were war veterans. But that's exactly what they were, fighting with courage and an uncanny instinct for survival. I hugged each of them and they responded in kind. I stepped back to signal the final goodbye, but the boys were not ready to leave. They stared at me waiting. I knew what they wanted and I gave them my pledge.

"I will find him," I said with determined conviction. Our eyes met and the boys knew they had my word. Joseph stepped forward to hand me Joshua's knife. His words were full of conviction. "He will be asking for this."

I smiled with my answer. "Yes he will."

They were satisfied. In the dim light of the end of the day, the boys made their exit. Each gave me a nod of respect, turned and left through the door.

Chapter 20 – Just Outside of Heaven

A Need to Reflect

I stood in the room not willing to move, feeling completely drained. A strange feeling began to overtake me and I had the sensation of floating. The white brightness that I had encountered when first traveling had returned; I was about to travel again. The sensation did not last long, but the energy around me was intense, and the bright whiteness felt as if it were pulsating through me. Eventually, it began to fade away, as it did, my feet found solid ground. My vision cleared to reveal a place that had the feel of somewhere I had been to before.

It was night time and the moon was out. A warm breeze ran through my hair. There were trees not far away and I was standing on plush green grass with plenty of open space. A softball park lay to my right with lights on but no one playing, familiar tennis courts to my left. It all clicked: it was the park near the college that Ham and I attended, the spot of many talks.

In the distance I could see Ham. He was sitting on the bench adjacent to the tennis courts, dressed in old baggy jeans and wearing a white t-shirt with a Jerry Jeff Walker label on the front. He threw his hands in the air and gave a big smile, waving dramatically for me to come over. Approaching him, I wondered if we were really back in the park, it all looked so real. I asked. "Where are we, Ham?"

His eyes twinkled as he answered. "Well, buddy, we are somewhere between heaven and earth. But I thought you might feel more comfortable if it looked like the park.

I wondered. "I can see you."

He grinned and said, "Yeah, I can do a lot of things here that are pretty cool."

I asked, "Where exactly is here?"

He answered, "This is in the dimension that we are able to share. It's the reason we can talk, and the thing that allows you to travel."

I had a lot of pent-up feelings that were begging to come out. "Ham, why did you send me to do this? That's the most evil place on earth."

He became very serious. "Rusty, that time is not mine, it's history to me just like you. My time started when I was born on earth. You can move back before your time because you have a host sending you back. That host is from that time period, and can place you. I can't, I can only watch. I didn't send you."

I was confused, "If you didn't send me then who did?"

Ham spoke cautiously. "All of this is very complicated, buddy, and the reason so much care has been taken with what you know and what you don't. Rusty, you need to understand how all this works and what's at stake. You are changing history with every action that you take. It is vital to keep Joshua safe, but you gotta be really careful with your impact on surrounding events. There are many here that are watching, and are rooting for you on this mission. This is a very important time, and so far you have been fantastic."

"Ok fine, I know I'm there to help Joshua and I know the other traveler is obviously there to kill him. But why did Sara have to die? Why couldn't I save her, Ham? She was such a sweet little girl and she didn't have to die."

Ham became noticeably focused. "That was her destiny. This is a very big picture, Rusty, and all that happens is a part of that picture."

I answered, "So big that a little girl had to be sacrificed?"

He said, "No, so big that everything is involved, including the little girl."

He paused for a moment, as if he were debating on whether he should comment further. "Rusty, it was Sara who sent you back."

"What?"

Ham continued. "Sara's destiny had been determined before you traveled. She had already crossed the threshold. She sent you back to counter the other traveler, and save Joshua. She sent you to keep hope alive."

That news stunned me. I sat frozen; tears trickled down my cheeks. I gasped for breath, realizing I hadn't taken one. Ham said nothing, and let me sit quietly thinking. My mind was racing through all the events over the last week and the agony of losing Sara.

I flashed back to the pain of losing Donna and my kids; then I realized they were alive and ok. I skipped to Sara and the shock of seeing her lifeless body on the street, holding her and having to say goodbye.

Then it occurred to me what Ham was saying; she was alright. Sara was alive and part of this whole thing. A flood of relief and thankfulness filled me. I looked to the stars above the park; I knew she was out there somewhere.

Tearfully I said, "I will find him, Sara. I will find him and help him." I don't know if I'd ever meant anything more in my life.

Ham decided it was time to speak. "You ok, Rusty?"

I gathered myself. "Yeah I'm ok."

Ham continued. "Rusty, do you remember talking about the feeling that you were going to be part of something big in your life?" I nodded. He continued. "Well, buddy, this is it."

Ham told the story of the ancient traveler and the gene that carries the beacon, being inserted into the bloodline of Joshua. He explained the Nazis role in the plan of the dark side to eliminate the carriers of the gene within the context of the Holocaust; and one more very important fact: Joshua was the last in the line.

I asked, "What does the beacon do?"

Ham was careful with his answer. "It's gonna guide travelers through a shortcut in space, a wormhole between the dimensions of the realities that exist."

I asked, "How short?"

"Very short," he said.

I continued. "And what happens if these space travelers don't have a beacon?"

Ham frowned. "They'll exit the wormhole at an incorrect angle, ripping a hole in the protective dimension of your reality. That would be a real bad deal, destroying earth and starting a chain reaction through the wormhole that would destroy all attached worlds that share the connection. The effect could alter the structure of the total universe; and I'm talking everything. If the universe expands at an improper angle, it will create massive black holes that will cause it to feed on itself. That would be the beginning of the end; you, me, everything that is. The dark side doesn't see the big picture; they are totally obsessed with stopping the wormhole."

I had more questions. "Why is the dark side so worried about a short cut in space?"

Ham answered. "The revelation of all of these worlds and making a connection between them would revolutionize the earth like nothing else in history. All of the discoveries ever known would pale in comparison to the advancement that would come about with this one breakthrough. The insight and understanding in all life forces would be unprecedented, and that doesn't fit the current patterns within hell.

"Souls would enter with way more knowledge and understanding. All kinds of new dynamics and thinking would come about. They would gain more understanding of the world around them and the better choices that are out there to be made. Billions of souls would discover new ideas and opportunities. The controlling forces of the dark side would be turned upside down, and a massive power shift would occur. They have fought this for thousands of years, and fear it more than any other event."

I asked. "Why does heaven care about what happens in Hell? It seems like a big risk to take if the wormhole travel fails."

Ham scratched his chin like he always did when he contemplated; then he spoke. "You're asking two separate questions. Rusty, the dark side isn't inherently evil. It's creating evil due to the actions of the guys in power. There are billions and billions of souls in the dark side who are being used and victimized.

"If it hadn't been for you, I would be one of them. I was drawn that way and would not have chosen the light if we had not talked about it. Think of it, Rusty, all of those souls just like me who will suffer for eternity if we don't do something. We have a chance to help. The dark side will never be like heaven, but it doesn't have to be the evilness that it is right now."

Ham was now up and pacing as he continued. "As for the wormhole, we don't control how the earth develops. We are involved only in stopping the dark side from interfering. The natural process of gaining knowledge, and the development of understanding of that knowledge, is the building block for the meaning and purpose of the universe. The stabilization and use of this wormhole is a natural evolution in the development of mankind.

"You were brought in because of your gift, and only to minimize the effect of the other traveler. I feel bad about what this has done to your life, but in the big picture there was just no choice."

I stood there not knowing what to say. Ham looked at me and gave me his big goofy grin. "Kind of piled on with information didn't I."

I nodded my head and just stood there for a few more moments.

"What now?" I asked.

Ham pointed at me and started talking like a Baptist preacher. "Son, you go get that boy."

I felt the whiteness wrapping around me, and I prepared myself to travel again. I said. "By Ham, I'll give it everything I've got."

Ham answered. "I know you will, partner; adios, muchacho."

Chapter 21 – Poland WW2

In The Midst of Evil, Goodness Brings Hope

It was a frigid night and activity in the streets was light. I knew this would ease Joseph and Daniel's plan of making it to the river undetected. I began my quest by weaving my way through the streets, and back toward the camp. I approached the guard post by the barracks and found it empty, then continued past my destroyed hut and on in closer to the camp. I left the roadway near the crest of the hill, not wanting to be seen, at least not yet. It was important to know who was down there first.

Topping the hill behind a cluster of trees, I looked down into a beehive of activity. A train was being loaded with all types of equipment. There was a perimeter of security about two hundred meters around the camp but that was it. They were preparing to leave and it appeared to be almost done.

The security force was the same unit that occupied the barracks. I looked for the captain but did not see him. It was essential to get permission to enter the camp and offer my help inside, but it was hard to tell if anyone was in charge, and if the officers were even still around. The only decision to be made was go down and find out.

I walked back to the road to make my entrance. Being fairly well known by these guards, it would help my chances if they were given a legitimate request. So the upfront approach brought me directly to the guard station.

"Halt, Cart Man, what do you want here?" The question came from the soldier in charge. I did not recognize him but he did me.

"I'm here looking to help," I said, continuing to move closer.

"We are leaving, Cart Man, so we have no need for you to take things to the city."

"I can see that," I said. "I don't want to return to the city, there is nothing for me there, I need to leave just like you." I was now among them and they all were very casual with their demeanor.

A familiar voice came from the side of my vision. "Where is it you intend to go?" It was the captain and he appeared through the dark mist of the cold evening air. I turned to him and gave a respectful nod.

"I have family in the west. I can't stay here and be considered a Nazi sympathizer. I would like to travel with you and help where I can."

The captain smiled and circled me with a slow analyzing walk. "You always show up, Cart Man, at the most unusual times. Why is this?" He stopped and engaged me in a stern gaze, knowing I was up to something. He would make sure that it was nothing that would affect him.

"Our paths have crossed out of necessity, Captain, but I assure you I only need the opportunity to travel." My only chance to be on the inside rest in the hands of this man. I returned his gaze with a determined one of my own. We had established an unspoken relationship with each other and I was putting it all on the line at that moment. The captain turned his gaze toward the camp and became thoughtful. He remained silent for what seemed an eternity. Finally he turned back to me.

"There is a need for supply personnel to keep the caravans moving. You will come with me; we shall go talk to the supply officer." He turned and offered his hand in a gesture to walk with him.

We strolled towards the camp as he continued. "The camp will begin to move tomorrow at sunrise. The prisoners will walk and be kept in units of three hundred men. Each unit will be divided into three marching groups. Each group will have guards moving with it, two guards on duty at a time." The captain was offering up a lot of information that I was not expecting. I intently listened.

"The guard will change three times daily, and that is when you will supply the lines." He turned his head and looked at me. "This time will be the only rest for the prisoners; any that cannot continue will be disposed of. Many of them will not make it through the mountains. Cart Man, you might be one of them. You will have to walk most of the time. The trucks will be for supplies and for the guards to rest."

The captain was laying it out for me. He knew I was there for Joshua but he was letting me know about the danger to me. I remained silent and just listened. "The boy is in a unit on the north side of the camp. It will be up to you to arrange to supply those units. If you are able to do that, the boy will see you often."

We walked a bit further and then I had to ask. "How did you know I would be here tonight?"

"I didn't," he said. "But, I would have been disappointed if you hadn't come." He continued to walk with his eyes focused straight ahead. He had the slightest of grins on his otherwise stern face. "He's a good boy. I can see it in him." His eyes glimmered with moisture in the light of the approaching camp. "I have one just like him waiting for me."

The thought of the captain having a family had never occurred to me. He was just a father stuck in the apparatus of a monster. We came to a tent where the supply officer was located. The captain went in first and talked to the man. He came out and motioned me inside. The officer looked me over and nodded his head, then requested the captain's help to show me where to go, and we left the tent.

We walked toward a campfire with men sitting and warming themselves. The captain explained that these men were in a similar situation to me. They would also be supplying the lines. "Cart Man, the units are all organized with supply trucks that will service them. Each truck will supply a unit." He pointed to the far north end of the camp. "That truck is the one you want."

I nodded my head and turned toward him. I could not thank him or make any kind of gesture. He looked straight ahead into the night air, but continued to speak.

"You need to get some sleep and rest your legs. You will probably not see me from this point; I am in charge of all security, and will be coordinate this massive march from a central location. One more thing, the soldier that shot the girl is new to my unit, and was not under orders to shoot. He has also shown a special interest in the boy. Cart man, he is an evil one, I have seen enough to know. Be very aware of him, he will be one of the guards."

Turning his back, the Captain prepared to leave. "Good luck, cart man." He walked away with an officially brisk pace. I kept my eyes on him until he disappeared into the misty night, just as he had arrived. I was sure that he had just warned me of the Dark Traveler. He had done as much as he could; giving me a chance, a chance to save Joshua.

The Book of Thomas

Chapter 22 – Poland 1944

The March

I was up early and at the gathering point, wanting to insure the best chance at being assigned to the truck that the captain had pointed out. The other men supplying the trucks couldn't care less, so I was confident of getting the assignment I was wanting.

Soldiers began to mill around in anticipation of the move. In the distance I could see large groups headed toward us escorted by Nazi soldiers with rifles. As they came closer I could see the men being escorted. They were not the same detainees that I had been seeing. They were all men with a more physical presence to them, and they had better clothing.

These guys are prisoners of war, I thought to myself. The captain had arranged for Joshua to be put with these men, probably in an attempt to improve the odds of saving his life. From my vantage point I could see in the distance, thousands of prisoners being organized for a massive movement. This was it, the final move back to Germany.

Joshua was in a group headed my way, but walked with his head down, which prevented him from seeing me. It was important for him to know I was there. Figuring out some way to get his attention became high priority. I spotted who might be the commander of the escort unit.

"Sir, is it time for your squad to get a ration of water," I said in a loud voice.

He answered, "You will be told when its time."

"Yes, sir," I said, while looking at Joshua. It worked; he raised his head and looked my way.

I stared at him intently. His eyes were dark and sad. I kept eye contact with him and nodded my head firmly as a sign of commitment and support. He maintained eye contact as he passed, but his expression never changed. He was not emotionally in a good place. I knew exactly how he felt and had to find a way to talk to him.

The march began to take shape. Hundreds of POWs moved into view. Multiple marches were being organized with three units per section. The prisoners had no restraints and I thought that was a good thing for any plan of escape. It took most of the morning to get organized, but eventually my unit was on its way. The guards were on a rotating schedule of three hours, and sat in the supply truck while they rested. The only rest for the prisoners was during the changing of the guard. At that time, I would be in charge of supplying water to one group of prisoners. That meant that a prisoner would only get a drink of water twice in one days march.

The first day was about getting the routine down. I was not allowed to supply water because it was only a half day march. Night had arrived and it was getting very cold. The commander of the unit guided us to a farm just of the road. The prisoners were herded, like cattle, toward a large barn. Three hundred men and a little boy were stuffed shoulder to shoulder into a wooden structure meant for farm animals. This allowed the guards to keep only a two man rotation on the exits. The rest of the guards were in the farmhouse resting. My job was to get rations of food and water to the men in the barn, consisting of hard biscuit and a tub of water.

The men were to rotate one at a time to my position at the entrance of the barn, then obtain a biscuit and ladle full of water. This process was hurried along by the attending guard, so when Joshua came by I could only look at him. His eyes met mine with the same stare as he had that morning. I did my best to give him a look of determination and commitment as he moved past; and continued eye contact until he was out of sight. I at least had his attention.

There were multiple problems to deal with; I needed to come up with an escape plan and communicate that plan to Joshua. I also had to deal with the brutal schedule of the march. It would not take very long before the prisoners were worn down to nothing. The move had to be made while Joshua had enough energy to escape. The other concern was if Joshua had the will to escape. It would be vital to talk with him in the morning. The other problem was the Nazi soldier that I presumed was the dark traveler. He was the biggest threat of all.

I finished with all the prisoners and headed for the truck, it was my quarters for the night. The march would continue at dawn and I needed to get off my feet and in somewhere that was a bit warmer than the freezing night air; a blanket in the truck and the boxes of food were available for warmth. I snuggled in between the boxes and wrapped up in the blanket; trying for as much insulation as possible. My thoughts were on Joshua and the men in the barn. It had to be below freezing temperature outside and the barn was nothing but a drafty wood shell. It was very cold in the truck but manageable. These conditions left me very little choice on how soon to act. If not tomorrow, it had to be the next day. I had to get Joshua out of there.

A long night ensued, and sleep did not come easily. The sun was about to bring light to the day, when I heard movement coming from the house. Opening the flaps to the truck, I hopped out. The guards were headed for the barn and told me to have water ready as the prisoners came out.

In single file the men shuffled out of the barn, briefly stopping for a quick swallow of water. Joshua moved passedme. There was something different in his look; some of that determination was back. I couldn't tell too much from the brief encounter, but his mood had seemed to brighten. It gave me hope; he would need all the resolve and grit that could be mustered to be able to pull this off.

The march continued. While walking, I monitored the routines that the guards were setting; plus attempting to ascertain which one was the Traveler. I wanted to know his location at all times.

It came time for me to give Joshua's group their drink of water; thirty thirsty men hovered around me, which provided for the opportunity to grab Joshua and pull him close to me.

As I poured water I talked to him. "Tomorrow afternoon we will make the escape." He looked at me with a blank stare. "Joshua, are you listening to me? Tomorrow I need you ready to make the break." His stare now posed a question and I could tell he was thinking.

The guard change was complete and they were forcing everyone back in line. Joshua continued eye contact. I couldn't tell what he was thinking but it was a different stare than the day before. I would have one more chance to talk to him that day and another in the morning; then it would be time to make the move.

I noticed the guards, while resting in the truck, were sleeping and had their rifles stored to the side. I also noticed, as the march went on, the line had a tendency to stretch out. Two guards were assigned, one at either end of the long line. Right before the changing of the guards in the afternoon would be the best time to go.

The day extended on and I was exhausted, but it was time to give Joshua's group their water break. We followed the same procedure as before, and I pulled Joshua to me past all of the huddled men. I poured and talked.

"Joshua, I want you alert and ready to go tomorrow afternoon. Do you understand me?" My talk was tough and precise, there was little time and limited chances to get through to him.

He grabbed my arm. "I'm ready," he said. I saw it, the look, the one I'd been waiting and hoping for.

I smiled. "Alright then, here we go." Joshua looked at me and blinked. I could tell I had him back.

The day ended badly. The march came to a farmhouse with a burned-out barn. The prisoners were placed inside the destroyed structure for security sake only. The walls were pretty much intact, but there was no roof and no protection from the cold night air. The men huddled tightly together and took turns moving to the middle for warmth. There would be no sleeping on this night, just survival. These were military men and they knew how to survive. I hoped they would include Joshua.

I was exhausted walking back to the supply truck, just managing to climb in and fall between the boxes with my blanket. We had walked dozens of miles in the last two days and I ached in every joint. Needing to sleep, it didn't take long.

Suddenly it was morning and I jumped out of the truck, wanting to check on Joshua as soon as possible. The guards were moving around slowly and looked tired. They had been doubled up on the watch because the barn was not secure; that was a good thing for later on in the day and the escape. I had the water ready for the prisoners as they filed out. Joshua looked better than I thought he would. We made eye contact and I nodded my head. Some of the men had a rough night and were in physical trouble. There was no way they could take much more of this.

The morning routine stayed consistent and I was very glad for that. It came time for me to give water to Joshua's group. The men huddled in and Joshua slip in between them.

I began. "This afternoon when I give water to the guards, wait till I serve the one in the back and then make your break."

Joshua had new information. "Some of the men are going to run today. I heard them talking about it."

I thought for a moment, and then said. "That could be good, or it could mess up the plan. Joshua, you will just have to decide when the best time is to run. I will support you as soon as you make your break." He nodded.

The guards were back and forcing the men back into line. The stage was set and it all rested on the tired legs of the young warrior named Joshua.

Chapter 23 – Poland 1944

THE ESCAPE

My mind was racing all day. I kept thinking of the different scenarios that could happen when Joshua made his move. We were headed for mountainous terrain and the snow was deep on the side of the road and in the fields. We needed a ridge or embankment where the snow would not be quite so deep. Otherwise, Joshua would struggle and be too slow in his escape. Some positive developments were forming with the landscape. Trees were more abundant and locating closer to the road.

It was a waiting game through two guard rotations, till it was time for Joshua's water break. He came to me and we talked quickly. "Wait till I bring water to the guards, unless something happens earlier. When I serve the guard in the rear, I will force him to turn his back. Check the guard in the front; when he faces forward, make your move. I will try to time the water with a good location." Joshua nodded his approval.

The guards were back and pushing the men into line. The march was dragging and that was good. The men were exhausted and the guards were tired from pulling the double duty the night before. Those who were resting would probably be asleep in the back of the truck. The next objective was finding the best place ahead to start the action.

I saw it, a tight tree line and a rocky ridge at the top of the hill. It was time to make my move to the front of the line and offered water to the guard. Doing so, I then walked towards the back of the line. While passing Joshua, I shot him a look. He acknowledged with a blink. I made it to the second guard and served him the water.

At that moment, three prisoners in the front broke for the trees. Right next to me two men broke away. A third man threw himself into the back of the legs of the guard; who folded up and fell backwards. The guard in front saw the men break away and brought his rifle up to fire. He was tackled by a charging prisoner and knocked off of his feet. Three men broke away in the back and ran down the road. Three more took off in front and were running away up the road.

Joshua did not waste his opportunity. He was gone in a flash over the top of the ridge. The guards in the truck hopped out and began to deploy. The commander was screaming orders; the remaining POWs were told to sprawl on the ground. The commander ordered four guards to pursue the men who broke for the trees. Two motor cycles with side cars had arrived from the main group and headed down the road in both directions for the others. Joshua had broken clean except for one set of eyes.

The soldier that shot Sara had been in the truck resting. He peered out of the back and saw Joshua disappear over the ridge. He leapt out of the truck with rifle in hand and informed the commander that the boy had escaped then volunteered to go after him. The commander gave the ok, and the man who I assumed to be the traveler took off for the ridge in pursuit.

I quickly offered my help for the pursuit of Joshua. The commander was running out of personnel and was considering it. I urged him that I needed to leave immediately to be in position to help. He agreed, and without asking I grabbed the rifle of the injured guard and was gone before anyone could react. I climbed the ridge and found the foot tracks in the snow. Tracking them would be easy, but getting there in time was my biggest concern.

In front of me Joshua was charging through the knee-deep snow until he found another ridge where the depth was less. He began his climb and suddenly a bullet whizzed by his head. He dove behind a boulder. Not knowing enough details, he needed to determine where the shot came from. This would dictate how to proceed when leaving the cover of the boulder. Shuffling his feet in the snow, he came across a stick and pulled it free. Taking off his floppy cap, he stuck it on top of the stick, then raised the cap above the boulder into the sight line of the shooter.

A shot rang out, knocking the stick and hat to the ground. This gave Joshua the necessary information of the origin of the shot, and the angle necessary to leave and be out of sight of the shooter. He left quickly, crawling like a bear through the ankle-deep snow, knowing the shooter was probably advancing. His hands were frozen with no feeling in his fingers, but he knew to push on.

Reaching a tree line, he crawled until there was adequate cover to stand and run again. The snow once more was over the top of his knee, and he was tiring quickly; this pace could not be kept for long.

The pause of the boulder confrontation had allowed me to catch up. I wanted to stay out of sight, so my plan was to keep vision on the traveler and mirror his movement. I had the advantage of being the unknown factor, and it needed to stay that way.

The Traveler had advanced to the boulder but was unsure of Joshua's position, and slowed his advance on the side of caution. He thought he might have hit his target, so there was not a huge hurry. He edged toward the big rock, slowly sliding around the corner to find nothing. That angered him and he cursed at the tracks leading away. He had wasted valuable time.

Joshua continued to climb along the rocky ridges that had less snow. He was concerned about the terrain; the ridges had drop offs that were starting to look more like cliffs and canyons. He didn't want to get trapped. As he approached the top of a ridge, he noticed more sky on the far side than normal.

His fear was confirmed. He had walked onto the top of two merging canyons, with cliff-like drop offs on either side. He was going to be forced to double back toward the approaching shooter. If he hurried, some width could be gained along the edge of the canyon where the bluff widened on the way out. It would be a necessity to use the lowest and widest points of the terrain to aid in not being detected. This unfortunately would be precariously close to the jagged canyon edge, which was blanked with snow and ice.

His hands were numb balls on the end of his arms. He couldn't stick them in his pockets for warmth, for need of balance and support along the slippery cliff. One false step could be disastrous, but he had to quickly gain ground, or the shooter would see the tracks turn before he had the opportunity to move past him undetected on the way out.

The Traveler noticed the canyons forming and slowed the pace of his pursuit. He would entertain the possibility of a cliff at the end of this forming bluff, forcing the boy to turn around. He was tiring and couldn't keep up with him anyway; so the smart play was being ready for him when he turned. The problem for the Traveler was he couldn't watch both sides of the bluff at the same time. He would continue slowly, following the tracks but concentrating his focus toward the edges, searching for movement and listening for the slightest of sounds.

Joshua knew he would be approaching the shooter's position at any time. His pace slowed to a cautious and methodical advance. Each step was calculated and designed to make no noise. The blanket of snow actually was helping muffle any sound; he just needed to be careful.

The situation became a pressing one. *There he is,* thought Joshua. The Traveler's head came into view only twenty meters away. Joshua instinctively stepped down to a large rock, attempting to move further out of sight. Glancing down, he saw his boot only inches away from a thirty-meter drop. He was stuck and had nowhere to go but straight back up into view. If he were seen or heard it would be over. The canyon merged only thirty meters on down; if he could get past the shooter, there would be new open territory for his escape.

The Traveler was at a snail's pace, not seeing anything, but listening closely for any unusual sound. The snow was making it difficult to ascertain where sounds were coming from. Not aware of anything odd, he decided to advance.

Joshua desperately needed to know the position of the shooter. If he waited too long, the shooter would realize he had turned. If he showed himself too soon he would be trapped. His decision was to take a look. Carefully he rotated himself to face the rock ledge above, placing his foot firmly and slowly lifting until his eyes obtained a clear view. He surveyed the situation rapidly and lowered himself down to his original position. His observation told him that the shooter had moved approximately ten meters past and would soon be close enough to see the tracks turn. It was time to go.

He placed his boot in the identical print it had just left. Again he rose to eye level and saw the back of the shooter. Slowly he brought the other boot up and out to the next rock. The process was going to be slow but he could possibly be out of sight with a dozen more steps down the rugged path. He stayed as close to the edge as possible, it being the lowest level and providing the most cover. Six more steps and he could bolt for the tree line and the advantage of the woods.

A sudden movement stunned Joshua. He had flushed a winter hare from its hiding place. The hare race across the bluff toward the shooter as Joshua dove face down into the snow. He lay there completely motionless listening for the next sound.

The Traveler heard a click and turned quickly with rifle ready. He saw the hare racing toward him, then dart away when spying the Traveler in its path. He searched the landscape looking for anything out of place or moving. He wondered what might have spooked the hare and decided to investigate in the direction from where it had come.

I was well back from the Traveler but had almost accidentally overtaken him when he slowed down. Quickly backing off, I decided to wait. From this vantage point I could see that the ridge was actually a bluff and was narrowing. It made sense to wait and be in good position if the pursuit came back at me. I had yet to see Joshua, but my biggest concern was staying in contact with the Traveler. He would eventually take me to Joshua or give up and turn back.

Joshua's mind was racing. There was a critical decision to be made, run or wait. If he waited, the shooter might move on, but he would still have to run eventually. If he ran right now he stood the chance of being shot in the back. His father had always taught him to trust his instincts; he exploded off the ground and flew into a full sprint, spraying snow with each step.

Joshua! I thought to myself. I watched as the little warrior sprinted along the ridge on the far side away from me. I turned my head to see the Traveler raising his rifle, preparing to fire. I heard the shot echo in the canyon, and quickly turned to locate Joshua. Nothing, I couldn't see him.

The bullet sunk into the snow bank that Joshua dove into, about one nose length from his head. He looked around to see what was available for his next move. He was so close to the end of the canyon, and the ledge on the opposite side was only about three meters away. When he dove he landed in a natural bunker between two rock outcroppings. The bunker ended at the canyon edge about five or six steps away.

The Traveler fired, and pulled his head up quickly to see if he had hit his target. Being a good marksman, he was confident of not missing this time. Yet, he couldn't see anything. Where did the boy go? He moved in slowly with rifle ready.

Joshua couldn't leave the protection of the bunker. His only choice was to move to the ledge and jump to the other side. He walked to the edge and looked down to a drop off of at least twenty meters. He paced the steps back to the bunker wall, figuring to have only five good ones and then the takeoff. That told him he must step first with his left foot to allow for a finish with his left foot on the leap. On the far side he would be landing in snow, and he wasn't sure what might be underneath. Time was running out and he urgently cleared off a place to plant his foot for the important last leap. Stepping off the distance one more time, he then turned and faced the ledge. Joshua told himself he had done this dozens of times, leaping across buildings in the city.

The Traveler edged closer, and as he did, could hear the sound of movement. This angered him; he had missed again. He brought his rifle up to the ready position as he approached a large rock. Pausing, he assumed that the boy was on the other side. Gradually, with rifle barrel leading the way, he elevated, popping up in firing position in time to see Joshua flying through the air toward the far edge. Pulling his rifle down, he jumped into the bunker, then cautiously moved to the slick canyon edge.

Joshua's takeoff was strong, landing him flat out and face down. He collided violently with the snow covered cliff. The landing stunned him and took his breath for a brief moment. Quickly regaining his air, he scrambled for the cover of the rocks.

The Traveler watched as Joshua disappeared on the far side. He cursed and quickly turned back to the bunker wall, hopping out and surveying the landscape. His frustration continued, seeing Joshua weaving in and out of the rocks. There was not going to be another good shot, and he would easily be fifty meters behind the boy by the time he made it around to the other side of the canyon. He angrily deduced that he would not catch him now.

I was relieved to see Joshua climbing out of the canyon. The Traveler was learning again just who he was dealing with. I watched as Joshua headed for the tree line, cleverly weaving through the rock formations for protection. Suddenly I lost sight of him. I waited a moment. Still no Joshua; something was wrong.

Joshua was moving quickly now, making good progress toward the trees. The snow was deepening so it was important for him to find rocks and fallen trees to step on. He jumped from a rock toward a log, just a short hop away. As he did, the log gave way and sunk into the snow. It began to slide down a small ravine towards the canyon. Joshua felt himself being pulled along, his pant leg snared by a broken branch extending from the log.

It began to pick up speed. He shook his leg violently trying to free himself. The log had become a wooden sled skimming its way along the snow toward the edge of the canyon and a twenty-meter drop off. It crashed into a boulder near the edge, turning sideways and ramming the other side of the ravine, wedging between the two and coming to a violent stop. Joshua slammed into the log at contact, ending up pinned under the heavy wood and wedged against the ravine.

The Traveler watched the scene unfold and thought to himself he had finally caught a break. He swiftly headed towards Joshua's position, hoping to finish the boy and finally be ready to leave. He worked his way across to the other side of the canyon and was closing in.

I didn't know where Joshua was but I saw the Traveler cross to the other side. He was moving with speed and I worried about that. I quickened my pace to keep up. He began moving down towards a ravine, and I knew that wasn't good at all. I had to hurry. I saw the Traveler raise his rifle to fire and I wasn't yet close enough.

There was a voice. "Freeze, dirt ball."

I couldn't see who was talking but I knew it wasn't the traveler.

He ordered, "Drop your weapon or I will put you down."

Now I saw him, an American soldier.

The Traveler was startled and turned to see an American Lieutenant pointing his rifle ready to fire.

The Traveler advised, "American, this is not your fight. I just want the boy."

"You're not getting the boy, and I'm going to tell you one more time to drop your weapon," the lieutenant warned.

"American, you don't know what you're into here, it would be best for you to walk away. I can kill you." He paused. "You, on the other hand, can't kill me. I don't think you want to find that out the hard way."

"But Traveler, I can." He had not seen me move in; his preoccupation with the lieutenant had blinded him to my advance. I had my rifle fixed on the middle of his chest. He turned to see who would call him traveler.

"Cart Man, what a surprise; I see there still is another traveler. I should have known it to be you." He was glaring at me.

I demanded, "Put down the weapon like the lieutenant said or you will be dead." Rage was brewing in my gut. My finger tightened on the trigger, but I waited. I could not shoot him in cold blood. If he would only give me a reason, just make a move.

The Dark Traveler sensed my hesitation and used it to buy the time he needed for travel to safety. "Cart Man, you have me at a disadvantage and I shall gladly lay down my arm." He dropped the rifle to the ground and stood stoically looking at me for a few moments. Then, a wicked smile slowly edged across his face.

"I will kill the boy just as I did the girl. But alas, it appears my time here is done." His image was beginning to fade; he was about to travel and I realized it was too late to stop him.

He had a final message for me. "You should have killed me when you had the chance, next time I will not fail to kill you."

Then, he was gone.

Chapter 24 – Poland 1944

THE RESCUE

I turned to see a rifle barrel pointed at my chest; the lieutenant wanted some answers.

"Who are you?"

I said, "I'm Rusty."

He barked, "Well, Rusty, do you want to tell me what the hell is going on!"

I was trying to calm him but I needed to get to Joshua. "Lieutenant, I will explain, but we need to help the boy."

He acknowledged. "Ok, you go and I will follow; don't do anything stupid."

I reassured him. "I won't, we are on the same side. I just need to help Joshua."

We descended down the snowy ravine. The going was very slick, and it was a priority to find solid footing on the rocks; this was done by repeatedly sweeping away snow with my boot. Joshua was in sight, alert and squirming to get out from underneath the log.

I yelled, "Joshua, stay still we will be there in a moment to help!" Joshua looked up and I could see the fire in his eyes.

"Go away, Rusty! I can get out myself." I realized the fire in his eyes was meant for me.

I said sternly, "Joshua you stay still, you're right on the edge of the cliff." He was not deterred, spewing, "You could have killed that bastard."

By then I had reached him. I slid down close and braced my leg against the log. It gave against my weight and I figured we didn't have much time. I could see the canyon drop off just on the other side of our position. The side of the log braced against the large rock was just fine; the other side on the snow bank was becoming the problem.

The more Joshua wiggled the looser it became. He was furious with me, and as I slid next to him he pounded on my shoulder with his fists.

I repeated, "Joshua, stay still or we both will go over the side."

He answered angrily, "I don't care."

I wrapped my arms around his and pinned them to his side. "You can punch me all you want when we get on top of the ridge, but you stop it right now."

He was snorting with frustration, but stopped his assault on me. I turned the best I could to see where the lieutenant had positioned himself. He was braced on the rock outcropping, about five meters away.

"Lieutenant, I'm going to need your help."

He responded, "Tell me what you need."

I had nowhere to push from and nothing to grab. The only way up was to form a human ladder. The lieutenant was too far away but we could use his rifle.

"I'm going to push Joshua up toward you. I need you to anchor yourself as far down as you can, and extend the rifle and strap."

He said, "You're kidding, right? You want me to pass down my rifle to you."

"It's our only way out," I said with determination.

"Why don't you just disappear like the other guy?" he said sarcastically.

I was willing to make a deal. "Lower the rifle for the boy and pull him out and leave me here. Lieutenant, between the two of us we must save this boy." There was a pause.

"Ok, but I'm taking out the cartridge so it won't fire."

"Good," I said.

The lieutenant lowered himself as far as he could without losing leverage, and had undone the shoulder strap on the side of the barrel. The strap now extended down below the butt. He lowered the weapon and gave a quick slinging motion to extend the strap as far as possible down the snowy slope.

The lieutenant was bent at the waist reaching through his legs as far as he could stretch. "Ok, ready," he said breathlessly.

It was one of Joshua's boots that had trapped him, and it was definitely stuck under the log. I place my foot on the log toward the rock side for balance; trying to avoid any pressure on the fragile side against the dirt slope. I gently pushed Joshua's boot with my other foot toward an opening just a few inches away. I felt the log give and immediately stopped. I knew I could not do that again.

"Joshua, very carefully see if you can slide your boot free." I said this in a whisper, as if it would make a difference.

He did, and the boot moved ever so slightly. He was then able to wrench it free. I began pulling Joshua up toward the strap, using only my arms and the one leg braced on the secure portion of the log.

He was back to his focused self and climbed over me and upward toward the strap. He clawed through the packed snow, in search of rocks to grip with his frostbitten fingers, but that did not detour him. He was able to move high enough to place his boot on my shoulder. From there, he pushed with an available leg and extended himself within grasp of the strap.

He secured it with his frozen hand, and ran the other through the loop adjustment; then tightened the loop around his wrist for support while grabbing the strap to create a double grip support system.

I could not see, so I had to ask. "Joshua, do you have the strap?"

"Yes," he said.

I said, "Ok, Lieutenant, pull him up."

"No," came the answer. But it wasn't the lieutenant's answer; it was Joshua.

"Joshua, what do you mean no?" I questioned urgently.

He stubbornly answered. "We are bringing you out." As mad as he was at me, he wasn't going to leave me behind.

"Joshua, we need to get you out, I will be ok."

The lieutenant chimed in. "Come on, kid let's go."

"No," came the answer again. "Start climbing, Rusty; I'm ready."

I tried to turn to get a look at the stubborn malcontent that had chosen to make a stand on the side of a frozen cliff. "Joshua!" I roared.

"Start climbing," he said, unfazed.

The lieutenant, with irritation, said, "I hate to interrupt this family squabble but somebody needs to do something, and do it pretty damn soon."

I felt the log shift, and instinctively reached for Joshua's ankle. As I clasped on, the log began to fall away. I pushed hard with my planted foot one more time and swept upward with my free hand, latching on to the bottom of Joshua's coat. The added weight and pressure surprised the lieutenant. "Whoa; you better hurry!" he warned.

I took heed of the advice and flung my body in the other direction, creating space for my lower hand to move to Joshua's shoulder. My feet swung high and I felt for some kind of jutting rock to brace with, catching an edge just below the big outcropping that supported the lieutenant.

From there I pushed away from Joshua until I had a grip with my hand on the edge of the rock above my head. I was good for the moment.

"Ok, Lieutenant, pull him up."

"It's about time," he said with relief.

Joshua scrambled and the lieutenant pulled, making quick work of the process. Joshua was safely on top of the outcropping, but I was going to be a little bit different story. There was no way around the big rock except swinging back out onto the slope, and then up.

The lieutenant asked, "What do you suggest?"

I was thinking. "If you sling me the strap I can use it to swing over to the rocks on the other side. I can climb from there."

"You're assuming I can hold you with a grip just on the barrel of a rifle," the lieutenant offered with trepidation.

"Yeah," I said insecurely.

The lieutenant was ready. "Ok, we're burning daylight."

He extended the rifle and slung the strap toward me. I latched on and made sure my foot was secure enough to get a strong push. "I'm ready on three," I said.

I exploded and scrambled toward the rocks on the far side. The lieutenant had done his job and I landed belly down on a round boulder covered with snow. The impact knocked the breath out of me and I was momentarily disabled.

I felt myself begin to slide, and I couldn't move my arms to grab hold of anything. Below me was a quick slide to the bottom of the canyon. Just then a hand secured the collar of my jacket. "Hey, you're not going anywhere; you've got some questions to answer." The lieutenant had wisely crossed to my position, and held me to the rock.

My breath had returned. "You're a pushy kind of guy aren't you?" I joked with obvious gratitude.

He laughed. "Wait till you get to know me."

"I'd like that, I think," I said.

We moved back to the safety of the rocks and I checked on Joshua. He was sitting huddled with his hands in his pockets.

"You ok?" I asked concerned. He nodded that he was.

I turned to the lieutenant. "We need to treat his hands for frostbite."

We made a temporary camp site; the lieutenant found a protected overhang that would work. My science background took over and I started the process of treatment.

The lieutenant gathered nearby wood that was dry enough to burn, and with use of his survival training, had a fire in place and melting snow in a collapsible pan from his backpack. I took a blanket from the pack and wrapped it around Joshua.

"Ok, Joshua we need to warm your fingers slowly. Move your hands underneath your armpits. Stay as bundled as you can to keep warm, but most importantly your fingers." He nodded that he understood.

"You will move your hands to your pants in just a little bit." I made the motion of my hands going into my crotch. Joshua smiled; I gave him a good grief look.

Speaking to the lieutenant, I said, "We need that water just warm and not real warm."

"You got it boss," he answered.

We would rotate Joshua's fingers from his armpits to his crotch. Then we would fill the lieutenant's tin cup with the warm water, dipping his fingers into the lukewarm moisture. The process would repeat until I could see circulation returning to his fingers.

This gave us a chance to sit and rest, and the opportunity for the first time, for me to actually take a good look at the lieutenant. I guessed him to be about six feet tall with a very athletic build; definitely an athlete. Matter of fact, he would have been on a wish list for one of my teams. He was a handsome enough guy, kind of the rugged type. He took off his helmet to display a short dirty-blonde hair cut, with a strong chin framing an average mouth and nose. His eyes were brown and commanding, with an air of confidence. Our down time also created the environment for the questions to start.

The lieutenant began. "All right, Hot Rod, start talking; who the hell are you and where'd that ol boy get off to a while ago."

I began to laugh. "Where are you from?"

He said, "I'm an Oklahoma, boy, so what?"

"Really," I said mockingly. He gave me an impatient look. "Ok, my name is, Rusty, and that's Joshua over there." Joshua glanced and nodded as I continued. "I'm what is called a traveler, and have been sent back in time to help Joshua. The man you saw disappear is also a traveler. He has been sent to kill Joshua. That's all I really know, I'm hoping for an update anytime now."

The Lieutenant was curious. "An update from who?"

I knew how he was going to react, so I just told him. "An angel," I said.

He leaned back and spewed, "Oh good god, man; an angel! I'm serious; you better tell me what's going on."

I answered with frustration. "I should have known a cowboy from Texas wouldn't understand."

He leaned forward. "You didn't just say that. Them's fightin' words, boy."

I smiled and said, "Yeah, and the angel's name is Ham, and he is from Texas."

The lieutenant scoffed. "This keeps gettin better and better."

I took a lecturing tone. "Lieutenant, you better accept that you're dealing with a situation that is outside the norm."

He got an incredulous look on his face. "Buddy, I had that one figured a long time ago." He continued. "And by the way, what did that ol'boy mean when he said I couldn't kill him?"

I answered in a matter-of-fact manner. "He is from the future and would revert back to his time and out of harm's way. I could kill him because we are from the same time period, and any interaction between us is relevant, but he could also kill me."

I changed the subject to him. "Who are you?"

He boastingly answered, "Jason Thomas, the pride of Ardmore, Oklahoma."

I asked, "What are you doing way out here in enemy territory?"

He hesitated, as if he shouldn't say. "Ah what the hell; I'm part of a special force paratroop that dropped in behind the lines. We're here to disrupt supply lines and send information back to command."

I said, "I think Joshua and I have some valuable information for you."

"Let it fly," he said.

I explained that we had been part of a march of POWs toward Germany, then went on to say that our particular group was three sections of three hundred men, in addition to thousands more walking west. He pulled out a map and showed where we currently were, and I was able to give him enough information to determine where the march would be located. He said he needed to make contact with his unit by radio, and left to climb higher up the ridge for reception.

That left Joshua and me there alone, and I knew what was coming.

"He murdered my sister, Rusty." The boy was staring me down. I nodded my head and looked right back at him.

I said, "He was after both of you." Joshua and I weren't on the same page at the moment, and I was looking for some way to get back in his good graces.

"You could have killed him," he said.

I wanted very much to answer correctly. "Joshua, I would have murdered him just like he murdered Sara, and that's not the answer, at least it's not the answer for me. He murdered my family too. I just couldn't kill him for revenge. There will be more times ahead where the situation will be different. The Traveler is not going away and he intends to kill us both. That leaves few options and I see that more clearly now."

The lieutenant was back and had overheard part of the conversation.

"Kid, if it makes you feel any better, I was about to shoot the bastard."

I said, "Really, Lieutenant, that's all I need right now is a cowboy riding in on a white horse."

He started packing his back pack. "I'm just telling it like it is. And by the way, I got the word to move out. You two are coming, we're going to intercept that march, and we need your intel."

I suggested, "Let me check his fingers." I went to Joshua and motioned for him to show me his hands. He was still mad at me but he did as I asked. The fingers were showing improvement but there was still cause for concern. "He's going to need gloves."

Lieutenant Thomas stopped his packing, reached under his fatigue jacket and pulled out a pair of gloves. "First rule of survival training, two sets of gloves." He threw them to Joshua.

"Food," I said. "He hasn't eaten in days."

The lieutenant went back to his pack. "Joshua, my boy, you are about to taste the world-famous c-ration biscuit." He pulled out three and handed them to him. Joshua devoured them on the spot.

Lieutenant Thomas was amazed. "Damn," he said, and handed Joshua his canteen. "You're gonna need some water after that."

Joshua took a drink. "Thank you, Lieutenant, that was very good."

He said, "You can call me Jason; and really, you liked those?"

Joshua nodded.

"I'll be damned," he laughed. "First I ever heard of that liked them sumbitches."

He went to his backpack again and pulled out some packaged caramel squares.

He smiled. "If you liked those biscuits I can't wait to see what you think of these." he said as he gave Joshua a handful.

"Put those in your pocket and you can eat while we walk. We really need to get going." The lieutenant strapped on his pack. "We will be moving quickly, do you think you can keep up?"

I laughed. "Thomas, you best not underestimate this boy, he will be showing us the way."

The lieutenant turned with a sly smile for me. "I was talking to you; and you can call me Lieutenant; and I ain't from Texas." He turned and gave the signal. "If there's nothing else, ladies, move out!"

Chapter 25 – Poland WW2

A Talk with Ham

As promised Joshua took off to the lead. He had a good idea where we were going and knew the fastest way to get there, heading straight for the top of the ridge.

"Whoa, Joshua, come on back here," the lieutenant said.

Joshua turned and spoke with confidence. "Jason, the snow is much thinner up on top."

"Sure enough," he said. "But you are part of a covert operation now; I'll show you a little trick along the tree line where no one will see us. There was a reason you boys didn't know I was at the canyon, you didn't see me until I wanted to be seen."

We headed for the tree line. Lieutenant Thomas showed Joshua a variety of travel aids within the confines of the wooded protection. He explained that about three trees inside the line is where the snow depth decreases, and wouldn't get any better after that. It was the best of both travel worlds; far enough in for cover and not so deep that you lose your bearings.

He demonstrated the process of where to step and get the most consistent footing; plus the use of a lead stick to navigate through the forest floor. The stick gave support and warning, which allowed the holder to keep his eyes up scanning for danger ahead.

I thought to myself that Joshua was getting his first special military operation training; yet he had been living that very life over the last two years. I also noticed that he hung on every word the lieutenant said.

We were making big time through the trees and obviously were working toward a rendezvous point that the lieutenant knew. I began to feel strangely. My body was tingling all over and I was light headed.

"Lieutenant Thomas, can we stop for a moment?" I asked.

He turned his head back. "You gettin a little tired, Rusty?"

"Not exactly," I said. "I think I might be getting an update."

"You mean from that ol Texas boy?" he asked.

"Yes, I think this is Ham."

He worried. "How long do ya think?"

I said. "Well, I'm not sure, but you might not even know I'm gone. I just want to make sure it's him." I was starting to fade.

"I'll be damned; there you sure enough go." The lieutenant and Joshua stood frozen and stunned.

It was the same bright light that I had experienced before; pulsating all around and feeling as though it went right through me. I began to travel, but it wasn't to the park. I came to rest in what felt like a room, but with no sense of any walls or the feel of a floor. Yet it felt as if I were standing. In the distance, a figure moved toward me. As it got closer I was able to identify it as Ham. He wore long blue swimming trunks and a bright yellow Hawaiian shirt.

"Where are we exactly?" I asked.

Ham said, "You're in the pathway. I just didn't create the park this time."

"Oh I see," I said. "And you chose to wear that?"

He became slightly defensive. "Why? What's wrong with it?"

I said, "I'm not really sure, just doesn't seem appropriate."

"Maybe you were expecting a big long robe or something," he kidded.

"It's not that, we're just not headed for the beach; just seems strange," I reasoned.

Ham smiled. "I really didn't think of it that way."

I said, "We need to talk about the Traveler."

Ham agreed. "Yes we do. Rusty, the traveler will try again."

I acknowledged, "Yeah, he indicated that when he left." I said, "I know I have to protect Joshua, but how long before the beacon will be activated?"

Ham gave an urgent look and said, "Soon."

I pressed again. "How long?"

Ham smiled. "Sorry, bud, too much information too soon. We have to be very careful, it's for your safety and others."

I shook my head in disgust. "Whatever." Then I continued. "You know the dark side doesn't seem to worry about giving information to the other traveler."

Ham glared at me as he spoke. "Exactly; and countless people were murdered and millions more suffered. The dark side created multiple paradoxes that have changed history forever. They altered the natural path of countless destinies."

I just stood there like an idiot. Ham's timing was always one of his gifts; so he let me stand awhile to absorb the hit. He had more to talk about and finally broke the silence. "All of this situation with helping Joshua has gotta also include the lieutenant."

I worried. "I don't know that he will want to be involved."

Ham responded, "He's already involved, and the sooner he realizes that, the better."

I wasn't convinced. "Wouldn't it be better to just let me handle this?"

Ham responded quickly. "No, Rusty, the longer you stay in history the more you change outcomes. It is very dangerous to have you alter history more than is absolutely necessary." Ham was adamant. "You must convince the lieutenant to stay involved. When he understands more about the big picture he will step up. He is a good man."

I had a good point. "Ham, how am I supposed to show him the big picture when I don't know the big picture?"

Ham scratched his chin again, contemplated some more, and then conceded. "You're right."

"Wow," I said to the nonexistent crowd in the room. "I finally won an argument."

He gave me his go-to-hell smile of big buck teeth and squinting eyes. Then, continued to speak. "The beacon is gonna activate for the first time very soon in Joshua's time. From that point, it will activate and send a signal approximately every ten to fifteen years. When the time comes for the worm hole to be completed, a series of signals will go out over multiple days."

I asked, "When will it be done?"

Ham answered with a hint of urgency. "Completion is very near in your real time."

I tried to wrap my head around all of this information. "So I need to go back to my time soon; Lieutenant Thomas needs to help Joshua; and Joshua will send the first signal shortly."

Ham said, "That's the basics of it, but it will be a little more complicated than that."

"How so?" I questioned.

"The Dark Traveler," Ham said. "He'll be able to track the signal once it activates."

I said, "So, Joshua will be on the run until he reaches my time."

Ham said, "Yes, and you will be sent back to help as needed."

I sarcastically surmised, "Well, this all should be easy enough."

Ham was all business as he responded. "First things first; none of this matters if you don't keep Joshua safe right now; and you have a lot of talking to do with the lieutenant. So, are you ready to go back?"

I was in fact, and felt uneasy not being there with Thomas and Joshua.

"Yes, I'm ready," I said as the brightness began consuming me once again. It was such a strange sensation, but one I was becoming accustomed to. That was probably a good thing, because none of this was ending soon.

I heard Ham's voice. "Ok, dude, Sara's taking over; adios, muchacho."

Chapter 26 – Poland WW2

Joshua's Fate

"Lookie there, Joshua, he's back already."

The process was a bit disorienting but I knew I was returning. The surroundings were coming into focus. There sat Lieutenant Thomas, his butt on a fallen tree and legs sticking out in front. Joshua was standing and had a very anxious look on his face.

"How long have I been gone?" I asked.

Thomas joked, "Boy, I haven't even had a chance to pee." I saw Joshua smile, which was a good sign.

Thomas said, "You're like one of those new-fangled television sets; you fade out, then you fade in."

Joshua was curious. "Where did you go?"

I wasn't sure what to say. "Well, I went to talk with Ham."

He curiously asked, "What did he say?"

I explained. "It's a long story and definitely something we need to talk about, but probably not right now."

Joshua gave me his stubborn look. "I want to know."

I didn't know where to start. "Joshua, we talked about you, and we talked about Thomas."

"About me?" Thomas asked with surprise.

I got back to the pending matter quickly. "Joshua, I promise we will talk about it, but we really need to keep moving."

"Yep," said the lieutenant. "We need to move out."

Joshua relented, knowing time was precious.

We made a lot of progress over the next two hours; stopping every so often for the lieutenant to give Joshua more to eat, and communicate with his command.

We arrived at a hill on our right side, and a lake in front of us.

"Ok, boys, we need to bust it over that hill." Lieutenant Thomas emphasized with an alert voice. Not being comfortable traveling out in the open, he took the lead and set our pace at a jog. It wasn't long before we crested the hill. On the far side lay a meadow, and our destination.

At the edge of the snow covered meadow was a company of American Special Forces paratroopers. I figured maybe a hundred or so. We entered the camp and made our way to the command group. Thomas headed straight for a crowd talking with a Major. I assumed he was the man in charge. They spoke briefly and then Lieutenant Thomas pointed at us. The conversation continued. Finally, he waved for us to approach. The Major had a small portable table set up with a map on top. He wanted to know how the march was structured and how many Nazi soldiers there would be to deal with.

I gave him my best guess on the number of guards, and I had a pretty good idea about how the groups were organized. The next problem was to figure where they were currently located. I wasn't sure how quickly the march continued after all of the turmoil and escape. I also wasn't sure exactly of our location compared to where we had begun.

Joshua spoke up. "I know where they are."

The Major looked up from his map and gave Joshua a dismissive look; then returned his attention to the map. I caught Thomas's eye and nodded my head insisting that they listen to Joshua. The Lieutenant thought about it for a moment; he looked at Joshua; he looked back at me and rolled his eyes.

He reached for the major's arm and lightly placed his hand on it. "Sir, it might be a good idea to listen to the boy." The major turned and gave Lieutenant Thomas a stern stare. He looked again at Joshua and surveyed him closely.

He addressed the Lieutenant. "If you say so, Thomas."

He spoke to Joshua. "What have you got, kid?"

Joshua jumped into action. Knowing the area well from years of hunting and fishing with his father and having a good feel for reading a map. Going on, he explained that his escape had run due west toward the mountains. Our location was currently in the southern highland area and he knew the march would turn northwest toward the river valley.

Joshua theorized, "They probably haven't moved very fast today and that would put them north of us. There is a small hamlet about two hours from our position and I'm sure they would stop there."

The Major was impressed and asked for more information about the hamlet. Joshua knew there were nine structures in the general area. The terrain was a wide meadow with a small stream running through it.

The Major asked me how the march set up overnight and the deployment of the guards. I knew the guards would be trying to rest inside the houses so the deployment of guards would be light.

I surmised, "They will try to put the POWs in a confined space, like a barn. They are organized into 300 men in three separate groups."

The Major was convinced of the location of the march and it was time to get going.

Within the company, the Major had six platoons under his command. He met with his lieutenants and laid out the plan of deployment. Three platoons would deploy in front of the march and three to the rear. We had about an hour of daylight left, and that meant arriving in the dark. The Major decided to acquire strategic position on arrival, and wait till daylight before engaging the march, reasoning it was important to get a clear visual before any decision was made.

The order was given to move out and within moments six platoons were on their way. Joshua and I stayed with Thomas's unit, along with the major and the communication specialist. It was apparent that the Major depended on Lieutenant Thomas, and he was his right-hand man.

We swiftly moved toward the hamlet; not being concerned about being visible with the onslaught of the approaching nightfall. It was far more important to make maximum time.

We reached the hamlet about a half hour after dark. As Joshua had predicted, the march had made the hamlet and no further. There was a bevy of activity going on, and made it very easy to move into position without being detected. The platoons were set, and it was time to observe and evaluate the situation. It was also time to get some rest.

Our platoon was in the middle and far enough back so the radio specialist could do his job without giving away our position. We were just beyond the meadow along the tree line, and settled within a small depression, guarded by a fallen tree. It provided a bit of shelter but not much. Joshua was seated on Thomas's helmet and wrapped in his blanket. I found a small log and pulled it over to him and sat. The lieutenant positioned himself against a large branch of the fallen tree. His eyes were trained on the action in the hamlet.

I leaned over to Joshua to check his fingers. There was very little moon light and I couldn't see much. But, warmth had returned in them, and that was a good sign.

The Major strolled over to where we sat and placed a thin brown tarp in my hands. "Spread this over the top of the two of you, and it will keep your body heat in."

I thanked him and said, "Major, these POWs have been in horrible conditions for quite some time, and are in a desperate situation."

He said with concern. "Yeah, we'll see how this plays out in the morning, and try to help the best we can."

I pushed on. "There are thousands more walking toward Germany, and most are worse off than these soldiers. There are atrocities in the city that are beyond belief."

He questioned, "What do you mean?"

I paused for a moment to recount all I had seen and what Joshua had told me.

"I've seen thousands of bodies in mass open graves, being burned."

I pointed at Joshua and continued, "He tells me the count goes into the hundreds of thousands that he knows of. Major, it is very bad."

He said nothing, appearing to be contemplating the situation. He shook his head and spoke. "I don't know what to say, war is a nasty business, and bad things happen. We have a thousand men right in front of us that must be taken care of. We can only handle one fight at a time."

I knew he was right, but I felt the need to tell someone how bad it really was.

He changed the subject to me. "Thomas tells me you check out, but that still doesn't explain where the hell you came from, and why you're here."

I pointed at Joshua. "He needs to stay alive."

The major laughed. "And I suppose that's all the info I'm going to get."

I looked him in the eye. "That's the way I'd like to keep it."

He was really looking me over, trying to get a read. Finally he conceded. "Fair enough." Remembering something, he excused himself and walked over to talk with the communication specialist.

"Rusty," Joshua called out. I knew what was coming next. "What did Ham say?"

Thomas piped in. "I'm kinda curious about that myself."

I acknowledged the need, and began mentally gathering my facts, so I could give a good account of the situation.

I explained to Joshua, "You are a very important part of the future of the world." I paused for a moment to emphasize that point. "You carry inside the ability to guide people from other worlds to us. When the time comes, you will send a signal that they will follow."

Thomas started laughing. "I figured this was gonna turn into some kind of *H.G. Wells* deal."

I ignored him and continued. "Do you know anything about this?"

He nodded and said, "My father told us about it before they killed him. He told me to never reveal it to anyone."

I added my support. "That was good advice, but now we all know, and we know what we're facing." I had his attention, and he was intently listening to every word. "I've been sent by people who want you to stay alive, and use your gift when it's time."

Joshua had tears in his eyes. "I don't want this gift. All it has done is get my family killed."

I knew exactly how he felt, but had to press on. "Joshua, I lost my family too, the dark traveler killed them, and tried to kill me. I was just like you, I didn't want my gift. But people showed me how important it was, and it provided the opportunity to come help you."

He asked, "Who are these people?"

I said, "They are the people of heaven."

Joshua was trying hard to figure this out. "Are you from heaven?"

"No, I'm from America," I said.

He questioned, "So Ham sent you to help me?"

"Not exactly," I said.

I moved to one knee right in front of him, and placed my hand on his shoulder.

"I only talk to Ham; he is not from this time and can't send a traveler to a time that is not his. Only someone from this time can move a traveler back."

He questioned, “So who sent you?”

I squeezed his shoulder with firm support as I spoke. “Sara sent me.”

His initial reaction was a blank stare, but I could see the wheels were turning. His expression moved to surprise and then to distrust. He gave me a stern, questioning look, and I returned a nod of support right back.

He asked with an air of distrust, “How could she do that?”

I answered, “In heaven, she can. She sent me to help you. Her destiny had already been determined; I couldn’t help her. She knows you must live on.”

Thoughts and emotions began exploding through his brain. He was reliving every tragic event that had happened to him over the past three years. All of the pent-up anxiety was erupting from his core.

I could feel it; reliving my own experience, watching Joshua deal with his. Tears streamed down his cheeks and he began to shake. The little warrior was facing a personal crisis that had built into a volcano inside him. He was, finally, just a vulnerable twelve-year-old boy. Without warning he lunged into my arms and held on tightly.

Joshua wailed, “Sara, I’m sorry, I’m so sorry!” He cried in agony, venting his over flow of sorrow. “Rusty, it should have been me! I let her down!” He beat upon my shoulders with his fists.

“I should have died! I don’t deserve to live!”

It was time for me to step in. “Ok, that’s enough of that talk.” I gently grabbed his shoulders and held him out where I could see him.

“Joshua,” I said. “Joshua, you look at me.” He slowly raised his eyes.

“Now listen to me. You’re the finest man I have ever met in my life, and you are only twelve years old. I want to see what you will become when you’re seventy.” I shook him gently.

"Joshua, that's what Sara wants as well. She sent me for a reason." I pulled him back to me and hugged him tightly, and felt him relax.

Thomas joined in, "You should listen to him, kid; you have a lot of spunk, although I didn't know you were such a big cry baby." Joshua coughed out a quick laugh.

I chastised, "Thomas, would you please shut up!"

Off handedly he muttered, "He knows I'm kidding."

It seemed to help; Joshua began to get his composure back. We sat for a while not saying anything, and then I remembered something very important. Reaching inside my pack, I pulled out the dagger that I had been saving for Him.

I said, "Joseph, Daniel, and I thought you might want this back."

Joshua had the look of a father holding his newborn child as he took possession of the blade. Then he wrinkled his face with concern and asked, "Are they ok?"

I answered, "We parted at the cemetery after Sara's funeral. I made them promise to leave; in return I promised to find you. They headed for the rafts and off to find Joseph's people, and I came after you."

Joshua gratefully said, "Thank you for burying my sister."

I responded, "We were all there, and she was sent on her way with love and honor."

Interrupting our conversation, the major walked up. "Looks like we have some boys leaving the party over there."

Thomas inquired, "Who's leaving?"

The major answered, "Hard to tell in the dark, but C Platoon reports four bodies moving out."

Thomas said, "How we gonna handle that, sir?"

The major chuckled. "We're going to watch them leave, and see what they do; more than likely deserters. Meantime, everybody needs to try and rest, we will be moving to engage position in about three hours."

The rest of the night flew by and I tried to doze off. Joshua leaned against me and fell fast asleep. I was sure it was the only sleep for him in three days. Lieutenant Thomas stayed on watch with his platoon and alternated shifts. I sat, unable to sleep, thinking about Joshua and what was next for him.

"Rusty." Thomas was shaking me; apparently sleep had crept up on me again. "Time to go," he said.

I woke Joshua. He was up quickly and we stored the blanket and tarp. Thomas had C-rations ready for breakfast and Joshua devoured them as if he were eating a gourmet meal.

The plan was to move the platoons in close, under the cover of darkness. We set up further back with the Major, in position to monitor the action. Before long, all platoons reported that they were in position; now it was a waiting game for the Nazis to assemble.

The march had closed ranks to take advantage of the housing in the hamlet. This was a benefit to the American battalion; it was important to maintain visual contact over the entire area. The march was forming quickly into the three large groups that I had anticipated, each within a hundred meters of the next. I saw the captain for the first time come out and take his position in the lead car.

Thomas and his platoon were fifty meters in front of our position. There would be a series of warning shots, and then Thomas would do the talking. The Major gave the signal and one shot from each platoon rattled off. It was intended to give the impression to the Nazis that they were surrounded and outmanned.

Thomas yelled out to make that fact known. "We are allied forces and we have you surrounded. We are here to take control of your prisoners. Drop you're weapons and walk out. You will not be harmed."

I watched the captain leave his vehicle and give an order. Momentarily the canvas covers were ripped off of the three supply trucks exposing mounted machine gun turrets on each. The major said with a bit of surprise, "Looks like they were expecting us."

From behind the middle truck the captain spoke. "We are well armed with many hostages."

Thomas yelled back, "Don't be foolish, walk out of there and live."

The captain responded, "The foolish thing to do would be walking out to an enemy, unprotected, in the middle of a war."

Thomas turned and looked back at the major and shrugged his shoulders. We were at an impasse, and the longer it lasted the less chance of a non-violent outcome. I had an idea and I spoke to the major.

"You need to trust me. I know that captain and can talk to him. I need to go out there."

The major shook his head. "No way, you are not going out there."

"I figured you'd say that," I said, then abruptly stood and yelled toward the standoff. "Coming out, don't fire." Looking back I apologized. "Sorry, Major, but I know what I'm doing."

I began walking before the major could stop me, heading straight for the Nazi position. My hands were exposed above the waist as I approached Thomas, who was curled up behind a small snow-covered mound. My eyes stayed trained on the Nazi truck.

Thomas urgently whispered. "Rusty, what the hell are you doing?"

I mumbled under my breath. "I'm not crazy, Thomas, they can't kill me."

He agreed, to a point. "Oh yeah, that's true; unless that disappearing boy is over there."

"Yep, I thought of that too; no plan is perfect."

Continuing on, I came to within approximately twenty meters of the truck and called out, "Captain, we need to talk."

From behind the truck he responded. "Cart Man, what a surprise; has this been the plan all along?"

"No, Captain, the boy has always been the plan."

He said, "Very popular lad, that one. The soldier who covets him came back and warned of this force you come with; and with hope that the boy would be with them. Funny, then he deserted last night. I suspect that he waits out there somewhere for you."

"Thank you for the information, Captain, but we have a more pressing matter."

He responded, "Yes, we have a predicament. You've been brave to come out in the open, Cart Man; so what is it you have to say?"

I needed to convince him of the futility of any conflict. "If you fire at the prisoners they will scatter, and then you will be fired upon by a superior force. All of you will die. Too many will die, and it doesn't have to be that way."

He answered, "It would not be wise for a troop of hated Nazis to walk out unarmed to the enemy."

I thought for a moment and answered. "Captain, these soldiers are American paratroopers. They only want the prisoners; there are no Russians or Poles out here to deal with."

"Americans this far into Europe; the war will be over sooner than I expected," he said.

I was encouraged by his answer. "Captain, there is no reason to die here today. Turn over your weapons and walk home to your son."

He strolled out from behind the truck to face me. "How do I know you speak for these Americans?"

The statement of telling him he should trust me was probably not going to be enough. Suddenly, behind me Lieutenant Thomas stood up.

He declared, "He speaks for the American troops. Assemble your men, lay down your weapons, and walk out."

We were at a critical point, and the captain and I stood face to face. I could see his fatigue. Our eyes studied each other for clues. I had wounded his heart with the mention of his son, and gave him a reassuring nod.

He spoke. "A teacher of history; my profession, Cart Man, is a teacher of history. What will I teach about all of this; so much death, and for what?" He paused for a moment. "One day I wish to understand all of this; you, the boy, this godless war. For now, I shall attempt to walk home to my son." He smiled emptily as he declared, "I will probably be court-martialed."

The captain turned and gave the order, and the Nazi troops began to vacate positions and make their way toward him. As they condensed into formation, the prisoners behind them proceeded to rush the supply trucks. The realization of being liberated was spreading quickly, along with a chaotic search for food and water.

The major quickly ordered the American platoons to advance and aid as best they could. Thomas's platoon stayed in position as the Nazi unit completed assembling.

The captain gave the final order to discard arms. Dozens of weapons fell to the snowy ground. He looked my way, gave a salute, and nothing else was said between us. His attention shifted to Lieutenant Thomas. The lieutenant extended his arm, in a permission to leave manner. The captain in turn gave the command to march. He led his unit out of the hamlet and toward the desired destination of home. As he walked away, he left the war behind, but not the end to his nightmare. Leaving with him, an evil piece of history, with which he would forever struggle.

Chapter 27 – Poland WW2

Joshua Takes a Stand

The course of restoring order in the hamlet was going to take a while. The supply trucks were completely ravaged of all they possessed. The paratroopers gladly gave up their rations to aide any way they could. The major went through the process of identifying the command chain within the POWs. He would use them to restore order eventually. He had already arranged a supply drop for the men, and the open meadow around the hamlet was a perfect target for the supply planes to aim for.

Facing the major were many challenges. He had a thousand men in very bad condition; along with the Nazi army moving west to Germany, and Russians bearing down from the east. The first order of business would be to stabilize the hamlet. It would be best to stay put, to receive the supply drops and distribute supplies to the men. The hamlet provided water and some housing to allow the setup of aide and distribution stations. The process was going to take at least three days to get organized and functional. Eventually the plan would be to head southwest toward the advancing allied forces. It would be a tricky path trying to avoid contact with the Nazi retreat.

Mid-day had come, and the action around the hamlet was beginning to calm. I noticed Joshua standing by himself staring at me, as if he needed something. I walked toward him, while avoiding the celebrating that was ensuing all around me.

"What is it?" I asked.

"I must go find them," he said sternly.

I knew he was talking about Daniel and Joseph, but I had reservations. "We don't know where they are. Joshua, you are safe here, and the traveler is out there somewhere waiting for another chance."

He grabbed a dead tree limb from the ground and began to draw on a patch of moist dirt. "I know where they are. The river runs here and we are over here to the south. They would have headed for Joseph's people on the river. I know two or three places where they would be. It would make sense to stay east of the Nazis, which would put them somewhere here." He continued to draw. "They wouldn't go any further east than this big bend in the river, the Russians are probably there by now. In between this point to the west, and the bend in the river, is where we will find them."

The passion with which he described his plan to find the boys was inspiring. Not from just seeing it, but the understanding of its emotional weight. The feeling of being alone, and craving to reunite with what you know, can be a heavy burden to bear. I was continuing to understand more about this amazing boy. He had survived the last three years on his instincts, courage, and absolute loyalty. There would be no talking him out of this; perhaps holding him hostage, but the better idea was to have a talk with Lieutenant Thomas.

Momentarily excusing myself from Joshua, I set off to look for Thomas and soon found him struggling to organize the reception of the first supply drop that was due soon. He looked miserable trying to keep a bunch of celebrating men from injuring themselves or others. I asked him if he had time to talk.

He thankfully said, "You bet, let's go talk. I'd rather talk to Hitler than deal with one more of these lunatics." I just chuckled and pulled him aside.

I pleaded." I need your help; Joshua is determined to go find his two friends. I'm going with him and I think it would be best if we had you as an escort."

He frowned. "That's a little much at this point for two friends isn't it?"

I countered, "They aren't just friends, more like family, the only family he has left. Thomas he's going to go, with or without our help, and you and I both know the Traveler is out there." Thomas was fond of Joshua, and would be influenced by any chance of danger that might come his way.

He questioned, "How do we know where his friends might be?"

I replied, "Joshua knows where they were headed, and has a great understanding of the area. He believes he can find them."

Thomas contemplated the situation. "We're stuck here for at least three days. I can't send you two out there alone, that disappearing boy probably has three other guys with weapons helping him." He thought some more and made a decision. "I'm gonna go talk to the major, don't you two do anything till I get back."

"That's a deal," I promised, then walked back to Joshua.

Thomas strolled over toward the major and engaged him in conversation. He did most of the talking while the major patiently listened. When he was done, he gave a quick salute and headed toward us with a concerned scowl on his face. I had no clue if the news was good or bad.

"Well, boys, prepare to get under way," he said, then looked at Joshua and gave him a wink.

Joshua smiled and enthusiastically urged. "Let's go."

I rose from my seated position and asked the lieutenant, "What now?"

As I asked the question a soldier came up carrying two backpacks. Thomas took them, then handed one to each of us. He was taking charge. "We will all pack out of here with supplies for a three day trip. That will be the length of our search and no longer." He looked at Joshua and then me; his demeanor was one of complete seriousness.

Joshua nodded his head and answered with confidence. "We will find them by then."

Thomas remained stern. "You both need to realize that we are most likely walking into a trap." We acknowledged the fact.

He continued. "We will get troop support as we leave the valley and enter the woods. It will provide for a safe head start. I figure that ol boy doesn't know what we're doing, and all this will catch him by surprise. He'll have to keep his distance and we will move out quickly."

I was encouraged by the idea of an escort, no matter how long we had it. Thomas supplied me with a rifle, but did not arm Joshua. The plan was to provide Joshua with the best possible safety, and use Thomas and myself as the front and back men on the journey. We were ready, and our escort troops began to deploy.

Thomas loaded his pack and addressed us. "Let's go, gentlemen; we gotta make great time until we find our spot for the night. If he's coming after us, it will be tonight, and I intend to be ready."

I was concerned. "Thomas, there will be four of them."

He grinned. "Exactly, if there's just four, it won't even be a fair fight." I knew he was bragging, but it made me feel better. I had a suspicion that Lieutenant Thomas was no one to mess with.

Chapter 28 – Poland WW2

The Battle

We set out, with the Lieutenant taking the lead and me in the rear. Joshua was focused, and walked with a determined step that I had not seen for some time. Our group made the woods very quickly, and kept the escort for about an hour more. During a quick break, Thomas spoke to the escort leader. It was time for them to turn back, but they would retreat in a broad pattern to further secure our head start. This strategy gave Lieutenant Thomas the knowledge that the traveler either lay in wait in front of us, or was far behind and would not be a factor for most of the remaining day.

Continuing on, Thomas set a demanding pace. Joshua was doing fine, but my backpack was taking a toll on aging legs. My main job was to listen for any suspect sound, and periodically scan territory behind us. We were traveling in heavily wooded hill country and were gradually working our way toward the river valley. There was only two more hours of light, and Thomas was actively looking for a place to set up for a probable confrontation to come that night.

Cresting a small hill, we came upon a hunter's cabin, nestled in the trees between two larger hills to each side and beyond. Thomas came to a halt and began evaluating the structure. He liked the fact that there was only one window, and that it had a front and back door. The cabin had a high visual vantage point, and advancing enemy would most likely be funneled up the hill toward its front. The Traveler and his men would not know about the location until they were on top of it.

Thomas ordered, "This is the spot, we'll meet them here." We entered through the front door and found a broken wooden table with one chair. Thomas immediately began to break it into pieces; creating wooden wedges to insert at the doors to prevent unwanted entry. His plan was simple. Let the Traveler and crew come to us, then ambush them with a tactical advantage. The only problem I had with the plan was defending the cabin. It would be up to Joshua and me to hold the Traveler at bay, while Thomas did his work on the outside.

Darkness was descending and our plan was in place. Thomas was to move outside, and we would secure both doors behind him. The window was where I would make my defensive stand.

As the Traveler approached, my job was to immediately attack with the two rifles that the lieutenant had left with me. Joshua was to stay covered, and reload weapons as needed. Thomas would lay in wait for the Traveler's force; suspecting they would split up and surround the cabin. This would be the time for his attack, and take them one by one. I had to hold them off until Thomas completed his mission.

There was fire in Thomas's eyes as he spoke. "Ok, here's the deal: attack them as soon as you can, and make them separate. Concentrate on the front where you can see. Don't open either door for any reason unless you are trying to escape."

I indicated that I understood. He continued. "Joshua, you must stay down and out of the line of fire; let Rusty take the chances of being shot." I looked at him quizzically, although I knew he was right. He shrugged his shoulders and smiled. I had a one in four chance of surviving a fatal gunshot; if Joshua were hit the world could be in jeopardy.

"Stay alert and I will see you in a few hours." Thomas put his hand on Joshua's shoulder. "Take care of Rusty for me." Joshua grinned and Thomas gave his shoulder a big squeeze then exited through the front door.

Now it was a waiting game. The lieutenant took a position at the top of the hill where I could see him. He was scouting the approach and would signal when the time came. If it turned dark, which was only minutes away, he would turn on a flashlight that he had placed against a log. The light was a signal but it also created shadows allowing me to see movement. I needed that flashlight to stay on as long as possible.

Darkness took over as Joshua stood beside me staring into the night. He had a flashlight ready if needed, but for now it was best to stay dark. He had unsheathed his trusty knife and was mindlessly sticking the wood in front of him.

He spoke. "I will kill that man if I get a chance."

I responded. "The more important thing is keeping you alive. Joshua, you must remember; no unnecessary chances." I was sternly looking at him. He nodded his agreement.

He continued. "When my father told us about the gift, he said it was our duty to keep it alive. I will be careful."

"Yes," I said. "That's exactly what you must do."

Suddenly, the flashlight outside came to life. I felt the knot in my gut and the tension stiffening in my face. "Here they come," I whispered to Joshua while bringing one of the rifles up and anchored it against my shoulder.

The Traveler had recruited three soldiers to accompany him. A large payment of stolen gold jewelry had secured their temporary loyalty. He assured them that the task would be simple; after all it was just a man and a boy. He was frustrated that they had fallen so far behind, having to avoid the American troops. The pace of their travel had been extreme, and he had to believe that it had gotten them close. Finally, he thought; a dim light was emerging from the trees at the crest of the hill. He stopped and alerted the men to the sighting; they proceeded with caution and rifles at the ready.

Lieutenant Thomas flicked on the flashlight and swiftly took his position above and to the side of the cabin. Thomas was quietly waiting for the Traveler to approach; the natural curvature of the landscape was ushering the group to where he wanted them to be. He thought to himself, "Here kitty, kitty." Being well trained for just such an event as this, his blood was pumping with anticipation.

A figure topped the hill and I prepared to fire; hoping it wasn't Thomas, I was about to shoot. Firing into the night, shadows darted randomly in the dim light. There were hurried voices, but unintelligible to my ear. A rifle fired, sending a bullet that thudded into the wood of the window directly above my head. I ducked and moved to the corner of the opening for more protection.

After firing again, I took a quick glance. The shadows were separating, and it appeared that they were surrounding the cabin as Thomas had predicted.

Thomas watched as the Traveler's men moved toward positions to surround the cabin, one of them heading right at him. He stood motionless in the black, hidden by a tree.

The soldier was now even with his location, but all of his attention was focused on the cabin below. With the quickness of a cat, Thomas attacked and wrapped the man's throat with his powerful arm. He brought the other arm around the head and jerked with deadly force. In an instant, before he could make a sound, the soldier crumpled to the ground.

The Traveler decided to surround the cabin. He sent one soldier to either side and kept himself and one other in the front. It was obvious that the cart man knew it was him. He would try to talk him out with promises.

"Cart Man, you are surrounded. All I want is the boy; you don't need to die. I will give you two minutes to decide; then we come in. If we do, you will surely die. Leave the boy inside and walk out, I won't shoot you. There is more that you can do with your gift than this, Cart Man; leave the boy and live."

I shouted, "I don't need two minutes." With that, I let loose a barrage of bullets spraying the area in front of the cabin, empting my rifle, with Joshua handing me the other ready to go.

Thomas was working his way around the backside of the cabin in the darkness. The going was slow and deliberate; it was vital to make no noise. Visibility was only a few feet, and the surprise factor would continue to be his best weapon if he did not give away his position due to sound.

In silence, he stepped around a tree and came face to face with the other soldier, who immediately raised his rifle to fire. Thomas swung his left arm across his body, colliding with the barrel of the gun, as the right hand drew his knife from its case. The rifle discharged, sending the bullet just under the now sweeping right arm of Thomas; the knife it held on a deadly course. Its blade slashed through the soldier's throat.

Dropping his rifle, the man threw his hands to his neck to render aide. Confused and dazed, he stared at Thomas, gasping for air that was no longer available, and then sprawling lifelessly on the ground.

The traveler heard the shot. "What was that?" he wondered. He called to his men and received no response. He had been foolish;

a third participant was involved. The advantage was now with them; he would have to change the rules.

Thomas wasted no time moving on; the element of surprise was gone. His strategy turned to full frontal attack; knowing where the enemy was, plus the odds continuing to turn in his favor. He knew that Rusty was helping a great deal with the barrage of gun fire generated from the cabin; this kept the enemy focus away from his attack.

Carefully he advanced; able to locate the enemy by listening and observing the gunfire. The remaining two adversaries were still in front of the cabin, but he hadn't heard a shot from one of them in a while. This was a concern, his training required that he always know location of the enemy. He came to a stop about ten meters from the source of the remaining enemy fire. Drawing his sidearm from its holster, he readied his arm and waited. The flash at the end of the barrel would be his queue. Finally a shot; as it flared, he fired. Hearing a thud, he proceeded slowly, looking for any kind of movement; his weapon ever ready. A body outline lay motionless in the dim light.

He approached with great caution, and checked for signs of life. Turning the body, he discovered that it was not the Traveler.

Abruptly there was a commotion in the cabin; then a light. The hair on the back of his neck stood straight; he realized what had happened; it was the Traveler. Thomas bolted for the cabin window.

The Traveler knew his only card left to play was his gift; the cabin needed to be entered and he would travel to do so. He felt himself begin the process; his dark angel was on task and working with him. The move was completed quickly, but had left him surrounded by darkness and struggling to get his bearings. There was a loud gun burst and flash. The resulting light helped him realize his position inside the cabin. He was thrilled to see the cart man kneeling in front, firing his weapon through the window. He smiled at his great fortune, and raised his weapon to fire.

Suddenly, a bright burst of light flashed in his eyes. He was stunned by a sharp thud against his chest. Massive pain flooded through his upper torso and he dropped to his knees.

Joshua felt a vibration and heard the roof of the cabin rattle. He instinctively moved away from his position behind Rusty for a better look. The area by the front door gave him the best view. He wasn't sure what it was, but something was in the back of the cabin. He held the flashlight with his left hand and firmly clutched his knife with the right. Rusty fired his rifle, giving Joshua a glimpse of a figure in the flash. There was no doubt who it must be. He pointed the flashlight and turned it on. Seeing a gun pointed at Rusty's back, he drew his elbow back and hurled the blade.

Thomas came racing toward the cabin window shouting, "Rusty, the Traveler; look out!"

At that point I turned to see Joshua pointing his flashlight at a stricken Traveler. His eyes showed confusion and pain; torso slumped docilely over his knees; a knife handle protruding from the left chest.

Lieutenant Thomas flew through the window, shoulder rolling to his knees, and came up with pistol drawn and ready to fire. He surveyed the room, lowered his pistol and proclaimed. "Well, I guess I wasn't needed in here."

I looked at Joshua, standing there motionless and without facial expression. My eyes followed his to the Traveler, who managed an eerie smile as he began to fade.

In moments, he was gone, leaving the three of us to evaluate what had just happened. I wasn't sure what was next, but for now, we had won. I knew one more thing: Joshua had just saved my life.

Chapter 29 – Poland WW2

The Reunion

Thomas stood and walked toward Joshua. "Are you ok?" he asked.

Joshua acknowledged him. "Yes, I'm fine." Then turned and slowly walked toward me, giving a puzzled look as he spoke. "It doesn't make me feel any better."

I smiled. "Well it made me feel better; Joshua, you saved my life."

He smiled and accepted the praise with a bow. Turning his attention to Thomas, he asked, "What now?"

The lieutenant was thoughtful. "I think we should move out and change locale. We don't want that boy coming back at us later on in the night. He doesn't seem to be able to drop in unless he knows where we are."

I added, "I believe that's true, according to what Ham has told me to this point; it would be a good idea to change location."

It didn't take us long to pack up and move out. Joshua and Thomas talked about the direction we should head. Thomas was an expert in nighttime maneuvers; he needed input from Joshua on where exactly we were attempting to go.

Thomas took the lead and we headed out. It's hard to determine how far you travel at night, and even to know how long. It seemed as if we had been walking long enough for the sun to be rising soon. Thomas suddenly stopped us and indicated we would rest at this particular spot. I hadn't noticed but we were next to a running stream.

He commanded, "We need rest before daylight; get some food and water in you and bundle up. No fire, just food and sleep."

I was thankful for the break, collapsing into a blanket with my backpack as a headrest. My dreams were vivid and they centered on Sara. I spoke to her, and she told me she would see me soon. She skipped away, her platinum blonde hair flowing as if in a breeze. She turned, waved, and spoke, "Rusty, wake up." Thomas was shaking my shoulder; it was light and he was ready to move.

I asked, "How long have I been asleep?"

Thomas answered, "Not that long, but you were snoring and I didn't want to give away our position." He looked at Joshua and winked.

Joshua smiled and picked up his pack. "Let's go," he said. He was eager to get on the way, and looked at me with urgency.

I extended my arms defensively and said; "Ok, ok; I'm ready, let's go." It was good to see him excited, sensing that we were getting close to Daniel and Joseph. Overnight we had moved into the river valley, and the travel was dramatically easier. Thomas had his bearings, and was headed for the first location where Joshua thought the gypsies might be. The plan was simple: get to the river and follow it until we found them. Joshua knew specific locations to check; the rest of the trip would be dictated by Thomas, checking enemy movement and the best terrain to travel.

It didn't take long to get to the river edge. We stopped for a break on a small bluff overlooking the water. Thomas took out his binoculars and surveyed the area. The river had many auxiliary channels that would support a large group camping at its edge. Getting a clear look into these channels would take time; he didn't want to go to the trouble of checking an area unless there was evidence of the gypsies being there.

Thomas felt the need for more information. "Who are these people anyway?"

Joshua answered, "They live off the river, fishing and hunting. Some of them make goods for trade; others are performers, like in the circus."

Thomas continued, "So is there some big boat I'm looking for?"

"No," said Joshua. "Small boats, many of them, that can be tied together then anchored to the shore."

Thomas stopped talking and focused his binoculars downstream. "I see smoke on the river about two miles down." He handed the binoculars to Joshua. "Here, take a look and see what you think."

Joshua peered into the glasses and adjusted the focus, his eyes scanning the shore for the smoke that could be the gypsies. He brought the glasses down, turned to Thomas and shrugged. The lieutenant smiled then gave his trained analysis. "The lazy smoke pattern coming from multiple locations indicates an encampment. The big question is who?" He picked up his pack. "I guess we better find out."

Joshua tugged on Thomas's jacket to get his attention. "I know this area of the river well; my home is not far away. I can show you the best path."

Thomas looked at me, and then at Joshua. He stepped back in a manner to give Joshua control. "Lead the way, kid." Joshua did, taking the opportunity to set a hurried pace. The lieutenant followed, scanning for anything that might be considered a threat. Within an hour, we had charged our way to a grassy area next to the water, and across from the encampment. This area of the river was slow moving and deep, probably fifty meters wide. Joshua stood on the bank and scanned the far side. The encampment was as he had previously described, obviously a gypsy group. What wasn't known: were these the gypsies we were looking for, and had Daniel and Joseph made it out?

The boats were tied together in a flotilla, and anchored in a small channel off the main river. Dozens of tents dotted the shoreline, and a group of small children played in the meadow that lined the shore. One of the children spotted us and pointed our way. They all stopped their play, and stood staring in our direction. One child bolted for the nearest tent; quickly two adults emerged with rifles. The news was spreading through the tents and creating quite a commotion. Soon, many lined the shore wondering who we were and what we might want.

Thomas was uneasy but calm. Joshua stood motionless, studying the far side for anyone familiar. A boy stepped out from within the crowd; he moved close to the water's edge and was scanning us just as intently as we him. I knew him; it was Joseph. I heard Joshua gasp beside me; he stepped forward toward the water to be seen. Joseph dropped to his knees, overwhelmed with emotion. Another boy emerged; it was Daniel. He threw his arms above his head, fisting at the sky. I waved my arms back and forth above my head in a friendly gesture. Joshua remained motionless, but tears glistened in his eyes. The boys were fixated on each other; they had made it, against all odds, and that reality was sinking in.

Thomas decided to move things along. "Ok, are you going to look at each other all day, or is somebody gonna do something?"

I laughed. "You're right." I began waving my arm in a motion that indicated we wanted them to come to us. Daniel immediately understood and spoke to one of the men.

Soon a boat was being untied; one of the men took the rudder, while another manned the oars. Joseph and Daniel both hopped in the boat. It didn't take long for the experienced gypsies to navigate their craft to our position. Thomas entered the water; from the boat, Joseph tossed him a rope and the lieutenant pulled the boat to shore.

Joseph was the first out and raced toward Joshua. He attacked him with a giant bear hug. "I was scared I would never see you again," he blurted through tearful sobs.

Joshua spoke as his old strong self. "I was going to find you no matter what."

Daniel stood waiting for Joseph to finish his hello. Joseph step away and Daniel moved forward to speak, his eyes betraying his love and respect for Joshua. "I knew you would come."

Joshua smiled and embraced him in a warm gesture of unity.

The gypsy men were eager to get us back to the other side. We piled in the boat and Thomas pushed us away from shore, then hopped on board. The boys were all smiles, and Joseph talked non-stop. He was excited for us to meet the clan and bragged about the celebration that would take place.

As we approached the far shore, Thomas threw the rope to waiting helpers on land. There was time to look around as we waited for the boat to be secured, and I was impressed with the intricate design of the flotilla and camp.

The boats were connected in a way that provided easy access from one to the other. Onshore activities were housed under large tarps or tents. There was a large meeting area surrounding an open fire. Lights were strung in strategic areas along the tarp line, and along the area surrounding the open meeting space. A generator provided the power; it looked to be of military variety, and I wondered how they had come upon one of those. Lanterns were the other light source that I could see from the boat.

We stepped ashore and the young children ran toward us. The girls were all in long, colorful skirts or dresses; boys in wool shirts and pants. The adults were very eclectic in their dress, with multiple styles and colors.

Joseph was a social butterfly, trying to introduce us to everyone he could. We gradually moved toward the center of the camp and reached one of the larger tents where the crowd began to part. From inside the tent emerged a medium-height, handsome man.

He was dressed in the theme of a pirate, with the puffy long sleeve shirt and colorful vest. He wore a wide-brimmed velvet hat, with one side pinned up and a feather protruding from its top. I viewed him as a cross between Zorro and Peter Pan.

Joseph grabbed Joshua and stepped forward to speak. "Uncle, this is Joshua, the boy I was telling you about, the one that saved my life." The man scanned Joshua from head to toe, as if he were inspecting him for a buy. He scratched his black goatee and smoothed his long, thin mustache. A smile eased onto his face as he raised his hand and readied himself to speak to the crowd. "Prepare a feast, for we must celebrate this warrior's victorious return from war." He turned to Joshua and stood at attention. He graciously bowed to him and spoke. "It's an honor to meet you, young man. We cherish the return of Joseph and our new son Daniel."

Not knowing what to do, Joshua bowed in return. The man smiled and acknowledged his response.

He turned toward Thomas and me for a formal introduction. "I am Sebastian, leader of this sometimes unruly and ungrateful group; and who might you be?"

I thought it best if I did the talking. "My name is Rusty, and this is Lieutenant Thomas of the American Forces."

Sebastian was surprised. "Americans?" His hand again stroked his goatee as he thoughtfully spoke. "Americans this far into Europe; the end of this war is at hand."

I said, "This is a very unusual situation and I hope you will gift us with your understanding." Thomas gave me a look, wondering where my current linguistics were coming from.

Sebastian was amused as he spoke. "We are gypsies; we understand everything." He winked at Joshua and turned to the crowd with hands raised. "It feels good to celebrate after so much sorrow. We must show our new friends the gypsy way."

Two women came forward and Sebastian ushered us toward them. "These women will take you to your tent. Joshua, you will stay with Joseph and Daniel. I must take your leave, for I have much to do." He pressed his palms together in front of his chest and gave a slight bow.

"Thank you," I earnestly said.

He stepped away with a confident gait. Thomas and I were unsure what to do, and I thought to myself that things move quickly around this place. The women pointed the direction they wanted to go and escorted us to a small tent, just big enough for two and our packs. I placed my pack on the dirt floor and sat against it. Thomas took a seat; it was time to rest and reflect on the ever changing events of the day. It was also a good time to have an important talk.

I began the conversation. "Thomas, we need to talk about Joshua."

He replied, "Hey, you can call me Jason if you want to; I was just giving you a hard time before."

I smiled and said, "I actually prefer Thomas."

He gave me a sly smile and said, "Well ok then, Cart Man, go ahead."

I laughed but quickly moved on. "Joshua is going to need a lot of support over the next several years."

Thomas responded, "It looks like these people are ready to do that."

I shook my head. "He can't stay here, he would be easy to find and all of these people would be put in danger. The Traveler knows we were headed in this direction. He would quickly deduce that fact and locate Joshua. I'm hoping you are beginning to understand how important Joshua is."

Thomas nodded sarcastically and said, "Yeah, I think I get it. You're from the future and your job is to keep Joshua safe. His job is to stay alive and be some kind of human signal for some kind of H. G. Wells travel machine. What's not to get, seems real simple to me."

Smiling, I said, "I know this is way out there, but you have seen plenty to justify the story."

He agreed. "No doubt about it. I'll do whatever I can to help you two out of this mess and be on your way."

We were getting to it, and I knew it was not going to go down well. "Thomas, I can't stay in history very long. I must go back to my time, and Joshua can't go with me. I need you to guide him when I'm gone."

His demeanor changed as he realized my intent. Giving an incredulous look, he pushed out his palm. "Now wait just a second, just wow!" Shifting to his knees, he continued, "I'm in the middle of a war and I can't be in charge of some kid."

I countered. "Thomas, you already know he's no ordinary kid. He doesn't need much help, he needs opportunity and guidance. He won't hold you back, he just needs a chance."

He acknowledged. "I would like to help, but I can't swing this. How am I supposed to be in the military, during a war, and drag along a kid?"

I attacked back. "You and I both know this war is over and there are going to be millions of refugees. Joshua is just one of them. I'm only asking you to get him in the system and have the ability to stay in touch. Just get him started, Thomas, Joshua will take care of the rest."

He started shaking his head back and forth. "I knew I shouldn't have come on this trip."

I encouraged. "Come on, Thomas, you know you like the kid."

He said, "Of course I do, what's not to like."

I pleaded. "There is nobody else. He can't stay here; he would be a sitting duck."

Thomas raised his head and looked at me with resigned eyes. "Well we can't have that, can we."

I smiled at him and answered, "No we can't."

I stood and offered him my hand as help up. His powerful grip revealed the strength in this rugged man. As I was finding out, he was also a good man.

We left the tent and took a stroll around the encampment. Excitement was in the air with the hustle and bustle of preparation for the celebration. The group was beginning to gather in the main area. The fire now had a spit that was roasting a carcass of unknown game. The men stood in a group passing around a jug that I suspected was full of moonshine; while the women hustled the children to their assigned spots.

Our three boys sat with a group of older children, across from us on the far side of the fire. I could see Joshua sitting quietly, listening to Joseph ramble on with excited chatter. I notice that his attention seemed to drift often toward a pretty dark haired girl a few feet from him. She would catch him staring at her and smile; Joshua then quickly would turn his head and act as if he had no knowledge of the incident. It was really funny, and I had never seen that shyness from him before.

Soon she was sitting next to him and forcing conversation. I wished I could hear, but from what I saw, for the first time Joshua was clueless on what to do. This pretty little girl had him tongue tied and speechless.

I jabbed Thomas in the ribs. "Take a look at Joshua; I've never seen him so uncomfortable."

Thomas speculated. "That's more than uncomfortable, that's love."

The night progressed quickly into a big party. Everyone took their turn dancing and performing. The talent among the gypsies for special tricks and circus acts was amazing. Joseph put his talent on display as well. He was a masterful juggler of all types of objects; the most impressive being the handling of many large bladed knives. He possessed a fabulous sense of balance, and demonstrated that fact with acrobatics on a tree branch that hovered about eight feet off the ground.

Daniel took a keen interest in what apparently was a still for making moonshine. The men hovered around it, and this gave Daniel the opportunity to ask many questions about how it worked and what went in the mixtures. Always the curious one, he had a natural flair for such things and would know all about the still before the evening was over.

Joshua's night was being consumed by his fascination with the pretty dark-haired girl. They kept to themselves and continued to talk. She even convinced him to share a dance.

Sebastian had been overseeing the events of the evening, but ascertained that he no longer had any meaningful control. Deciding to join us, he strolled over, smiling and shrugging his shoulders. "I told you this was an unruly group."

I asked, "Sebastian, who is the young girl that Joshua is sitting with?"

He smiled and said, "She would be my daughter, Victoria."

I said, "She certainly has Joshua's attention."

Sebastian answered, "I hope there is nothing to worry about there."

I laughed. "Victoria looks to have total control."

Sebastian wryly answered, "Perhaps you're right; she's just like her mother."

He turned his attention to us, and was curious about our plans. "So what is next for you Americans?"

I said, "We will head back soon; the lieutenant must rejoin his unit."

Sebastian questioned, "And what about you, what are your plans?"

I said, "That's a long story that I should probably keep to myself."

He thoughtfully said, "You are quite the mysterious one."

I smiled and changed the conversation to Joshua. "It is important that Joshua comes with us."

Sebastian looked disappointed as he spoke. "I had just assumed that he would be staying."

I explained, "He is in great danger, and having him here would put all of you in danger as well. He would be an easy target if he stayed here. He can come with us and disappear into a big world, until the time comes for him to use the gift he possesses."

Sebastian asked, "Am I to know what gift he has?"

I said, "I'm afraid not, but I can tell you it is of worldwide importance. He must stay safe."

He was concerned. "Now I know why you are here, but I'm not sure Joshua is going to want to leave."

I answered, "Yes, that has been my concern as well, but I think when he realizes the danger he would put everyone in, he will understand that leaving would be the best thing to do."

The lieutenant had been listening but was becoming increasingly distracted. He interrupted the conversation. "Gentleman, I would feel a lot better out there patrolling the area. I don't want any surprise appearances from our friend."

Sebastian was quick with a response. "Lieutenant, I should accompany you so that there is no confusion. I always have lookouts and they are armed. I would not want a mistake to be made tonight."

Thomas smiled and said, "Well thanks, Sebastian, that's good information to have."

They left together, leaving me free to roam the camp. Daniel had joined up with Joseph and the other boys; they were playing some type of game involved with the throwing of sticks. Joshua and Victoria were seated on a fallen tree, still deep in conversation. I should have left them alone, but my curiosity pulled me over. As I approached, Victoria looked my way. She smiled and said, "Hi."

I returned the greeting, "How are you?"

Joshua figured out that he needed to make introductions. "Victoria, this is Rusty; Rusty, this is Victoria."

I said. "Very nice to meet you, Victoria, I believe I've been making friends with your father."

She said, "Yes, my father makes friends very quickly, that's why he is always in charge."

I complimented, "He seems to be very much in charge and a gracious host as well."

She smiled and grabbed Joshua's hand. "I've been telling Joshua all about our clan and our traditions."

I said. "How interesting, I know it must be, because Joshua can hardly take his eyes off of you."

Joshua glared at me; Victoria slightly blushed and giggled.

I gave Joshua a sly smile, and stayed a bit longer, making casual conversation. Finally, I put him out of his misery and announced my departure. "Victoria, I will let you get back to your education of Joshua, it was a pleasure to meet you." I gestured with a short bow.

Victoria answered warmly, "My pleasure, sir."

I walked away from the couple relishing the small victory of embarrassing Joshua. Chuckling to myself, I realized that hadn't happened in quite some time. It felt good, and I wondered about the origin of this warm emotion.

I surmised that the catalyst of my feeling was this clan of fascinating people. In the midst of war and the Holocaust, their spirit had survived. There was joy in their hearts. Sure they felt sadness, but they were careful to cultivate moments of celebration and happiness. They understood their situation and would not settle for hopelessness.

I strolled down the grassy path that led back toward my tent. Suddenly I heard a scream; it was coming from where I had just left Joshua and Victoria. I turned and ran to them, thinking that the Traveler had returned again. As I approached I called out, "Victoria, what is it?"

She responded in an urgent voice. "Rusty, please help him."

I turned the corner around a clump of trees to face a brilliant light. Shading my eyes with my forearm, I searched for the two. I could make out the image of Victoria standing and looking upward. I followed her gaze and discovered Joshua suspended in mid-air, about ten feet off the ground; a familiar pulsating light surrounding him. His arms were extended perpendicular to his chest, his head tilted straight back.

Not knowing if he was conscious or not, I yelled, "Joshua, can you hear me?"

He responded by slowly lifting his head and rotating his body toward me. He said nothing, and his eyes were glazed over.

Sebastian came running down the path behind me, while Thomas stepped out of the cover of the woods and positioned himself by Victoria. We all stood watching, not knowing what to do.

Daniel and Joseph were the next to arrive, Joseph shouted in a panic. "Rusty, what should we do?"

Still stunned and looking at Joshua, I answered. "I don't think anything; just wait."

The suspension of Joshua seemed like an eternity, but in reality was probably about a minute. Slowly, he lowered and the brilliant light began to fade. I could see his eyes open with recognition, as his feet lightly touched the ground. He searched for balance as Victoria rushed to him to deliver a supportive hug.

Lieutenant Thomas wondered, "What in the hell was that?"

I answered with an assumption "I believe the beacon has just activated for the first time."

Moving over to Joshua, I asked, "Are you ok?"

He smiled and said, "I guess I know how you feel now."

I grinned, seeing he was fine. "I believe you do." I was curious. "What did it feel like?"

Joshua had a puzzled look as he spoke. "The light was inside me, beating like my heart. When I closed my eyes I saw numbers flashing in front of me."

I reasoned, "I'm sure that was the beacon activating inside you. I'm not sure what the numbers might mean. For now, we know that the process has started; we will deal with what comes next."

Many of the clan had drifted out to see what was going on. Sebastian took charge. "Ok everyone; the show is over, go back and get some sleep." He ushered all on their way; then came back to me. "Well that was interesting," he said.

I replied, "Yes, it really was."

Sebastian's demeanor turned official. "Rusty, we should talk later."

I agreed. "I think that would be appropriate."

It had been a long night and I suggested that all three boys should say their goodnights and go to bed. Daniel and Joseph returned to their tent, although I doubted much sleep would take place. They were abuzz with excitement, and I was certain that questions would rain down on Joshua when he returned to the tent.

Joshua took some time to debrief with Victoria, their relationship was bonding quickly, and there's nothing like a levitating experience to help bolster things to talk about. They eventually said goodnight and headed their separate ways.

I admired watching Victoria exit through the trees that guarded her path. She was graceful in her movements, and had an elegant air about her; that of a princess flowing down a royal hallway.

I noticed Thomas standing near, and walked over to talk. "The Traveler will know where we are now."

Thomas agreed. "Yeah, I figured that." He asked, "Do you think he's coming?"

I had been mulling over that very thought, and decided that he would not come by himself. There was no more support personnel from the Nazis, and the odds would not be in his favor. I reasoned, "I think he will wait and reorganize. He knows he can track Joshua when the beacon activates again."

Thomas asked the obvious question. "How soon will that be?"

I said, "According to Ham, somewhere around every ten to fifteen years."

The lieutenant got an anxious look on his face and asked. "And that's until when?"

I gently explained, "Well, I'm from over sixty years in the future and nothing has arrived yet."

Thomas starred out to space, his voice quietly drifting as he spoke, "A lifetime of this?" He shook his head with dismay.

I said, "It will be for Joshua, everyone else has a choice." The lieutenant gave me a look. It wasn't a nasty or angry look; it was one of a pondering thought. It was as if he were considering his commitment.

I thought it best that we continue later and break it off for the night. He needed time to think, and there wasn't much left to say. I suggested it was time for sleep.

Thomas spoke cautiously. "Ok, I believe the Traveler probably isn't coming, but just the same, I think I'll go back out on patrol."

I said, "Thomas, I have to say, I appreciate that."

He nodded, turned, and headed back into the woods. Watching him leave, I couldn't help but wonder what was going through his head. I stood for a moment more, then attempted to head for my tent for a second time that night.

Strolling slowly and thinking about the situation we were in, my thoughts were centered on the upcoming talk I needed to have with Joshua. It would be about his life changing again, and the burden he would carry for the rest of it.

I felt great concern for how lonely all of this was for him, and realized that I was one of only a few who could understand how he felt. It was also apparent that the people here were those few, and I knew they were good for him. He had to leave with us, but I was developing a growing understanding for the need to keep him in touch with this clan. I would talk to Thomas about that. A nagging feeling kept tugging at me; this was something that needed to get done.

We stayed with the gypsies for an additional couple of days. Lieutenant Thomas didn't seem to mind. He realized that Joshua needed the time, and I believe he really liked being around the clan. More than once, I saw him laughing and joking with the men; he also attracted much attention from the younger single women.

The extra time gave me an opportunity to further talk to him about Joshua, addressing the issue of maintaining a support system. He agreed that Joshua needed a family that understood his unusual circumstances, and this group was that family. The lieutenant was developing a real affection for Joshua, and that's exactly what needed to be. It was also apparent that Joshua felt the same way.

After my conversations with Thomas, came the search for Sebastian; wanting to meet with him as promised. That meeting needed to take place before sitting down with Joshua for our talk. I had an idea, but would need Sebastian's blessing before implementing my plan.

My search found him fishing by the river, sitting on a wooden dock that was attached by two wire cables to a large boulder lodged in the sand of the river shoreline. He seemed very relaxed, and that provided for an opportunity to approach him with my plan. I started the conversation. "Have you caught anything yet?"

He laughed. "No, Rusty, not yet, I'm not sure I really try to catch anything when I'm out here. It's just a good place to think."

"I didn't mean to interrupt your quiet time, but there is something I need to speak with you about."

He laughed again. "So you did mean to interrupt me after all." Motioning for me to sit down, he continued. "What can I do for you on this fine day?"

"It's Joshua, I'm worried about him."

He acknowledged. "I can see why. I think it might be time for all of us to know what is going on with him."

Agreeing, I opened up to Sebastian about Joshua's gift, also telling him my story and ability to travel. We spoke about Ham, and about heaven and the dark side. Also my concern, that due to circumstances beyond his control, Joshua was going to be isolated from any kind of normal support and friendship.

I was asking for his assistance, but there also had to be a conversation about the consequences of being involved in Joshua's life. "Sebastian, before we talk any further about Joshua, I must tell you about the other traveler and the danger involved." He nodded his head as a signal to go on.

"He has the same abilities as I do, and is looking for Joshua. He represents the interests of the dark side, and his intent is to kill Joshua. There is nothing but evil in his heart, and would not hesitate to kill anyone in his path." I looked for a reaction from Sebastian. He was stoic but attentive.

I decided to press on. "Getting involved with Joshua could mean danger, and a long term commitment to a very unusual lifestyle; living on the move, avoiding detection, staying to yourselves."

That brought a smiling response from Sebastian. "You have just described the life of a gypsy."

I continued. "Joshua needs to know that he has a family. I can only be around during certain moments in his life. The lieutenant is going to help him, but that is not enough. He needs to know that he has people out there that he can turn to if need be; real people he can trust."

Sebastian raised his hand in a gesture for me to stop. He spoke in a calm, yet emotional tone. "We have suffered much here, and know the hatred in the world around us. We accept all who have a good heart. Here is a boy, who has suffered great loss, and you tell me he is the key to the survival of the world. He is one of us, one of the survivors from this evil time. Of course we are his family; I was hoping you would ask us to be." Sebastian's response felt like a weight being lifted from my shoulders.

After sincerely thanking him, we talked on about my plan, and discussed how it would be possible to track the clan, and periodically keep Joshua in touch with them. Being comfortable with all of that, there still was the issue of talking to Joshua. I finished up with Sebastian and went looking for him.

I found him in the woods, sitting on a large tree stump, midst a gathering of bushes that framed the area around where he sat. There was sadness evident in his eyes as he spoke. "I knew you would be coming soon."

Taking a seat beside him I confessed. "You know me too well."

He stared at his feet as he replied. "I know I can't stay."

The knot in my stomach returned. "Joshua, I really wish you could." Putting my arm around him, we sat silently for many minutes. There weren't any words that would help. Joshua once again was sacrificing for the good of others. Finally I said, "Let's get some sleep; it's going to be a long day tomorrow." We strolled back to the camp and said goodnight. Walking back to my tent, I knew the lonely emptiness that Joshua would be feeling all night. Another thought came to me while walking away: Joshua might be the finest person I had ever met.

The next morning came quickly and we packed our gear for departure. I left the tent and walked down the tree covered path to get Joshua. There he sat, backpack at his feet and ready to go. I motioned for him to get up and follow me. Reversing my tracks, we returned back down the path from where I had come, all the way to the main tent of the camp; a large canvas structure similar to what you would expect at a circus. We stopped and I explained to Joshua, "Before we leave, we must go in here for a moment."

Joshua answered with a questioning look on his face, "Ok."

We entered with me in the lead. After going in, I stepped aside to reveal a gathering that had assembled for him. In a casual semi-circle sat his would-be; included were Joseph, Daniel, Lieutenant Thomas, Sebastian, and Victoria.

Joshua seemed confused as he surveyed the group. Looking to me, he asked, "What is this?"

I smiled and said, "They have something to tell you."

Joshua returned his attention to the group as Daniel stood to speak. "Joshua, we are your family and will always be. Whether together or apart, we will always be with you."

He sat down and Joseph stood for his turn to speak. "We took an oath, and we will do anything it takes to honor that oath." Joseph's emotions overflowed as he proclaimed, "Family forever!"

Sebastian was next; he stood and articulated his message with the authority of a master of ceremony. "Joshua, I hereby pledge what is known as the Heart of the Gypsies. You will be a part of us, one beating heart together. Wherever you are, we are."

The lieutenant took his turn next. "That's right, kid; we're going to make it happen. All of us are with you, and I will make sure that you see these guys again."

Joshua stood motionless; his expression was one of thankfulness. He still exhibited great self-control; that is until the pretty dark haired girl stood up. Victoria took a step forward to speak. "We love you, Joshua; I love you."

Tear welled in his eyes. Victoria moved closer and took his hand. "Come back to me, Joshua," she said, gazing intently at him.

Joshua managed two words. "I will."

The family circled closer, with each resting a hand on Joshua's shoulders. Sebastian looked at me and nodded his head, as a signal for my time to speak.

Like a minister at a baptism, I gave the final blessing. "All in this room have pledged their support for this young man Joshua, who carries within him this hope for our world, and for whom we care so very much about. It will be a lifelong commitment to him and to each other, and an opportunity to save the world."

The group hovered in the moment not knowing what to do next, until Lieutenant Thomas decided to speak. "Well that about wraps it up I think," he said with a smile. "Time for us Americans and the savior to get on the road."

I disgustedly asked, "Could you have chosen anything more inappropriate to say?"

He winked and said, "Probably."

The time had come to go and we said our goodbyes. The boat was waiting for our ride across the river. The lieutenant and I boarded quickly, but Joshua stayed on shore with Victoria. They stood hand in hand talking. Thomas shook his head and mumbled something about love. Joshua slowly leaned toward Victoria and placed a kiss gently on her lips. This immediately brought loud oohs and ahs from Daniel and Joseph. He stood erect and smiled, then boarded the boat; and as we floated away, kept his eyes fixed on Victoria for the length of the trip across the water.

We unloaded and climbed our way up the embankment to a grassy ridge. From there, the gypsy gathering was in full view on the other side. There they were, all waving to us; every man, woman, and child. All of them, with the exception of Victoria, who stood there as a statue, just as she had while watching Joshua cross the river to leave.

When Joshua topped the ridge, he positioned himself to our front, similar to that of a leader addressing a crowd. As if on cue, he extended his arms and waved them boldly above his head. It was in the fashion of a signal or message. For the first time since Joshua left shore, Victoria reacted, raising her arms in a similar fashion. I looked at Joshua, then back across the river to Victoria, and realized that this was their final goodbye. There was no doubt something special had developed between them.

The gypsies continued to wave and show their enthusiastic support for us, a testament to their supportive way, and joyous lust for life. The moment for me became a living picture, framed within the picturesque river valley. It painted a poignant portrait of family and love, of hope and survival midst the crushing oppression of evil. As Sebastian had stated earlier, it truly was a feeling of one heart beating together. It would be a picture and a feeling that I would never forget.

Chapter 30 – New York City – Post WW2

A New Coalition

The Traveler was aware that he would need a new strategy to find and kill the boy. He could be patient; the beacon had activated and would now give him immediate information on the location for the hunt. He was not ready to act on the initial activation; having learned a lesson in making himself too vulnerable. But, he had a plan, and would be ready the next time. After all, he had years to prepare his trap. What he needed most were resources. That's why he had come here at this time.

It was a dingy little office in the bowels of a towering office building, in the heart of the bulging financial district. The Traveler had been searching for a candidate to be a surrogate in his quest for the resources it would take to find and eliminate the boy. It was late, and most in the building had gone home. The office housed a young intern desperate to break into the financial scene of the stock exchange. His puffy eyes suggested late nights ending with multiple glasses of alcohol; the Traveler's guess was Scotch. He was of medium build with light brown hair. His small brown eyes and weak chin gave him an Irish look. The intern's demeanor provided evidence to the Traveler's assumption that this man could be manipulated. Yes, finally he had found the perfect one: a spoiled and only child, with very little conscience, if any.

A product of an overbearing father, along with a weak and submissive mother, he would do anything to make it, to show that he could be a force in the market. The Traveler had watched him for weeks to be certain that the target could be controlled. His plan was to offer him the opportunity for more power and wealth than could possibly be imagined. It was time to meet, and he approached the office ready to snare his prey.

The young man was busy with papers in hand as the Traveler opened the door. The man looked up and quickly asked. "Can I help you?"

The Traveler couldn't help but smile as he answered. "Yes, I believe you can." His cold, dark eyes pierced through the young intern.

The man was unsettled as he asked another question. "So what is it I can do for you?"

The Traveler bore down as he moved closer to speak. "No, my young friend, the question is, what can I do for you?"

The intern shifted nervously behind his small metal desk. The intensity of the moment made him very uncomfortable. He extended a hand as he offered his name. "I'm Robert; Robert Forrest."

Without making an attempt to shake hands, the Traveler answered. "Yes, Mr. Forrest, I know who you are. You are why I am here." He spoke in the darkest of tones. It amused him to see young Forrest struggle for composure. He sensed his fear, and it was intoxicating.

Forrest lowered his hand and picked up the phone. "I believe I will call security," he weakly threatened.

The Traveler wickedly smiled as he reassured him. "No need for that, Mr. Forrest; in fact this is a most fortunate day for you." He reached inside the breast pocket of his black trench coat that covered him from shoulder to boot, and pulled out a folder housing three single pages.

Forrest considered making the phone call, but the folder had sparked his curiosity. He brought the mouthpiece of the phone to his chest and gave the Traveler a questioning glance. His hand slowly moved toward the loose folder, and he opened the cover to expose the three pages. He scanned the documents for a moment; then began to slowly relax. He put the mouthpiece back on the base of the phone and turned his total attention to the paper bait that the Traveler had cast.

Forrest finished his analysis and dismissively dropped the papers on his desk as he spoke. "You have a list of companies and commodities; so what?"

The Traveler had his fish sniffing the bait. His manner was deliberate as he explained the contents. "Yes, Mr. Forrest, as you can see, the first two pages of the list contain companies that will make great gains over the next six months. The third page contains those that should be avoided or sold. I have provided these to you at no cost."

Forrest had an incredulous look on his face as he responded. "Sir, I don't know who you are, and you obviously have been misinformed on who I am. I don't have any money, nor do I have access to other people's money. I am an intern. Even if I did have money, I would not invest it on the advice of someone I just met for the first time."

The Traveler loved this part; he would give the line plenty of slack and let the fish run with the bait; then wrench the rod hard to set the hook deep. He turned away from Forrest and spoke to the barren walls of the mostly empty office. "Mr. Forrest, this list is just for you, no action is required. You will see the developing data over the coming weeks and make your own analysis of the value of my information." He turned back to the intern to make his next comment; the one that would set the hook. His intense stare caught Forrest's eyes as he continued. "In six months' time, you will have plenty of money to invest."

Forrest sat back in his chair and closed his eyes as he gently shook his head. With a wishful tone, he whined. "I only wish that were true. Like I said already, mister, you have the wrong guy."

The Traveler answered. "But I do have the right man, Mr. Forrest. You are the only son of a wealthy couple who have a worth of over a million dollars. Are you not, Mr. Forrest?" The Traveler placed his hands on the desk and leaned in for emphasis.

Forrest wrinkled his nose and answered with confusion. "What's that got to do with anything? That cheap bastard won't give me a dime. He says I should make it on my own."

The Traveler prepared to bore in deeply with his next offering. "Yes, Mr. Forrest, your father is a difficult man to work with. That's why I believe you should be the one to invest that money."

Forrest was laughing as he spoke. "So you know the old bastard; that also means you know he won't cut me in on any deal, and I doubt seriously if he would ever work with you on one."

The Traveler removed his hands from the table and stood erect. His eyes focused on a picture of the Empire State Building that hung on the wall behind the desk, the only picture in the tiny dark room. He spoke quietly but intensely. "I have no intention of working with your father, Mr. Forrest. I will only work with you."

Forrest looked up at the Traveler and positioned his palms to represent a question as he spoke. "How exactly do you propose to do this miracle?"

His eyes burned with cold dark energy. He was feeling the moment, and his inner most passions were being aroused. He answered the young man with great anticipation of the reaction he would get. "Your parents have only two months to live."

Forrest was stunned as he answered. "What, how do you know? You don't know that. Is this some kind of con?"

The Traveler coldly responded. "Mr. Forrest, your parents will die at my hands."

Forrest became panicked. "You need to leave right now; I'm going to call the police."

The Traveler answered calmly. "You are in no danger; this is strictly a business transaction." He continued. "For you to become wealthy and powerful beyond your wildest dreams requires the elimination of your family."

Forrest resisted. "I can't let you do it. I'm going to warn them and bring in the police."

The Traveler countered. "There is nothing you or the police can do. They will be dead when I will it. But, my young heir, if you warn them, you will never see me again. You will see the amazing results of the information I have provided in the coming months. This type of information, I can provide at will. With it, in half of your lifetime you would grow to be the wealthiest man in the world, with more power than you can possibly comprehend. I will leave it to you. The decision is yours."

Forrest sat dumbfounded in his chair, not knowing how to react. The Traveler turned and headed for the door at a slow lurking pace, he was giving young Forrest time to think. The intern did have one final question. "Sir, are you the devil?"

The Traveler did not turn around as he answered. He smiled to himself, knowing he had set the hook. "No, young man, I'm not the devil. I'm not interested in your soul; I simply want to share your power." With that, he gracefully swept out of the office, and into the darkness of the night.

Chapter 31 – Poland – WW2

Heading for Home

Lieutenant Thomas came down from the ridge that provided a tree filled back drop for our camp. He had scaled it to gain radio contact with his battalion. It had been a long day of walking since we left the Gypsies, and I was gladly off my feet; relaxing against a boulder that formed one side of the encampment. Joshua was back from collecting wood for the fire that would get us through the night. The weather had been good to us, but it still was very cold when the sun went down.

I asked the lieutenant. "Did you make contact?"

He nodded and said, "Yes, we should reach them by tomorrow or the next day."

I askedv "How are things going?"

Thomas answered with good news. "Apparently, the war is mostly over. The Nazis are in full retreat, and rumor has it that Hitler is dead." Thomas sat down for the first time and leaned against his backpack. Joshua had the fire going well and sat to join us.

He had been fairly quiet for most of the day, and I knew there was a lot on his mind. He was staring at his boots and shuffling them back and forth on the ground in front of him. I decided it would be a good time to talk. "Joshua, what's on your mind?"

He looked up and paused for a moment, looked at Thomas, and then back at me. He asked, "When will you be leaving?"

"Soon," I said.

Joshua nodded his head thoughtfully as he asked, "Then what?"

I didn't hesitate. I wanted to promote as much confidence as I could; although I was honestly lacking it myself. "You and Lieutenant Thomas will push on." I stopped right there because I didn't want to say too much. It was important to push this particular conversation away from me, and focus it on the two of them.

I waited, and Thomas came through. "That's right, kid; we will take it from here."

Joshua turned to face Thomas. This was going to be the test. Joshua was a veteran survivor and a guy who was accustom to being in charge. He asked his question as a challenge. "So what's the plan, Jason? How are we going to do this?"

Thomas was completely honest. "I have no idea, kid. We will take it day to day." He smiled; then pointed at Joshua. "But I tell you, Joshua; between you and me, that's a hell of a team."

Joshua's eyes widened, then he smiled. He shyly diverted his gaze to the ground. "You're right," he acknowledged.

I flashed a quick smile at Thomas, recognizing his well-played comments. We talked on into the evening. Many points were addressed on what the ultimate plan would be. Thomas's goal was to stay in touch with Sebastian; at least enough contact to know approximately where the clan would be. He knew the next couple of months would be tricky, dealing with the military and how Joshua would fit in. He was sure the major would cooperate; from that point on they would deal with each situation as it came.

The ace in the hole was Joshua himself. He could survive on his own, and Thomas knew that. It was simply a question of staying together, or at least in touch; until the opportunity to join as a family could be arranged. After talking through the evening, we came away with a course of action to follow. Joshua would blend in to the fabric of the world and temporarily be hidden from the Traveler. Lieutenant Thomas and the Gypsies would support him; and they would all wait for my return. The commitment around that campfire was strong. It was important, because we all knew the next phase of the plan was at hand. There was an unspoken component that also loomed in the air; this would be a lifelong commitment for all.

The next morning we packed up camp and prepared to leave. Thomas had his coordinates and was discussing the terrain with Joshua while looking on his military map. I was a few feet behind them and trying to figure the best way to put on my pack. I suddenly felt my head begin to swim, and a familiar tingling throughout my body. It was clear; I was about to travel.

I called out, "Guys!"

They both turned to look. Thomas clued in as he asked his question. "Is it time?"

I answered. "Yeah, I think so." I looked at Joshua. Tears were forming in his eyes as he stood quietly with arms at his side.

He was trying to hold on as he weakly cried out, "Rusty?"

Tears trickled down my cheeks as I extended my arms toward him. "Come here quick." Joshua ran toward me and rushed into my arms, holding on tightly as I squeezed him close.

With his head buried in my chest, he asked, "When will I see you again?"

Pulling back, I looked him in the eyes to answer. "I don't know yet; but you can count on this. Joshua, I will be back, I will see you again."

"Ok," he said as he wiped the tears off of his cheeks.

I said, "I'm going to miss watching you grow. You're going to look so different when I return. I hate to miss that."

Joshua asked, "What will you look like?"

I laughed. "I won't look any different at all."

Thomas quipped, "That's too bad, I was hoping for some improvement." Joshua laughed but I completely ignored the comment.

I continued. "Joshua, I believe in you, and can't wait to see what you will have become when I return."

He placed his hand on my forearm and caught my eyes as he spoke. "I won't let you down."

I smiled and placed him in a big bear hug. "I know you won't."

Thomas interrupted. "Are you going or not?"

I released Joshua and he stepped back. I conceded, "Yes, I'm going."

Thinking for a moment, I wanted something final to say. I smiled and said, "Let me leave you with this: May the force be with you." They both stared at me blankly.

I dead panned my answer. "That will be funny in about forty years."

Giving Joshua a final look, I declared to the open air, "Ok, Sara, I'm ready to go." I felt the process begin; keeping my eyes on Joshua, I gave him a wave. He waved back as the brightness engulfed me. I kept my focus on his intense brown eyes as the picture faded away. He was gone but the image of those eyes remained with me. I thought to myself. *Joshua please stay safe.*

I found myself in what appeared to be a hotel lobby, and facing the entrance to the bar. Looking around, the lobby was empty, and I figured the bar was my destination. Walking in, I found Ham. He was standing behind a huge, western-style, long bar and dressed as a bartender wearing a long white dress shirt covered by a sleeveless black vest, topped with a red bowtie.

He enthusiastically greeted me. "Hey there, Rusty, come on in, partner; belly up!"

I walked toward him shaking my head as I questioned, "A bar, Ham?"

He said, "You bet, buddy, the best margaritas in town. What can I get you?"

I took a seat on a stool as I answered. "Some water would be just fine."

"I have that too," he said, grinning at me.

The fatigue of all the walking, and spending the night on the hard ground, was catching up with me. "I'm tired, Ham, I just want to talk."

He boasted, "Partner, that's why I'm here; bartenders are the best listeners."

I smiled at that and admitted, "Ham, I'm glad to see you and glad you're here."

He answered earnestly. "I'm always here for you, Rusty; let's talk."

I rambled. "I'm not sure what I want to know. There's so much out there that I don't understand. Let's start with the people that do such terrible things?"

Ham responded, "It's really not that complicated. Evil is continuous action taken without understanding."

I answered with frustration. "You keep talking about understanding, but I don't get how that solves evilness."

Ham was patient. "When you truly try to understand something, you put effort into it; that my friend is intent. If your intent is to wise up and develop greater understanding of what you know and share it; that is considered virtuous. Greater understanding of knowledge is what virtue is. When you share that with somebody who does the same; then virtuous knowledge expands at an increasing rate."

He looked at me to see if I was staying with him. I nodded for him to continue. "Evil exists from using knowledge without virtuous intent. It doesn't create; it only consumes. Virtue doesn't solve evil, they co-exist together."

That spawned a question from me. "So why do people choose evil over virtue?"

He was quick to answer. "When we're created, we jump into a world of choices. We learn from the stuff around us, and right away we start making choices. We decide what we like, how we feel, and what we want. The world you're in is a big ol'melting pot. Folks who develop virtuous understanding follow one path, and those that just use stuff for themselves start down an opposite path."

I was confused. "So are you saying that we know who is evil from birth?"

He rolled his eyes at me as he answered. "No, man; like you and me for example. You've led a life with more virtue than I ever did. You understood all the stuff and the benefits that come with it. I struggled to see all that and made bad choices accordingly. I didn't understand, so I chose to manipulate rather than cooperate."

I said, "So this whole thing is about choosing good or evil?"

Ham shook his head. "Not exactly, it's all about understanding. I was lucky to finally understand. The whole deal about life is virtuous intent. When you understand better, you learn and grow. Evil just uses and consumes and doesn't try to understand, it has no pathway to enlightenment. Without the guidance of virtue, intent turns self-centered and dark. If you add layer after layer of self-centered intent together, evil exists."

I wondered about the Dark Traveler. "Ham, there is nothing good in that guy; you can't tell me there is."

Ham replied, "When virtue doesn't get a chance to exist, then guys like him develop. The forces of the dark side rely on that fact; it's why they fear the beacon so much. Virtuous enlightenment is there biggest threat."

We talked on about the dark side's fear and how a cosmic connection between worlds would create a new backdrop for the further development of purpose within the universe.

The enlightenment that would occur within the dark side would change it forever; a new universal order would begin. It was very heady stuff. I now had a much deeper understanding of what was at stake.

But that's not all Ham wanted to talk about, he had some important news for me. "Rusty, you're headed for some strange times. We have been careful with your travel because of what it does to history. But now you're gonna be traveling in your own historical time."

I acknowledged that, and wondered why it was an issue. "So what's the problem, Ham?"

He used his counseling tone. "Here's the deal, you're gonna create a new history parallel to the one that is already there, kinda like what the Traveler did to you. Sooner or later those two histories will begin to merge, making what we call a paradox. Events will blend and sometimes change as you travel. What you see once after you travel; may be different the next time you come back. You're gonna have to be careful when you're in current time."

I was concerned. "How will I know if things have changed?"

Ham answered straight forwardly. "That's the problem; you won't know till you get there. I won't know either, I can't predict the future."

I was thinking as I asked the next question. "What if you just kept me moving in history and didn't send me back?"

Ham answered. "No can do, buddy; you gotta physically come back before you travel again. You're also gonna need time to get yourself safe when you come back. As I said, things are gonna change. It will be important to figure out your situation and find a safe location before your next travel."

"Wow," I said.

"Yeah," he replied, then he continued. "The beacon is in Joshua, and is in your world. But, the worm hole is outside of that. It has no relationship with time as you know it. The request for the beacon signal will be sent as needed, and only one has been so far. When the request is made, it enters your reality at a specific time period. The elapsed time in your reality is significant, but is momentary within the wormhole itself."

I was beginning to understand as I posed my next question. "So the reason I was sent back at this time is because of the beacon?"

He conditionally answered. "Yes, but not entirely. The Dark Traveler gets the same information as you, and only knows what you know. He is why you were sent, and why you will be sent again. You and he will always share the same moment."

As was becoming the norm, my head was spinning. But, I was kind of getting used to it. I felt comfort in the fact that I was dealing with all of this with Ham's help. For all of his quirkiness, he was my friend, and I trusted him.

There was something else about him, now that he was an angel. For lack of a better description, there was a gentleness about him, so I asked about it. "What's different about you, Ham? It's something, but I can't quite put my finger on it."

He smiled as he poured a glass of water from the pitcher on the bar. He said. "I found the peace I was searching for all of those years. You know, during that time, I tried everything possible to fill the void I felt in my soul. Rusty, I didn't understand how to help myself. Then I met you and I saw a different way; I still didn't understand it, but I knew it was there. You were real, and became an inspiration for me."

I asked, "What is that peace? Where does it come from?"

He answered with conviction. "It's virtuous thought; thinking with your heart and your head." He slid the glass of water across the bar toward me; then continued. "The reward that comes from being virtuous is grace. The stuff created from relationships with virtuous intent. It's the tangible meaning to the universe. The understanding we get from each other is the true purpose of our existence, and grace is that sharing and acceptance of each other. That's what gives me peace, Rusty, just good ol'grace."

I softly shook my head in dismay as I responded. "I have to tell you, Ham, I'm not feeling any grace. I'm just worn down."

Ham straightened up and folded his arms in front of his black vest and thought for a moment. He then reached out with both hands and placed them on the table for emphasis. "Grace is the bond that anchors all that is good. You live in a world of free will, with many struggles and decisions. The path may not always be clear; so you work your way through and trust your instincts. With you Rusty, there has always been virtuous intent. And, when a guy looks back, friendship, love, and hope are what you see from your stuff. You're path is full of grace."

I was flattered by that, but I still felt inadequate with my responsibility to the world. "Ham, I'm not sure what to do, I don't know if I can help."

He looked at me and smiled, aiming his finger at me to make his final point. "I told you a long time ago that the world was lucky to have you on its side. And boy, you have come through like gang busters. Rusty, no one knows how to live life with certainty; we only can live it as it comes. It's how we deal with stuff that makes all the difference; and I'm sayin there is no one better for that than you." He gave me a wink and reached over to pat my forearm; it was his big finish.

That was it, we were done, and he was anxious to get me on my way. "Time to go, buddy. You need to get back and prepare for your next trip."

Ham had made me feel better. Really, for the first time, I felt secure about what I needed to do. In fact, I was ready to get to it. I stood and said, "I'm ready to go."

He spoke with a genuine look of respect on his face. "Sure am proud of you, boy."

I said, "Thanks, Ham."

He gave me a wink and a wave, and said, "Adios, muchacho."

Chapter 32 – New York City – Post WW2

THE WORLD'S RICHEST MAN

Robert Forrest sat in the front pew of the cathedral, wondering about what would happen next. It wasn't about the order of service in his parent's funeral which he was attending. He was curious about when he would be contacted by the mysterious man that had walked into his office months ago.

All of what the man said had come true. His parents were dead, and now he was a rich man. But more importantly, every stock and commodity that the man had offered was a winner. Forrest had never seen anything like it.

He had done as asked, and not warned his parents of their impending doom. It wasn't as difficult as he thought it might be. In fact, it wasn't a problem at all. He wasn't responsible for their death; and now the world lay at his feet. Yes, fate had finally been kind to him.

As the funeral procession exited the church, Forrest scanned the faces of those in attendance. The question kept cycling in his head; where is he? He sat by himself in the limousine on the way to the cemetery; having no interest in the family members that rode in the limo that followed. He had never been close to any of them, and knew them as the vultures that they were; poised and ready to pounce on the money that his father had left behind.

The limousine parked at the gravesite and Forrest stepped out. The grounds were gorgeous with massive elms providing cover for the lush bluegrass that framed the thousands of statuesque grave stones. He took a moment to drink in the view, letting his eyes wander the surroundings; and suddenly there he was. The man was fifty yards away, standing underneath one of the big elms. He stood stoically as they made eye contact. Forrest paused for a moment, and then was being ushered by the funeral director to his graveside chair. He turned his head to take a second look; the mysterious man was gone.

Forrest faced the large brick fireplace in the den of his parent's house. Finally, everyone from the funeral reception had gone. He rubbed his neck and downed a large gulp of scotch, then undid his collar and removed the confining tie.

A voice from behind startled him. "Good to see you, Mr. Forrest."

He whirled around in a panic and came face to face with the Traveler. Forrest was flustered as he spoke. "You scared the hell out of me. How did you get in here?"

The Traveler narrowed his eyes and intensely gazed at the frightened young Forrest, giving the slightest of smiles as he darkly answered. "Mr. Forrest, I can be anywhere I choose to be."

He had produced his dramatic entrance for this very effect, wanting the young millionaire nervous and vulnerable. The Traveler quickly got to the point. "It's time to talk, Mr. Forrest."

Still shaken, Forrest nodded his head and answered weakly, "Yes, you're right."

The Traveler felt totally in control and began to lay out his plan. "You will become a very rich and powerful man, Mr. Forrest; all you need do is take my advice."

Forrest was trying to regain his composure. "Yes, I have been monitoring your choices in the market; remarkable, simply remarkable." He continued. "So are you saying these results can be consistently reproduced?"

"Yes; that and much more. The world is yours, Mr. Forrest."

The young millionaire was leery, asking his next question. "What's in it for you?"

The Traveler manufactured a look of false surprise. "Why, Mr. Forrest, I assumed you understood we are partners."

Forrest answered still untrustingly. "Sure, I figured that; but what kind of partnership?"

The Traveler smiled and responded respectfully. "That is a very good question, Mr. Forrest. I'm not interested in sharing your wealth. I want resources and power. Over the years I will require these and must have them on demand."

Forrest had regained his composure and was thinking out loud. "What if I can't produce what you need?"

The Traveler answered confidently. "That will never be a problem. You will have unlimited resources. The issue will be timing, and that's what I will require from you."

Forrest had a bad feeling in his gut. This was all happening so quickly. He voiced his concern. "This all sounds too good to be true; I don't even know who you are."

The Traveler stepped toward his prey to emphasize his next point. "This is all very real, Mr. Forrest. I am your angel of fortune, that's all you need to know."

Forrest felt the hair rise on the back of his neck. He was becoming frightened, and insecurely asked, "Now I'm not saying that I don't want to do this; but what if I told you to find someone else?"

The Traveler wickedly answered. "You're not going to do that, Mr. Forrest; after all, we are partners. You will be the wealthiest man in the world. This is an opportunity you will not pass up." His dark eyes bore in on the young millionaire.

Forrest meekly answered, "Ok."

The Traveler continued, "We haven't discussed the final moments of your parents lives."

Forrest was confused as he answered, "What?"

The Traveler smiled as he spoke. "Yes, Mr. Forrest, it was quite a scene. Your father actually offered your mother to me sexually, and to take her life, if I would only spare him. I felt for her as she listened to him grovel and cast her away so easily. So I killed her quickly with no pain."

Forrest crumbled into a nearby chair as he listened to the morbid details that the Traveler was providing.

He continued. "Your father was very amusing, offering me outrageous sums of money; and was shocked when I told him I would have his money anyway. I told him of our arrangement and pending partnership. He wasn't a very good man, Mr. Forrest; I can see why you chose to let him die. You should know that I killed him slowly; a very dramatic man, your father; so much begging and screaming. At all cost, Mr. Forrest, our partnership must insure that your fate won't be that of your father's; a horrible death, such a weak and cowardly end."

The Traveler offered his hand to Forrest to help him to his feet then strolled over to the bar in the den and poured a shot of scotch into a glass. He turned to the new millionaire and raised his glass for a toast. "Here's to a lifelong partnership."

Forrest's hand was shaking as he brought the glass to his trembling lips. He guzzled the scotch as if it were water. Resigned to his fate, he dutifully answered the Travelers toast, "To our partnership."

Chapter 33 – New Mexico – Current Time

Home Sweet Home

The bright whiteness subsided and my travel was complete. I was back home, on the bench, looking out over the Rio Grande and the beautiful Bosque surrounding it. Checking behind me, I made sure the Sandia Mountains were still there; sure enough they were. It seemed like an eternity since I had been here, but apparently nothing had changed since I left. It was a very strange sensation. The school bell sounded, which brought with it the reality of heading back to class. It was hard to change gears so quickly; a surreal feeling as I rose from the bench.

I headed down the path that led back to school. While walking, I saw a man in a dark uniform approaching me. I thought he might be a UPS driver, but he was not carrying a package. His coat was draped over one arm, and I thought it was strange that he wasn't wearing it on this not-so-warm day. I prepared to say hi as he drew near. Abruptly he reached for his coat with his opposite hand, then suddenly lurched back, as if being pushed. He looked at me stunned. Blood gushed out of a new hole that appeared in the middle of his forehead and he lifelessly collapsed to the ground. The coat fell away to expose a pistol that he held in his formerly covered hand.

I heard Hal's voice yelling at me. "Rusty, get down!" He came from behind and tackled me to the ground. Above me bullets were whizzing by my head. I looked towards Hal for some answers, but he wasn't having any of that. He was all business and in a hurry. "Rusty, stay low, we must move quickly or die. We need to get down to the cover of the Bosque."

I gathered that we were under attack from someone who was farther up the hill toward the school. We were momentarily protected by the bench, because of its surrounding rock wall and canopy. Hal was carrying some type of military-issue rifle with an electronic scope. His full attention was focused toward the hill where the bullets had originated. I heard a buzzing sound coming from the sky and identified a small air craft flying into view.

Hal looked up and said, "Oh crap; move, Rusty, move!" He pushed me down the incline of the hill toward a shallow rocky cavity. He urgently shouted, "Jump!" We took off together as the canopy behind us exploded in a fiery ball. I scrambled behind a rock that protruded above the depression we were in. Hal pulled out a small radio from his pocket and was making contact. He barked orders in to it. "Activating Operation Joshua; authorization code Tango, Charlie, sequence numbering,7,5,0,3,4."

While giving commands and information to the radio, he was scanning the horizon. "We are under attack from an armed drone; at these radio coordinates. I need an immediate electronics buzz, and I mean now."

The voice from the radio acknowledged, "Roger that, we already have one in the air; ETA will be in less than a minute."

Hal braced himself against the rock that I was hiding behind and warned. "Get ready, we're about to have an F-15 about a hundred feet above our heads."

I could hear the drone but I wasn't going to pick up my head and look for it. Suddenly the ground was shaking and a deafening roar engulfed us. The F-15 had arrived; I gathered it came from the air base on the south side of Albuquerque. The heat of the engine burn was intense as it screamed over the top of us.

The next thing I heard was the explosion of the drone smashing to earth, just below us at the edge of the Bosque. I assumed that the F-15 had caused the crash. Hal radioed the contact that the buzz had been affective. In the meantime, his belted work radio was blaring with the voice of Officer Washington from the Tribal Police. "Hal, is that you I see down there with my binoculars?"

Hal took the radio from his belt holder and answered. "Yeah, it's me, Jonah. Where are you?"

He said, "I'm here at the school, parked on the outdoor basketball courts. We just put the school in lock down; you playing with fireworks again?

Hal ruefully answered, "I wish." He continued. "Hey, Jonah, how many hostiles do you see up there?"

Jonah answered, "Well, dude, I see two groups of three; one on the north side of school, and one on my left about two hundred yards. Who are these guys?"

Hal warned, "Jonah, do not engage. These are black ops guys, and some real bad boys."

Jonah paused and thought before he answered. "Well then we have a bit of a problem. There will be a boat load of EMT's and cops here in about five minutes."

Hal countered that thought. "Hey, maybe that's a good thing if they all pull up to the school." Hal thought some more, then radioed. "If you can keep them at the school; that would probably keep everyone safe, plus make these guys back off. It would give Rusty and me a head start, and a chance to get out of here."

Jonah rolled his eyes as he answered his radio. "Yeah, and leave me behind to answer all the questions."

Hal laughed. "Ten four, buddy, that's what friends are for."

Jonah turned serious with an important question. "What do I tell them?"

Hal looked toward the school as if he could see Jonah. "Just play dumb, buddy, just play dumb."

Jonah heard the sirens as he replied to Hal, "Pretty easy for me to do that since I don't know anything. By the way, after you leave, when will I see you guys again? Because Lucy, you have some real 'splaining to do," he said in his best Ricky Ricardo voice.

With sadness, Hal answered, "Not real sure, Jonah; the crap has just hit the fan." He paused for a moment, and then requested. "Jonah, will you tell Tinley…" He stopped short, emotion preventing his being able to continue.

Jonah responded. "I got it, buddy; you love her."

Jonah resigned himself to the facts at hand. "Ok, my brothers, you better get going. Stay safe, and may you fly with the eye of the eagle, and be as crafty as the fox on the run."

Hal smiled. "You just made that up, didn't you?"

Jonah dryly answered, "Yeah."

Hal quickly changed gears and spoke to me with urgency in his voice. "This is our chance, let's go." We sprinted out of our shallow bunker and down toward the river, about a hundred meters away. Reaching the tree line, Hal gave me the signal to stop. He moved to an opening between the trees and brought his rifle to firing position. He was actually using the scope to survey the hill. Completing the scan, he appeared to be satisfied that we were out of immediate danger. We moved on further through the thicket that was the Bosque. The path we followed was surrounded by salt cedars and tall grass. The trees were mostly towering cottonwoods that blocked the sun and prevented any visual contact that might be provided by any other aerial drone.

After a couple of miles at a jogging pace, I was in great need of a break. I breathlessly called out to Hal, who had no intention of stopping. He assured me that we were close to our destination and continued on. I held on for what seemed forever; finally he slowed to a walk as we approached a small cinderblock building.

It looked like a garage with a heavy metal door. Anyone walking in the Bosque would have assumed it to be associated with some type of river conservation. Hal opened a panel on a small metal box that was affixed to the block wall. He entered a code on the electronic pad inside the box, and the door began to rise.

Inside was a type of all-terrain vehicle; it looked like a gator but it was obviously adapted for special use. The tires were oversized and that made the clearance underneath somewhat exaggerated. The cab was built for two bodies; a small compartment on the back housed tools and a type of pulley system. Hal urged me to get in, as he quickly did on the driver side. He drove the gator out as the door began to close behind us. We headed straight for the river, down a path that did not look big enough for the gator to pass through. Branches from the surrounding salt cedars were violently slapping against the frame.

We continued on a winding path for quite some time before finally breaking clear of the brush and to an area of soft sandy dirt. The Rio Grande lazily drifted only a stone's throw away. Hal took a sharp left and began to plow through the soft sand while paralleling the water's edge. We approached a wide area of the river with an island that split the water into two paths.

Hal turned the gator toward the river as if he intended to cross, and I became concerned. "You're not trying to cross this are you?"

"Sure I am. Rusty, you're assuming that I haven't thought this through," he said with a reassuring smile.

He was wrong. I absolutely was not assuming anything; in fact I was in total disarray. An hour or two before, I had been talking to Ham somewhere in another dimension. Now, I was running for my life with Hal; an ex therapist, turned conservationist, and now some kind of super trooper.

Sure enough we began crossing the Rio Grande, which of course is Spanish for Big River. The water surged against the gator's tires and began to spill in on the side of the vehicle at my feet. The gator amazingly sliced through the water with surprising power. We reached the island edge, churning through deep layers of mud until the gator found solid ground on top. The four-wheel drive slung mud like a pinwheel, as we crossed the island and entered the water on the far side. Soon we were on solid ground again and making our way back to the cover of the far side portion of the Bosque.

Hal drove until we came to a small clearing, surrounded by beautiful aspens, with leaves that had turned red and golden in the coolness of the late autumn weather. He slowed the high powered gator to a stop, then turned to me; knowing he would be answering a barrage of questions. He put his finger up, asking for one more moment. Reaching in his jacket pocket, he pulled out the radio receiver that he had used to call in the F-15. He again referenced Operation Joshua, and gave his clearance code; then began to converse. "Status is secure and on the move. We are active in the River Rat and awaiting instruction."

The voice answered back. "Roger that; what is the status of the target?"

Hal looked at me and smiled as he answered. "Well he looks a little confused, but besides that, we have a healthy target."

The voice responded. "Roger that; big dog says bring him home."

Hal was matter of fact in his reply; "Ten four; on our way."

He put away his radio and turned his attention to me. "What do you want to know?"

I scowled at him with incredulous disdain. "Everything!" I exclaimed.

We sat and stared at each other for a moment; then I started in. "Ok the guy with the bullet through his head; did you do that?"

Hal answered calmly. "Yes, or you would be dead right now."

I nodded my head and gave him an appreciative look. "Well I owe you a big thank you; but who were those guys shooting at us, and what about that flying drone?"

He replied, "They are a specialized unit with advanced technical weaponry. Their mission was, and is, to find and kill you."

I said, "Ok." My mind was sifting through everything trying to connect all of the events together. I came up with another question. "What is Operation Joshua?"

Hal hesitated for a moment. He looked at me and decided he should continue with his explanation. "It is a highly classified safeguard put in place for your safety, in the event you were ever put in danger. When that black ops squad found you I had no choice but to activate."

I asked, "Was that squad sent by the Dark Traveler?"

Hal abruptly cut me off. "Rusty, you're asking questions beyond my pay grade. I have orders to bring you in; you can ask the rest of your questions then." He swiveled his head around checking the area, then commanded, "Let's move out."

He started up the gator and gassed it. We began our exit out of the Bosque and on to the desert floor of the mesa, which rested on the west side of the Rio Grande Valley. Our exit point was just off the reservation and close to the outskirts of Albuquerque. Hal's plan was to take the back roads along the mesa until we reached the rendezvous point that had been arranged over the radio.

We covered a lot of territory in a hurry in the surprisingly speedy gator. The terrain was bumpy but we no longer had to deal with the heavy brush of the Bosque. As we climbed the mesa I looked back into the valley, remembering how beautiful the view was from this side. The Sandias formed a majestic backdrop for the big river that had carved its way through this land for thousands of years. It was a view that I never tired of.

We traveled for what I guessed was about two hours, now proceeding on the flat top of the mesa through grassland, and headed for one of the local airports. We entered the airport facility through the backside of the fenced area. There was an electronic gate portal and Hal punched in a code that caused the gate to open. We headed for a massive concrete slab that sported three military gunship helicopters. Hal parked the gator and quickly jumped out. He was greeted by a soldier, and they engaged in a quick conversation. Hal gave me a wave to come forward, so I joined him at the chopper.

As the engine of the chopper began to churn the blades, Hal gave his next command. "Get in, Rusty; it's time to get you home." I could barely hear him over the noise, but I nodded my head that I understood. While buckling in, I felt as if I had just entered a war zone. Surrounding me were soldiers in full battle dress and armed with mounted high tech weapons. We lifted off, accompanied by the two other gunships; I could see that the other choppers were manned and heavily armed as well.

Our flight took us south down the river valley and around the southern edges of the larger Albuquerque International Airport. We were close to the air base that I had rehabbed in so many years ago, but we weren't headed there. We turned east and headed for the sister mountains of the Sandias: the Manzanos.

The choppers landed in what seemed like the middle of nowhere. A jeep was there to greet us; Hal ushered me out of the chopper and into the passenger seat of the jeep. He hopped in the back and gave thumbs up to the driver.

The jeep headed straight east for the base of the mountain, traveling in and out of a few rocky canyons until we came upon a seemingly ordinary looking building. Hal punched me in the arm, giving me a thumb motion to signal our exit. We stepped out of the jeep, Hal gave the driver a salute, and we approached the structure.

The brick building was probably a thousand square feet and perfectly square. It had a flat top roof and a heavy steel door for an entrance. We drew near the door and Hal opened yet another box with a key pad entry. He punched in a code, and the thick heavy door slowly opened.

Once inside, the building revealed another huge door that ran the length of the far wall. The floor beneath us was concrete but appeared to be some type of large platform. A buzzer sounded, and slowly the floor began to descend. Hal did not seem surprised or concerned, so I quietly tagged along for the ride.

As we dropped, another large area was coming into view. After obtaining full sight, I realized the area was huge. It was more of an aircraft hangar, or some type of staging area. I estimated it to be the length and width of a football field, all underground. Three sides of the area appeared to be all concrete. The east wall was rock; I guessed it to be part of the Monzano Mountains that we had traveled toward above ground.

A jeep and driver waited for us just beyond the platform. Stepping off, we entered the jeep and took our places, then traveled the length of the large empty room and in the direction of the solid rock wall. As we approached, a huge portion of the rock began to slide; revealing a twenty foot high tunnel, that appeared to lead directly into the mountain.

The jeep continued through, and we drove for what seemed to be about a quarter mile, until we came upon another massive steel door. Two soldiers manned a post outside, and the driver pulled over to it. The soldiers saluted as the driver ran his security badge through the nearby sensor. He saluted back as the door began to slowly swing open.

Beyond the door was a vista that reminded me of the Carlsbad Caverns in Southeastern New Mexico. We drove into a cavernous space of at least two hundred by one hundred meters; with a ceiling that was easily twenty meters high; all of it completely carved out of the natural mountain rock. The room was supported by massive concrete pillars anchoring large steel beams that spanned the solid rock ceiling. Large wooden crates and steel pods were stack three deep in a series of rows, filling the area and creating paths toward additional tunnels that surrounded the room.

While traveling through the room to what I guessed was the north side; I recalled all the rumors I had heard during my life of the hollow Manzanos. It was speculated that these mountains were a high security holding area for the military. I was seeing for myself that the rumors were actually true. We entered one of the tunnels and continued down a path that passed by space after space of stored material. After about ten minutes, we slowed to a stop in front of an area with an enclosed front. It had a door and an electronic security pad to the side.

Hal tapped me on the back and spoke, "Time to go meet the man."

We got out and walked toward the door. Hal entered a code and then opened it. Inside was a woman in uniform sitting behind a small metal desk in what looked like a reception area. Hal saluted her as she picked up the phone on the desk. The woman casually saluted back while speaking into the phone. "They are hear, sir." She briefly listened to the answer and then replied; "Yes, sir." Looking at Hal she said, "You may go in."

Hal led the way toward the next door and we entered a larger space that was set up similar to a classroom. There were a dozen tables with chairs scattered throughout; in the front was a large whiteboard. Standing next to it, with his back toward us, was an elderly looking man in full military garb.

Hal spoke to the man. "General, sir, delivering Rusty Ryan as ordered."

The man said. "Thank you, Hal." He turned to face us as he spoke again. "But that's Retired General for anyone who's asking."

The old man had to be in his eighties. He was fit and stood strongly, but the years were revealed on his face. The crow's feet showed fatigue, but his eyes countered with intense purpose. There was something familiar about him; maybe the way he stood, or the way he looked at me. The old general had three stars on his lapel, and a plethora of other metals attached.

He had a knowing smile as he spoke to me: "Hi, Rusty."

I knew this man, I just had to think. I looked in his eyes and it hit me. I wondered out loud, "Thomas?"

Hal butted in. "That's General Thomas to you, Rusty!"

Not taking his eyes off of me, the general consoled Hal. "It's ok, Hal, we are old friends." He continued. "Yes, Rusty, it's me."

It was hard to unite this old man with the soldier I just left. I shook my head as I answered. "It can't be, it just can't be."

Thomas became interested in my answer. "So tell me, Rusty, how long has it been since you've seen me last?"

I said, "I just left you and Joshua. I had a talk with Ham and then I came back to world war three with Hal."

The old general thought for a moment and reflectively answered, "I see."

I was trying to get a read off of his face to what he was thinking. I just wasn't sure enough of what was actually going on to make a determination. I did have an important question. "Where is Joshua?"

Thomas leaned over and placed his hands on the desk in front of him. He intently starred at me as he answered. "That, Rusty, is the world-saving question."

I was shocked that Thomas didn't know where Joshua was. I analyzed the old man, while thinking everything through. Then it hit me; he was waiting for me to travel. I guessed, "You need me to find him."

Thomas slowly nodded his head and acknowledged. "Until this moment, I did not know how much traveling you had done."

I cautioned, "Ham warned me about traveling in my own time and the paradox of events."

Thomas answered, "Yes, it has been my concern as well. The fact that we have met at this time could be a concern; on the other hand, you would be dead if we hadn't."

I asked. "So all of this time with Hal; it's been you behind the scenes calling the shots?"

"Yes," he said. He walked around the table and moved closer as he spoke. "I knew there would be trouble from the Traveler, but I wasn't in time. My only choice was to make it appear that you were dead and hide you for as long as possible."

I was concerned. "All of this could get very confusing." I thought again and restated. "Who am I kidding; all of this is very confusing."

Thomas agreed. "It was wise to wait as long as possible for you to travel. But the time is here." The door opened and a man walked in carrying a clipboard. General Thomas introduced him.

"Rusty, this is Walter Nail. He is the head of our team that is researching the wormhole."

Walter reached out his hand as he congenially said, "How do you do."

We shook hands and the general continued. "His research indicates that the time is near." Thomas gestured towards Nail that he wanted him to join the conversation.

Nail began. "Uh yes, our data indicates a massive buildup of energy in our solar system that is not associated with the sun. This energy is centralizing around the solar space of earth. In addition, inner earth data from our planet's core is extremely unstable." He stopped for a moment to nervously adjust his glasses. He briefly looked at me, and then toward General Thomas to get his ok to continue. Thomas motioned for him to proceed.

Nail continued. "This energy in space is something we have never dealt with before. It is unclear where it is from and what it is attempting to do. Our best guess is another dimension is revealing itself through this extreme buildup. It doesn't have a consistent pattern and is becoming a global threat; it seems to be searching for something."

I interrupted him. "It's searching for Joshua's signal."

Nail politely answered, "Yes, Mr. Ryan, that's what I'm told."

I turned my attention to Thomas. "Ham said I would travel as soon as I was secure back here in the present."

Thomas responded. "Good, we are running out of time."

I continued. "He warned that I could trust no one. My history and present status will be altered with every trip."

The general conceded. "The fact that I am here now, and that the Traveler has gone to your past to kill you, is an indicator of stranger things to come. We will do our best for you, Rusty. Your safest bet is to trust Hal." He turned very serious as he continued. "You might have difficulty determining what has changed when you return; you will be the only one who is aware of the difference. Already, there is conflict and confusion caused by the Traveler.

The men who attacked you are from a global company called Forrest Industries. It is a Wall Street front for the largest private army in the world. All of it is controlled by the Traveler. He has his hands in every facet of government; even in the military."

General Thomas's demeanor became one of secrecy as he moved in closer to speak. "That's why we have Operation Joshua and why I'm still here. I've been retired for ten years but not from this operation. It is the highest security priority at the highest levels. Only the most trusted and important of people have any knowledge or clearance to the inner workings of what we are doing."

He moved to my side and placed his hand on my shoulder as he continued. "You, my friend, must stay on the move and stay safe. But most importantly, you must find Joshua."

I was positive with my response. "I'm sure I will travel soon."

From the doorway Hal politely butted in. "General, sir, I think it's time for Rusty and me to go."

The general stepped back and paused for a moment to think, then he spoke. "Yes, Hal, you're right." He offered me his hand with a glimmer in his eyes while speaking his parting words: "May the force be with you."

The old man caught me by surprise and I gave a soft laugh. I grinned at him. "How many years have you been waiting to say that to me?"

Thomas said soulfully, "Too many, way too many."

I turned and headed for the door. From my side I heard Hal say, "Good bye, General, and thank you."

I paused, but did not turn around as Thomas responded. "No, Hal, thank you. You've made me very proud. Stay safe; you will take your orders from Rusty now."

Hal answered with an emotional voice, "Yes, sir."

I followed him to the jeep, and we set off. I sat in the passenger seat reflecting, while Hal navigated through the maze of tunnels in the hollow mountain. Looking over at him, I wondered again about this guy that I thought I knew. "Hal, are you going to tell me what all that was about with the general?"

He had regained his composure and was matter of fact. "The general knows that you and I must stay insulated with each other until this is done."

I asked, "How long have you known him?"

He suddenly stopped the jeep and turned to look at me. "My full given name is Henry Jason Thomas. He is my grandfather."

I was shocked, and for some reason the fact that I didn't know this information offended me. Submersed in self-pity I whined. "Is there ever going to be anything I know first?"

Hal countered, "Don't go there, Rusty, all of this is about you."

I acknowledged, "Yes I know that, Hal, but every once in a while it would be nice to know things at the same time as everyone else."

Hal counseled, "From here on it's me and you, and until you say different, we do what you say. The general has put you in charge of all decisions. I will get us out of here, and then it's your call for our next move."

I wondered about what was next; how was all of this going to play out? One thing I knew for sure, the key to it all was Joshua, and I had to find him.

To be continued...